The Janus Murder

The Janus Murder

an Anyway Books® novel by

John Nicholas Datesh

**Published by
Loiseau Media**

The Janus Murder

An *Anyway Books*® novel by

John Nicholas Datesh

Third Print Edition Published by
Loiseau Media/Anyway Books 2016
ISBN 978-1-940227-15-3

e-Editions Published by John Nicholas Datesh, Jr. 2009
Original Print Edition Published by Nordon Publications, Inc. 1979
Second Print Edition Published by Loiseau Development 2013

John Nicholas Datesh is a
pseudonym of John Nicholas Datesh, Jr.

This novel, its characters, their thoughts,
actions, and dialogue, are fictitious.

The Janus Murder

Chapter One

My head had been on the desk for a couple of hours by the time the phone jangled me awake. The night before I had spent outside an eight-dollar-a-night motel this side of Chambersburg, keeping my eye on one room in particular. Somebody else's husband went in with somebody else's wife at 12:30 AM and came out again at 6:15.

For twenty-four hours work, I billed $100. About four bucks an hour. It doesn't sound like much, but it's a fortune compared to some criminal work I indulge in for a couple public defenders I actually like. It's not pro bono, but it pays that way.

"What is it, Cath?" My mouth tasted like twenty-four hours of stale bread.

Cath Mays, who works for an accountant and takes care of my phone but nothing else, snapped, "It's Pete Kline again."

"Again?"

"He called an hour ago, but you didn't answer, Carmichael. What do you do, sleep the day away?"

Since she didn't even work for me, I cut off her sharp little voice. "Hello, Pete?"

His secretary answered. "Mr. Carmichael, Mr. Kline will be with you in a moment."

Pete Kline was a partner in a small probate firm I did some work for. Not much work really, searching for an heir occasionally, trailing a runaway. Kline's practice didn't involve divorce or much process serving—he did no criminal work—so he had little reason to call.

When he needed a detective, though, he used me.

"Carmichael," Kline said when he got on the line, "Do you have a couple minutes? I have a little something I'd like you to help me on."

The shrug must have been for my benefit. "Sure. Come on over."

"Fine," he cleared his throat. "And take a minute to fix up your office. I'll be bringing one of my clients."

The idea of having one of Kline's clients in my office threw me a bit, enough so that I forgot to say good-bye. Kline dealt with the kind of people who have enough money to leave behind to someone when they die. I don't usually meet that class of people, not face to face. I decided to follow Kline's advice about the office and started by hanging up the phone.

Not too many people would refer to my little place in the Haller Building as an office. It consisted of a single room off the corridor of one of the city's less distinguished buildings. Not that it was dirty or anything, but "office" seemed like a fancy word for it. My name, Casey Carmichael, was painted on the door in black, but there was no room number to go with it. Sometimes that made me seem lost even when I wasn't.

Straightening up didn't take long. I threw out everything I couldn't drink or write with, and made it look empty. That done, I stepped next door and hustled a couple of chairs from Fred Tindale. Fred was the accountant who shared Cath Mays with me. I let him think that gave him an "in" on the exciting world of the private eye.

Kline's knock came about two seconds after I had positioned Fred's chairs opposite my desk. I shoved mine behind the door, because I didn't want my guests to sit in them. Fred's were uncomfortable, bare wood, but solid and clean. Like Fred.

The attorney appeared a bit tentative when the door opened, uncertain of what he'd find. Pete Kline didn't quite reach six feet and had never seen 141 on the scale. Something about my 206 pounds bothered him.

"Good afternoon, Mr. Carmichael." His voice was as firm as usual and more formal. Usually he called me Carmichael like everyone else, but, of course, he had a client with him.

"Come on in, Pete," I offered, backing away from the door. As I did, I could see a second figure waiting to be introduced. "Invite the lady in, too."

She didn't wait for Kline's glance, but came in on her own. "How do you do, Mr. Carmichael."

I felt okay and admitted it. She seemed satisfied and volunteered her name. "I'm Diana Winter. Of the Winter National Bank." She didn't bother to elaborate.

She didn't have to. Winter National's the big bank in the counties north of Pittsburgh, so she had as much money as she seemed to have. Her clothes were expensive and didn't hurt her looks any. The small, unlined face had been just cute, but was making real progress toward pretty. Her makeup consciously worked for the former.

Under the ankle length fur, was probably a figure that deserved some attention, but she didn't disturb the buttons. When I asked them to sit in Fred's chairs, she didn't worry about the coat. Or the way it embarrassed the tiny engagement diamond she wore.

Kline lowered himself onto the varnished wood gently. He spent his time on soft leathered seats and didn't have enough portable cushion to make the wood comfortable.

I kept them waiting as I circled to my chair. "So, Pete. What can I do for you and Miss Winter?"

"Miss Winter came to me originally for some local work on her father's estate," Kline explained. "Now she has decided that she needs a private detective." The very thought made him frown.

"I like the way you think, Miss Winter."

The young woman smiled. She wanted to talk, but Kline made sure she didn't.

"The situation is somewhat delicate," he went on. "And a little unusual."

I hear the work "delicate" five times a week. No one bothers with a private detective when a public scene will do. I had expected something out of the routine this time and let my disappointment show. "I see."

The lawyer shook his head in a way that told me I didn't see at all.

Miss Winter spoke up anxiously. "I am afraid you'll think it's very strange, Mr. Carmichael," she said, sounding proud of it. "I want you to exonerate the man accused of killing my father."

"Oh?" was all I could think of.

The grimace on Kline's pale face indicated that his client had departed from the script. "It's not quite as lurid as it may sound," he hastened to say.

My mind tumbled back a few months and located an article detailing the coffin's lid of a case the State of Pennsylvania had presented against one Tony Hiller, to indict him for the murder of a banker named Harold Winter. The dateline on that story read September 21, 1975, almost nine months ago.

"Tony Hiller was my fiancé." She caught herself. "Is my fiancé."

"I wouldn't boast about it, Miss Winter. Not for the next twenty years."

"Ah, Mr. Carmichael," Kline interjected, "He hasn't even been to trial yet."

Diana Winter lifted herself out of the chair and walked somberly to my small window. "Tony has been in the hospital for nine months. He's not supposed to be sane enough to stand trial."

"At least he wasn't," Kline elaborated, "until yesterday. The court reviewed the case and this morning ordered a competency hearing for next week. That's why we're here."

"He's going to plead guilty," she said to the unwashed glass.

Which didn't surprise me. "It's easier on everybody. Don't get me wrong," I added to quiet her reaction. "I don't know what's involved, but I don't remember reading that anyone thought he was innocent."

The girl shuddered. "Innocent? The word never came up. Not even to me."

"There was no evidence to support him," Kline reminded her gently. "You couldn't be expected to believe the story he was using."

Her shoulders went up and down, exaggerating an already deep sigh. "Mr. Carmichael, I want you to find out if Tony's story has any basis," she said quietly. "If not for him, for me."

The brown eyes she used on me would have shamed my cocker spaniel, if I still had one. She wanted someone to tell her that there was no way she could believe the one man she was supposed to believe. The someone was supposed to be me.

It was all so dog-gone pathetic. "Okay," I agreed coldly. "I'll do it for you, Miss Winter. I'll do it for you, because it won't do your fiancé any good to pile up more bills he can't pay. And I'll want a hundred and fifty a day and expenses."

"One-fifty!" Kline was out of the chair. "Why that's half again your normal rate, Carmichael!"

"Yep," I said. "But wasting my time costs more."

She stared at me, more interested than angry. "Why are you so mad?"

I didn't know why just then, but I didn't let on. "Because I get frustrated chasing my tail for facts that don't exist, Miss Winter. Besides, if I'm going to feel guilty taking your money, I may as well take a lot of it."

Miss Winter's eyes brightened with her sudden smile. "Why not?" she said. "I've got plenty."

Kline, upset by the bizarre turn of conversation, suggested quickly that I drop by his office for the facts of the case.

"I know a guy at the Press," I demurred. "I'll go over their accounts first. I kind of like the sensationalism."

He shrugged. "That's just as well."

Miss Winter shook my hand. Her small hand had a sure youthful character. "Come to the Bank tomorrow, Mr. Carmichael. In Huntington," she enthused. "I'd like to have you start there. With me." She handed me an embossed card at the same time that she withdrew her right hand.

"Call if you need directions."

I let them out the door with an "Okay."

Once they had gone, I pulled out my favorite deck of cards, to help me think. Solitaire lets my mind wander around the possibilities of a given situation.

No. Not "situation". That was Kline's term. One I'd heard too often before, in the fifties. I hadn't used that word in twenty years. It made everything sound so messy.

Chapter Two

Pittsburgh that particular April wasn't a bad place to be. A late snow had cleared the air some and made the rains welcome. Leaving my office, I walked to the Press through a light haze suspended under some clouds trying to rain. The people in the street moved about full of the anticipation that spring is made of. Like the rest, I kept an eye on a particularly menacing bundle of gray that hovered over the Boulevard of the Allies.

Harry Blair stood waiting for me outside the Press Building. The five cigarette butts scattered around his feet told me that he had been there for about two and a half minutes. The Winstons hadn't been smoked down very far, the tobacco shredded by a relentless foot. Blair's face lit up when he spotted me shuffling his way. Maybe it was the match.

"You look nervous, Carmichael," he said.

I accepted the lit one he offered, mostly to prove to him that he could smoke the damn thing to the filter with some effort. "Sure," I replied. "I'm waiting for rain."

"Rain?" Harry checked the sky and looked surprised. "It does look like it."

It had looked like it for over an hour, but to say so would have cost Harry another Winston. After stowing his matches, Harry led me inside the building and along the tortuous path to his office. The room looked smaller than mine and more cluttered. It wasn't either, but he was busier than I was.

In the middle of his desk sat a pile of newspapers. The top date was August 18, 1975. "These for me, Harry?" I asked picking up the first copy.

The former reporter nodded vaguely and sat down. Before he hit the seat of the chair, he was up again. Nerves were a part of Blair's makeup, but I'd never seen him as jittery as he was that afternoon.

Trying to ignore him, I looked over the front page of the old paper. The lead had something to do with recession or inflation. The other columns meant nothing to me, until I reached the bottom right hand corner. There I found the first mention of what became the Winter murder case. Winter's Huntington, Pennsylvania, bank had been robbed minutes before the issue had gone to press. It was a very prosaic story, typical newspaper grist.

"The shit gets better," Blair told me.

Returning the paper to the top of the pile, I said, "I hope so."

Harry almost said something, but threw away an unlit Winston instead. "There's a little room you can use on the next floor up."

The papers were heavy and my back had aged faster than the rest of me. "Jesus, Blair, I thought you guys microfilmed this stuff."

On his way out the door, Harry said, "We do."

He wouldn't even wait for the elevator, making me tote fifty pounds of newsprint up the stairs. Harry opened the door of a tiny reading room as I puffed up next to him.

"I can't go in there," I warned him. "I get claustrophobic in my office."

He shrugged. "I'll come and get you for that free dinner promised me."

With that reminder, Blair went back to his business of re-writing other people's copy. It was a task he hated. He was a born reporter and his new editorial position drove him nuts. Eleven months before, the paper had rewarded Harry for his long career on the street by moving him up. A nice, logical gesture, it hadn't worked. Not, at least, for Harry Blair who hadn't adjusted to getting his news second-hand. high-paying, impressively-titled job had turned his hair gray and his temper short. It had also doubled his cigarette bill.

Harold Winter's murder was the kind of story Harry would have liked to cover. By the time it had happened, however, he was already saving ten bucks a month on shoe leather. I could tell missing it bothered him. It was a story everyone else in town had covered.

The killing itself had produced enough gore to keep Technicolor in the black for years. Harold Winter had been shotgunned in his study from very close range, by a murderer with a weak stomach who left most of his lunch on Winter's desk.

To get the publicity that the Winter murder had, a case has to have a good gimmick. This one had several. The first, and really the best, was the "Party-line Confession", as the Press banner put it.

The receiver of Winter's party-line phone had been set to let a couple of Nosy Nellies in on the entire pre-murder conversation. In the course of that conversation, a voice clearly belonging to Tony Hiller spilled out what he intended to do and why.

More damning, he went over "how", how he intended to get away with Harold Winter's murder. Hiller detailed his whole scheme for Winter and, via the eavesdroppers, eventually for the DA. He would be found by the police in the basement of his own house, tied up and helpless; he would innocently claim that a suspicious drifter, named Weil, had forcibly put him there; a respected member of the Huntington community, his word would not be remotely questioned.

Sure enough, the police discovered Tony Hiller, tied to a chair in the cellar of the creaky house he shared with his uncle. Expressing amazement at his arrest, Hiller earnestly related a story about being slugged from behind and tied up for hours. His own fiancée didn't believe a word.

Through the days of questioning, Hiller held steadfastly to his incredible alibi. He was so adamant that he frustrated three sets of polygraph operators and four psychiatrists. The only conclusion was that he had suffered a complete breakdown and had come to believe his own lies, making a trial impossible.

The whole thing was so ridiculous that I began to understand Diana Winter's dilemma. I couldn't dream up even a dumb reason to believe Hiller. She couldn't either. Now, all she wanted was for me to prove she was justified.

Just as I was rubbing black ink from my hands into my eyes, Harry stuck his head in the door.

"Dinner time, Carmichael."

There was more to read, but I couldn't focus anymore, so I agreed. We left the little room and the newspapers for the Press Club. Harry bought three packs of cigarettes on the way.

"I didn't do anything on the case, Casey," he admitted, "so I asked that looker from WPPA to meet us. She was in the town where it happened, Huntington, half of August." He dropped a newly lit Winston and added, "The story didn't even get to my desk."

Shrugging, I said, "It never came up for trial, Harry. That's when you would have gotten on it. You're a big shot now."

Blair snorted in disgust and lit another cigarette. "Yeah."

There being no point in going over it with him—without the looker to fill in the gaps, I let him brood in silence. We had a way to go, but he needed the walk. The raid had held up somehow for over an hour and the clouds grumbled about the delay.

"It's going to rain," I told him.

"I'll read about it in the paper." Harry buried his hands in his coat pockets.

Sensitivity to moods is one of the things I get paid for. "What's wrong with you, Blair?"

Harry Blair stared at me as though I'd asked a silly question, or worse. "Have you ever needed a girl detective for a favor?"

My smile went sly. "Sure," I said.

"You know what I mean," he snapped.

Stopping to look at the clouds, I said, "Harry, you idiot, I'll ask anybody who has a watch for the time. I'm not as proud as you are. My whole damn business is based on begging idiots like you for information. Christ, it doesn't bother me that you know what I don't."

Harry grunted. He didn't say another word, but he smoked more of his cigarette than usual.

~ ~ ~

Half way to the Press Club, those frustrated clouds got their way. We picked up our pace a little but not enough to avoid the worst. A good suit would have been ruined. Mine wasn't.

The Press Club maitre d' gave me a skeptical look as my coat dripped on the carpet. As he came over to me, I pointed to Blair and was welcomed as a brother. There was a table with a striking bluish green blouse and we were steered immediately toward it. In the blouse was one the best looking women in town—any town—waiting for us.

The detective hones in on the green blouse. And notices the color of her skirt...

Oh, yeah. She wore slacks.

Janice Simmons was less than twenty-seven, I knew for a fact, but age didn't seem important. The girl stood up as we approached, staring at Blair. "Hello, Harry," she said, in a voice much nicer than the one she used on the screen. "Are you Mr. Carmichael?" she asked me.

I nodded at her green eyes and located her outstretched hand by its magnetic field. She had managed to become the local glamor girl as a features TV reporter. That's how good she was. In person she was even better.

And the green blouse, deepening her eye color, signaled that she knew it perfectly well.

"Thank you for joining us, Ms. Simmons," Harry said, as formally as I've ever heard him. His face had changed, the basset-like droop to his eyes had, if anything, deepened. "Casey, here, has some use for you."

The line must have meant something to her, because she smiled warmly and looked at me with more interest that I deserved. "Harry told me that you were involved in the Winter case."

The nod came again. All by its stupid self.

"Wow, Casey," she said evenly, "aren't you taciturn."

She thought I was comical, I suppose, because only my head seemed to work. That wasn't the impression I wanted to convey, so I said, "I just like your voice."

"Thanks." The dual greens blinked to Harry and after a second back to mine. "It's the real one."

"How about something to drink?" Harry mumbled. He waved and a waiter appeared.

Then nothing happened. I was busily categorizing shades of green, looking for the right one.

"Casey?"

She turned a few degrees toward Harry and I had to start all over again. "He does drink, doesn't he, Harry?"

"Shit. Get him a damned bourbon."

"The same," she said.

Blair then ordered something with vodka in it and started talking loudly about Ms. Simmon's credentials. She stopped smiling and looked serious about it. A newspaper in Arizona, a TV station in Oklahoma City, one in Toledo and finally her job in Pittsburgh. We all knew she was being groomed to anchor the evening slot when the local favorite retired next year. A year or two and she'd be in New York. Maybe, she'd have to stop in Philly for one last rehearsal.

Once my bourbon had come and was half gone, I began to feel more at home. Except there was wallpaper. "You covered the Winter business, then?"

Her right eyebrow went up. "From start to unfinish. I even did a bit on it for tonight's show, but someone cut it. Not enough time. Yesterday's news." It bothered her and she didn't hide it. "Hiller's going to plead guilty," she added, "so I think it's dead now."

"Maybe," I made my voice sound doubtful. Her interest had become important to me. "Someone doesn't think so."

Janice Simmons spent a moment sizing me up. Done with that, she cocked her head slightly and stated, "Diana Winter."

I said nothing, probably out of professional ethics, confirming her guess.

"She's a little flaky, Mr. Carmichael. If you want my opinion," Janice Simmons offered, "she's responsible. Not for the murder, maybe, but for Hiller's break-up."

"Funny, I liked her better than most." I did, too.

"How about that." The brilliant green eyes flicked meaningfully to Harry and then back. "So did I. Much, much better."

Blair, feeling lonely by this time, snorted and crushed a cigarette. "You two have so much, much in common."

Janice didn't bother to look at Harry. She gave me her full attention. "We do, don't we, Mr. Carmichael?" The smile that played on her face warned me that she was smarter than I was and was after whatever information I had. Or was going to get.

I responded with my worldly frown and bluffed, "If you're interested in murder, Miss Simmons. We might get along."

She did my frown one better. Much, much better. "We'll get along, Mr. Carmichael. We'll get along."

Chapter Three

Janice Simmons had a nice little apartment in Shadyside, which is the trendy place for someone her age to live in this city. It took us three cars to get there, a trip half as long as the hunt for three parking spaces.

Her third floor, one-bedroom had big windows and a nice view of the area. She had less than her share of carefully arranged furniture and strategically placed, if few, nick-knacks. Plants, on the other hand, were everywhere.

"Green," I said as she went to make up some coffee. "Probably a coincidence."

Nobody heard me, or it least, pretended not to. Miss Simmons set on her coffee maker and headed for her bedroom. Harry stood, awkwardly fingering one of the plants, a tall, potted ficus, I think it was.

He shook his head and said softly. "How did she get this thing to grow?"

It looked like a nice little tree, not a depressing one. "Her thumb is shockingly green, too, I suppose."

Harry started. He was almost surprised to see me when he turned around. It took him a minute to say anything. "When the Winter case first broke, Case, she picked up and moved to the Huntington area right away. She has real instincts for this. Best I've seen in years."

"She has the best everything I've seen in years, Blair," I replied in a stage whisper. "And I thought she was something on TV."

He grunted. Could have meant anything.

The smell of coffee shut us both up and a second later, she swept around the corner with a tray. It was my first real chance to look her over and I took it without much finesse.

Janice Simmons had a good figure, if you liked slender, mild curves—and I did, now—It wasn't showy, just very nice. She wasn't as tall as she looked sitting down, because her legs were a little shorter than they promised, which might have been the flaw I was looking for. Maybe it was the two inch heels.

The slacks, by the way, were a less-than-navy blue.

I needed a color wheel.

She set the tray in front of me, watching my eyes finish with her. As she had all evening, she seemed amused by me. At least, there was a sparkle in her eyes that didn't come across on television. "You'll have to add your own cream and sugar, Mr. Carmichael. I only go so far, as a domestic."

Circling the knee-high coffee table, she took a seat next to me on the sofa. "I didn't tell you much at dinner, Mr. Carmichael. I apologize for that, but I had forgotten too many details. Over the months, I have formed my own theories, and have ordered the facts to suit myself. I know that isn't what you're after. So I took a couple minutes to checkout a few things I have written up in my room while the coffee was on."

From his chair across the room, Harry grumbled, "It's not exactly dinner conversation anyway."

Her smile was too intelligent to be indulgent or warm, but the one directed at Harry came close. "I was afraid your Mr. Carmichael was losing patience with me."

With my first mouthful of coffee, I swallowed my feelings about the profitless if enjoyable table talk. Miss Simmons had chatted amiably about a number of harmless subjects while we ate, none of them being Tony Hiller. I didn't mind, but I had the uncomfortable feeling that she was waiting for me to let her in on a secret I didn't have. If she was convinced that I had something interesting to hide, I didn't want to discourage her.

"All right," she said. "It began with the robbery of the Winter National Bank in Huntington last August. The robbery occurred at noon in the plain view of customers and personnel, none of whom was Tony Hiller, who was out at lunch. The thief had a thorough knowledge of the bank's security system and its layout. He also had a stocking mask and a shot gun."

"Once he had gone through the vault for about $20,000, he locked everyone in the vault and fled. At about 1:10, Tony Hiller returned from lunch and alerted the police."

Harry wasn't listening very hard, but he still said, "Too damn easy."

"Very easy," she agreed. "But the robbery is only interesting to us in light of what happened later. One wrinkle that may interest you, Mr. Carmichael. No one noticed anyone unusual coming into the bank. A guard stands by the only customer entrance and he swears the robber didn't come in that way. He's not a dummy either. He said all the back doors were well locked. I talked to him personally and I believe him."

"Then where did he come from, Janice?" I asked, slipping in her first name unconsciously. I called everybody I saw on TV by their first names.

Her hand on my arm and the expression on her face told me she could live with the familiarity. "That is one of the questions I answered, Casey," she replied. "He seems to have come in through an unlocked window in one of the offices. Jack Pazinsky, Winter's number two man, was out at one of the branches that day, but his window was open."

"Bank air-conditioned?"

Her long eyebrow went up in appreciation. "Very comfortably."

"Go ahead," I said, as if I were running the show.

The reporter paused, ostensibly to nibble at her upper lip, but maybe to take the show back.

"That evening, at about 10:00, Mrs. Alma Purcil and Miss Suzanna Wycick were talking, at length, on the phone. In the

middle of a recipe for something involving strawberry yo-
gurt, they heard a click, indicating that someone else was on
that line. Like a few other people in the area, they were still
on a party-line."

"Still...?" Harry buried the thought.

But I knew where he was going. "Harry grew up with the
hand-crank..."

He shot me a look so searing look that I gulped down a
couple words.

Janice smiled that near-gentle smile again and continued.
"Before either of them could say anything, they heard Harold Winter's voice. It became obvious that he wasn't using
the phone, because his voice was distant and he didn't say
anything to either of the women."

Holding up my hand to stop her, I asked, "Harold Winter
could have owned his own phone company. What was he doing with a party-line?"

"His daughter told me that he was sentimental about it,
hard as it is to believe that of him. Actually, he had owned
the phone service in that area, in the forties. He sold the
company and kept the phone."

"There's a small town joke in there..."

Janice laughed. "He had another phone on his desk with
about two dozen lines, if that makes you feel any better."

"Much much better."

Blair shifted in his seat. "Tell him what Hiller said."

She leaned toward me and then away again. Planting her
elbow on the back of the couch she twisted some of her hair,
still damp from the rain, around a slim finger. "Depends."

"On what?" I asked cautiously.

"On how interested you are."

"Do I seem that bored?

After sucking in her cheeks, she answered, "No. But I'm
doing all the talking. This is my story and I'm being pretty
generous. What do I get back?"

Harry seemed to jump out of his chair. "Shit!" He glared at
Janice for a second and asked, "Where's another ashtray?"

Wide open, her eyes redefined "emerald". She swallowed. "On the kitchen counter, Harry," she said, abashed. Once he had gone out of the room, she whispered to herself, "Wow." To me, she said, "He's a good guy."

"Yes."

"Why is he mad at me?"

It was the first mark of vulnerability on her. Up to that point she had been very wise, in command, omniscient.

"He says 'shit' a lot," I said.

"It's expressive enough." Her gaze dropped from me for a moment.

"Harry's been jumpy for a whole year, Miss Simmons. And you, you're a reporter and you're good. Harry used to be better. Much better," I echoed.

"Oh, I know." She seemed to know more about it than I did. "Much, much better." She laughed lightly. "A verbal tick. I have to watch that one on camera, too."

"It could be 'shit.'"

"Wouldn't that get me promoted?"

"Your face will get you promoted." Trust Harry to get us back on the track.

"Thanks a lot, Harry,"Janice Simmons said, conceding the point. Her lips pursed and her eyes dimmed. "Shall I go on? Or just sit here looking pretty for you two?"

"Can you do both?" I asked.

"Just Tell him about Hiller," Harry ordered, still cranky.

"Hiller insists first of all that he didn't say anything. He claims the whole thing didn't happen," she continued. "Mrs. Purcil, on the other hand doesn't doubt for a moment that she heard his voice. She's older than Miss Wycick but both her hearing and her mind are much, much better."

"Did you test her hearing?"

"That would have crossed a line, don't you think?"

"I don't want to bother if you did."

Her nose wrinkled. "Let's say, I talked to her an extra three times on the party-line phone..."

"...you liked her so much."

After a bite of her lip she went on. "Mrs. Purcil says that Tony Hiller had quite a bit to say about Harold Winter and none of it was complimentary. Winter coldly—it's funny how often that kind of association came up—interrupted him with the news that he had uncovered Hiller's embezzlement of over $100,000 from Winter National."

"The embezzlement," I broke in, "came to his attention because of the robbery."

She nodded. "Winter personally ran a special computer check and the books didn't square. That kind of check doesn't usually take place until the routine audit due in September, so Hiller was caught short."

"Hiller said he didn't care that he had been discovered. He had a plan. So he laid it out for everyone to hear." She thought that was funny. "It was very melodramatic of him. He was going to kill Winter, which he said was just as well for everyone concerned. With Winter dead, the embezzlement would remain a secret until Hiller could steal away. In the meantime, he would throw suspicion onto some bum who had been hanging around town for a couple weeks—who was suspicious enough already in a place like Huntington."

"All Hiller figured he had to do was fake a story about being tied up in his own basement by this handy tramp and let the police draw their own conclusions."

"And this tramp is the 'old, gray man?'" I asked.

With a sharp breath, Janice rose from the couch and deliberately caressed one of her plants, the one that had bothered Harry. "That was her description," she said. "Diana Winter's. 'A little, old, gray man.' A little girl's description of a stranger out of place in her small town." She bent closer to the plant, talking to it instead of me. "A stranger in a strange town; the most conspicuous of God's creatures."

An annoying stillness filled the room. Janice had her plant and Harry had something, too, something in the distance behind her. Whatever was going on, it did not include me, so I broke it up. "What happened to the little old gray man?"

"Gone," was all she said. Then she stood up, with a graceful curve to her back. "Just like that, you can disappear. He'd been in Huntington for two weeks and then..." She swept the air heavily with her hand. "I looked for him. Christ, I looked for him."

"And then," she added, "They lost interest." She turned to explain.

"My first story here, my first real story! And I was way ahead of everybody! The minute Hiller was committed, they pulled me off it. Just like that. To do some political puff piece on our peanut farmer..."

"Who may be our next President." Harry finished.

"A puff piece on Jimmy Carter?"

"A politician who won't lie?" she asked. "Please."

Harry grunted. "After Nixon, it's a good pitch."

"Maybe, but I could have killed someone myself. I almost quit." She laughed before correcting herself. "Hell, I did quit. Didn't I, Harry?"

An idea filtered through the confusion. Janice Simmons, the gem of WPPA, had bolted over the station's handling of the Hiller story. They had taken it away from her. They had taken something very important to her and casually dropped it in the garbage.

It had been a mistake. Carl Thomas, WPPA's news director and an old friend of Harry Blair, had made the mistake and probably had done what he usually did when he goofed up. He took his fiery star to a man who knew reporting from obit to byline, from passion to drudgery, to a man who desperately needed contact with his old life.

I let out my conclusion. "And that's when you met Harry Blair."

Her eyes drew widely defiant. "Yes.

Harry slumped in the chair, staring through her. He wore a look that told me there was more to it than that, more to him, more to her. Between the two of them, they had made a fine fool out of Casey Carmichael.

I laughed. "You've done some good work for this town, Blair, but I think you may have topped it all." To her, I said, "I'm glad you stayed around. I'm going to take advantage of that, of you, if you'll let me. I'm lucky I found you. You saw things when they were fresh. I won't."

Looking me over, twice, she asked, "How can I resist?" A note of suspicion entered her voice. "And if you find anything new, I'll take advantage of you. Deal?"

There was no point in being coy. Not with this one. "What's your number?"

She jotted it down on a small phone pad. Slipping the paper inside my shirt pocket, she almost whispered, "Don't lose that. It's unlisted and you won't get it again."

I nudged Blair out of his state. "Let's go.

We said good-byes, but Janice led us to the narrow elevator. There was something on her mind and she allowed me to see it. She waited until we were inside the elevator

"Casey," she said. "Diana Winter is a snake. Watch her."

The doors slid in front of her face before I could think of anything to say. The elevator hummed slowly down all three floors before either Harry or I spoke.

"Wow."

"Yeah, but who says that?"

"Me. As of now."

Harry grimaced. "Don't be afraid to use her, Case," he said. "But she'll use back."

There was more to that, but Harry lit up a Winston and walked off toward his car with it. I watched him get in and maneuver out of the tight space like he was used to it.

The rain had started again, but wasn't too hard. Not hard enough to think about.

Chapter Four

The next morning I rented a car. Renting simplifies my expense account which Fred Tindale assures me is important. Besides that, my 1968 Buick went through Arab oil faster than beer at a Steeler tail-gate party. The car I got was a sippier Granada with enough room in the back to accommodate forty winks in a pinch.

Cath sounded relieved that I would be out of Fred's hair, and wallet, for a couple days and promised to take good messages. When I mentioned the name Janice Simmons, she breathed in loud enough for me to hear.

"Keep that to yourself, Cath," I said.

Her voice quivered over the phone. "How did you get to know her, Carmichael?"

"Not very well," was my response. "Well enough to know that everything she says is important. Exact words, Okay?"

"Okay."

Annoyance tried to bubble to the surface after I hung up. Cath didn't think I was good enough to know someone like Janice Simmons. To Cath Mays, I was a photo-copy of the lowlifes she had known as a kid on the South Side. Janice Simmons, princess that she was, surely had something better to do than call Casey Carmichael.

Which may have been true, but who was Cathy Mays, ex-Mayszech, to say so?

Once on the highway, I forgot all about my resentment. Spring had turned her other face my way and the sunshine felt good. Not the warmth of it—it was still too early in April for that—but the brightness.

Western Pennsylvania is a joy to drive in a fine spring day. The rolling countryside hugs you close as you head north. The green of farmlands and intermittent woods remind you of how you could live weren't for the city. Cow instead of buses, horses instead horses asses to keep you company as you go.

My thoughts drifted as the Granada sped through the country, replaying my favorite versions of the previous evening. Obviously suffering spring-inspired euphoria, I even speculated what the nights to come might bring if I could just keep Janice Simmons interested.

It had been a long time, I thought, wandering into the past.

The hell with that. I swung my attention to the task ahead.

Not many miles off, slightly west of Oil City, lay the town of Huntington, Pennsylvania. By next week, I would have made that town my past, too. Diana Winter was there, waiting for me. She would want me to grind my heels into dust to soothe her conscience. That was fair enough. What made it seem unfair, I suppose, was that for her it would work. And that she could so easily afford it.

All I could think of, shamelessly, was how I could drag it all out. But not for the money.

Money, the Winter's had. They had their own and banked everyone else's in the area. They had started small. Clarence Winter graduated from the Huntington oil fields to found Winter Coal, Oil and Feed Bank. With the help of the local baron, Wilbur Huntington, the bank made good.

As Wilbur Huntington build Venango County into his own private fiefdom, Clarence Winter and his bank tagged along. That comfortable alliance lasted only as long as Clarence ran the operation: The sole surviving son of that successful first generation banker, Harold Winter had ambitions that did not include friendship with his Huntington equivalent, Willard.

It had taken Harold Winter forty years, but he finally eclipsed Willard Huntington. Now it was his Winterbank, Inc., that ruled over northwestern Pennsylvania. Until August of 1975, Harold Winter was unquestionably what he had set out to become. He was king of the kingdom.

At its zenith, however, the house of Winter was pretty damn empty. Harold Winter had had only three children, of which only Diana lived in the state. Tom and Bob Winter had long since escaped. And as for Diana, she had less interest in banking than a panhandler in Market Square.

So Harold Winter's murder looked like the end of the line for more than just Harold Winter.

His town, still named after Wilbur Huntington, was much cleaner and smaller than I had expected. Main street, as it was inventively tagged, contained all of the businesses in town, including the massive old bank. The Winter National Building, as a matter of fact, divided the place into two sections. To the south lay older buildings, struggling businesses and rundown homes. To the north of the bank, I could see the busy shops, the renovated houses.

As the Granada made its way toward the bank, it drew the outright scrutiny of anyone on the street or near a window. I felt like some strange animal wandering too close to their campfire. The bold glares said "you're an outsider, get used to it."

I grinned back it a couple of them. I was a leg up. I was already used to it.

The inside of Winter National Bank would make anyone shiver. The marble walls and the high dome probably had meant grandeur in past ages, but they left me cold.

The marble didn't stop with the walls. It ran over to an island of teller windows and up to the bars. Desks of lesser bank officers ringed the customer area, guarding access to oak-doored offices.

As I stood it the door taking in the view, a uniformed guard looked me over. Amateurish, but thorough. I recalled Janice Simmons' remark about him. He didn't look quite stupid or blind enough to miss a stocking-masked customer strolling past him with a shotgun.

"My name's Carmichael," I let him know. "I'd like to see Miss Winter."

The magic of my name brought a huge grin to his face. He became visibly excited just talking to me. "Oh, yes, Mr. Carmichael," he enthused. "Miss Winter is expecting you."

He pointed out the office in which I'd find her and watched me walk over to the secretary sitting outside the door. It made my stomach tighten to be so damned obvious, even if it were only with an aging bank guard in Huntington, Pennsylvania.

Before I could speak to the secretary, Diana Winter opened her door. She looked prettier than the last time I had seen her. She was done up with a care that worried me.

"Mr. Carmichael," she said, with her cheery smile. "I hope your drive was pleasant."

"Passable," I replied following her into the office. Once the door was closed, I demanded, "Exactly what the hell did you tell that guard?"

Surprise flashed across her smooth, white skin. "What do you mean?"

"He acted like I owned a circus."

She flushed. "I'm sorry," she said. "I only told him that you were a private detective. He thought that was wonderful."

"He should try it sometime." People got the screwiest ideas in springtime. "Let's keep my profile a little lower, okay?"

"I'm not ashamed of you," she said defiantly.

"Thanks. Try not to be so proud of me."

The defiance evaporated. Her head bowed a little. "I'm sorry, Mr. Carmichael. I suppose I was silly to hire you in the first place."

She looked up at me, for forgiveness, I guess. She made me feel like what Cath Mays thought I was. "That's all right, Miss Winter. You do what you want with me," I told her. "But you're new at this, so take my advice."

Eagerly, she nodded.

"The less obvious I am the better."

The girl came over to me, buoyant again. Her face had a youthful transparency that advertised the mercurial shifts of mood. Somewhere in there Janice Simmons had seen a snake. I couldn't and I knew snakes.

"I have a little surprise for you," she said cheerfully. "We can see Tony, if we go right now."

That was a big surprise. I had more or less resigned myself to groping about without any help from Hiller, at least at the beginning. Hiller was still locked in a mental ward awaiting his hearing. The DA would want him surrounded by the right kind of people and I had assumed I wouldn't qualify.

"Would you like that?" she asked uncertainly.

"If you can arrange that, Miss Winter, you could save yourself some money."

She recoiled. "Oh, no! That's not important!"

I studied her as she got her things together. To her the money itself was not important. The fact that she was finally spending it, that was important.

~ ~ ~

The Venango County Hospital had taken all the land it had wanted to build its psychiatric wing. The wing itself was relatively small, but the grounds encouraged the sane to re-think their position. Lawns, trees, gardens and patios combined to sell crazy as smart.

Inside, appearances were more normal. They hadn't disguised the hospital on the interior. The halls were clean and straight, the people neatly dressed in uniforms. Even the smell, while less distinct in this wing, said 'hospital.'

Diana Winter and I did not have to wait for our audience with Tony Hiller's doctor. Hanna Kish was a handsome woman in her well tailored white jacket and close-cropped hair. The serious intensity of her fair, square face reminded me that she was under thirty-five.

She ushered us off the floor and into an ante-chamber adjacent to her office. "How do you do, Mr. Carmichael," she said warmly. "Are you a friend of Tony's?"

Diana intercepted the question. "They went to school together."

Dr. Kish shot an annoyed glance at Diana and then said to me, "That's nice. Tony doesn't seem to have many friends."

"Can we see him now?" Diana snapped. "You said we could."

"Unfortunately, Miss Winter, I was instructed to tell you that," Dr. Kish retorted. "I would never have done, otherwise. You will upset him."

Obviously, Diana had used her influence to get us our visit. To avoid more hostility, I decided to level with the tall, stern doctor. "Listen, Dr. Kish," I explained. "Miss Winter didn't tell you that I am a private investigator. I'm trying to dig up something to support his case."

Disgust took over Dr. Kish's frown. "That explains it, then," she said, glaring at Diana. "Mr. Carmichael, I can't tell you how sorry I am to hear that."

"What if he's telling the truth?"

Her brow furrowed with disappointment, so she must have thought I looked passably intelligent before that comment. "I have worked very hard on Tony, Mr. Carmichael. He has finally begun to accept reality after almost nine months. I beg you not to jeopardize that."

There was an off note to her concern. It was in her eyes and she knew it. Away it went.

I hoped she was on Hiller's side. It sounded as if he needed someone. "Doc, I don't see the bonus in moving Tony from this garden to a place with thugs and concrete on all sides."

After uttering an unconvinced "All right," Dr. Kish took us to Hiller's room. She glanced through the small window in the door, her face troubled. Diana went up on her tiptoes to see over Dr. Kish's shoulder. We all went in together.

Tony Hiller stood at the rear window of his room, gazing out over the grounds. He had very broad shoulders and the remnants of a strong body. He was bent forward the way older people sometimes bend forward. Not dowager's hump, but a deep slump. His hair had broad streaks of gray running through the shock of midnight brown bristles.

Hanna Kish's voice became soft and gentle. "Tony," she said, moving up behind him. "You have some visitors."

Hiller's shoulders heaved as he snorted at the window. "Already," he said without the tone of bitterness I'd expected.

Diana spoke cheerfully. "Hi, Tony."

That sound made his head jerk up and he spun around. Dark circles framed his slightly wild eyes. His face had lines in a youthful skin that looked scary. "What are you doing here, Diana?"

The hard tone of his voice arrested her forward progress, dimmed her expression. The smile weakened and her voice broke. "Tony," she said. "Please don't be angry with me. I tried to come several times, but Dr. Kish didn't want me to see you."

A breath escaped Hanna Kish's body and she excused herself. She went through the door with haste and force. The door swung for a time, in memory of her.

Diana advanced toward Tony once Dr. Kish was gone. Her voice added a note of apology. "She said it would set you back, Tony. I was afraid."

Her fiancé unclenched his teeth and waved his head from one side to the other. "Yeah, I guess so," he said. "I understand."

By that time, Diana had her hand on his. "I brought someone to see you. His name is Carmichael and he is a detective."

"A detective?" he asked. "Why?"

I did the answering. "Because Miss Winter here, seems to think that you didn't make everything up."

"Didn't I?" he asked skeptically. "I must have."

"I'd like to talk about that. How about you?"

Hiller shrugged helplessly. "Sure."

I sent Diana Winter out of the room. She did not have the effect on him that I had anticipated. She made him nervous and unhappy. Instead of encouraging him to tell his story, she would only retard him. Besides she was a symbol of both sides of the messy business and that would not help.

When she had gone, Hiller began to speak spontaneously. "She hasn't been here before, Mr. Carmichael," he said. "I don't blame her, but..."

"Mind if I sit, Hiller?"

He grinned, shaking his head. "I haven't been called that for ages. Not since I moved in here. It's always 'Tony' or 'Mr. Hiller.'"

"A little patronizing?"

"God, I'll say it is. I suppose they're trying to be nice."

"Were you lying, Hiller? Before, I mean."

Hiller's hands ran over his face hard. "I didn't think so at the time. Dr. Kish says I wasn't. Not lying at least. She said I had some kind of breakdown."

Plainly part of his story had been sealed off by this time. All of it would be soon. I was damn lucky to be there before that happened. "Tell it to me."

He looked frightened, like a kid asked to steal cookies. "I'm not supposed to, Mr. Carmichael."

"They'll make an exception."

A sly smile stole across his tired mouth. "Okay. But I'll blame you."

"Fine," I agreed. "That's how it works best."

The decimated young man took a chair and turned it around. He settled against the back of the chair and rested his chin on his arms, again, just like a kid.

"First the bank was robbed," he began. "That was bad enough. Everyone was going crazy. 'Where was I?' 'How did

I miss it?'" He shrugged. "Even I have to eat. No one was impressed. It seems that I should have stopped it."

"Or at least suffered through it," I suggested.

"Exactly. I was the President of the bank and that made me different." His eyes twinkled as he spoke. "It was a joke. Me being President. I'm only twenty-nine. Why should I be president? Mr. Winter had plans for me."

"That's nice."

"Shit," he retorted. "All I wanted was to have my own gas station." The memory amused him. "That's all. Just a lousy little four pump station. I worked for years for a guy name Joe Kawoski in Huntington. That gas station you pass as you come into town from the south?"

"Yeah." I remembered the station. It had a couple of old Mobil pumps, with broken glass and stained plywood as decoration.

"But, Mr. Winter up and decided one day that I should be a banker," Hiller went on. "Just like that. The next thing I know, I'm on my way to college. I didn't mind. College sounded like fun. It was, too."

"It's supposed to be," I said. Not my experience, but maybe it could be.

"Then business school and back to Huntington and the bank. That was six years ago. And now I'm president. Or I was."

The guy was rambling. There was no telling when Hanna Kish would come roaring through the door to protect her charge, or whatever he was to her. "Let's get back to August."

"August," he repeated thoughtfully. "Oh, August. August 1st, I became president of the bank. Mr. Winter remained CEO of Winterbank, the holding company. He said he was getting ready for state-wide action and wanted out of operations. I said okay, but I knew everyone would hate me. And they did, too. Everyone resented me. I didn't blame them," he said quietly. "I remember once Joe brought another joe in ahead of me at the station—his name was actually Joe, too—Anyway, it really bothered me. Of course, I was part-time."

"Then," he said, "Then, all hell broke loose. The robbery. And that same night I was supposed to meet with that stranger. He said he had information on the robbery. I never saw him. The next thing I knew the police came and took me out of my own basement to the station and read me my rights."

"That's it?" It was a flimsy damn line to try at this stage of the play. "Nothing else?"

His eyes became terrified as they bore into me. "Honest to God, Mr. Carmichael, that is the only thing I remembered."

"Remembered?"

"At the time."

"What about now?" Tony was holding something back. Maybe everything. "Do you remember more now?"

"Dr. Kish has helped me remember more," he explained. "Now, I kind of remember going to Winter's house and argu-ing with him about something."

"Embezzlement?"

A strange, uncertain look of shame came over his face. "I guess so."

My stomach began to act up. A knot twisted it tightly until I had to stand up. "What else?"

"I might have been carrying a gun," he added.

"Might have?" I stared out the window.

His body shook. "Must have. I'm sorry."

The grounds of the psychiatric wing looked pleasant from the window. Definitely a place you'd want to be, try to be.

"Let's get back to your... fabrication," I said, selecting my term carefully. "Who was the stranger?"

"I'd like to forget it, Mr. Carmichael."

"Sure, Tony. Only this one question," I said reassuringly.

Waving back and forth in capitulation, he said his last few words to me. "It was that old man that had been hanging around town. I hadn't seen him before. He called and said he

could tell me something about the robbery. To meet him behind my house. I did wait there for him, I know that. For
sure."

Through the glass in the door, Hiller was staring at Dr.
Hannah Kish. He didn't say another word.

I put my hand on his shoulder before I went out. It gave
way and he almost fell out of the chair. Only my leg held him
up. The touch of his body against me sickened me. I've felt
guys go that limp before and they didn't end well.

It took all my strength to return him to an upright position
before I could leave. Dr. Kish viewed the scene from her post
in the hall. Her glowering didn't help any.

We faced off in the hallway. Hate shone vividly in her clear
brown eyes. The muscles in her jaw worked overtime to
maintain her stern professional expression. I could see the
whiteness of her knuckles as her hand clenched a clip board.

"Are you satisfied, Mr. Carmichael?" she said, with effort.

Annoyed, I returned her stare. "As a matter of fact, Dr. Kish,
I am," I said. "He's all yours now." I turned on my heel and
headed for the end of the hall where Diana Winter stood
waiting, but Dr. Kish caught my arm.

"At least, I tried to help him," she said through her teeth,
"when he needed it."

"Maybe you'll get to keep him."

~ ~ ~

Since Venango County Hospital was on the other side of
Oil City, the drive back to Huntington took a while. Because
I didn't feel like talking, it seemed to take forever. I let Diana
Winter run the conversation. I listened, but not much.

She exhausted her spleen on Hanna Kish. Most of it was
unimportant and the rest did not complicate my life, so I let
her go on about it. That Dr. Kish was married and childless,
"probably barren", as Diana put it, may have had some bear-

ing on her attachment to Hiller, but her motives were unimportant. She had compromised Hiller's memory. For that, she could have a slice of my spleen, too.

The remainder of the trip Diana passed by apologizing, at length, to me for not visiting her fiancée. Pressure had been very strong, she said, to dump Hiller. He was, after all, the murderer of her father and even though they had not gotten along well lately, well, he was her father. And her brothers were angry with her.

Only our arrival back in familiar territory calmed her down. We checked at the bank for someone else she wanted me to see, but found that he had gone to "the house" to look for Diana. Whoever it was shared his last name with the town. I could hardly wait.

The Winter house proved to be a magnificent old frame mansion hidden away outside of the town. Like most estates, this one had a wall around it, but it was a low stone job, not designed to hide anything from anyone. The forest of trees took care of that.

The drive wound through the trees like a country road, rambling over a couple small hills in the process. It was not paved with anything, which would have ruined the effect. I expected a palace at the end of the trip.

Splendor is a word that combines expense and taste, and it applied to the Winter's house. It was modest in size compared to some places I've seen, but it could easily have handled the five members of the Winter family, and any attendants they needed. The fact that it was made of wood impressed me. All we see in Pittsburgh is brick, so wood always comes across as the richer material. Especially when applies as well as at the Winter place.

We pulled up in front of the door and Diana hopped out. She hurried me out of my seat and into the foyer. Her impatience moved her from one side of the hall to the other, as she glanced into each of the rooms opening off it.

Finally, she called, "Lewis! Are you here?"

"Lewis Huntington?" I asked. The scion of her father's rival, in her house? It seemed queer when I thought about it.

"Of course," she replied not looking in my direction. "Lewis!"

A thin, handsome fellow with sandy hair wandered out of one of the rooms. "Diana," he said reprovingly, "Your voice carries rather too well."

Diana bounded over to him and dragged him the four feet over to me. It looked ridiculous. "Mr. Carmichael, this is Lewis."

The display did not embarrass him. He smiled warmly at Diana, hugging her shoulder lightly.

I looked him over and he let me. "Mr Huntington." He looked too much at home in the Winter house for my liking. If I had gleaned one thing from my research, it was that the Winter's and the Huntington's had been feuding for years. About seventy-five of them.

"How do you do, Mr. Carmichael?" he said with a reduced, less warm smile. He offered me his hand which proved solid and dry. "Diana has told me a little about you. You're the detective?"

"I'm not that exclusive." It came out unexpectedly brusque.

Huntington smiled at some internal joke. Maybe city manners amused him. "With Diana, you will be. She is very loyal. Speaking of loyalty, did you talk to Tony?"

"Yes."

"And," Diana interjected with scorn, "his 'nurse,' Hanna."

Raising an elegant finger, Huntington scolded her. "Hanna is, as you know perfectly well, my dear, is a doctor. And, despite her sharp dislike of you, a very good one. Tony is lucky to have someone in her class."

Diana was pouting, so I asked Lewis, "How's that?"

His eyes studied me for a moment before he spoke again. "Come into the living room, Mr. Carmichael. You can grill me there."

"Lewis!" Diana cried.

"Mr. Carmichael wants to ask me some questions, Diana," he explained. "And I want to be comfortable."

With that, Huntington spun about and led us to the living room. He moved lithely, almost precisely, proceeding to a bar in the dining room to fix us all a drink. "Do you drink bourbon, Mr. Carmichael? Don't all detectives drink bourbon neat?"

"Would ice disappoint?"

"Another myth dashed," he said turning back to the bar.

Diana settled in an overstuffed chair that swallowed half of her. "Lewis is staying here," she explained without a touch of irony, "This house is very lonely now."

"Sure," I replied. "That's nice of Mr. Huntington."

Lewis dropped her drink off first, then mine. "That is practical of Mr. Huntington," he corrected. "You see, Mr. Carmichael, the rivalry has declined in our generation, along with Huntington wealth and pride. Conservatism, when it overreacts, means disaster in the financial world. My grandfather finally joined the conglomerate rage in 1968. By 1970, he was out of them—and our money. It killed him, luckily."

"Lewis!" Diana objected. "That is terrible."

"Terrible, Diana, but true."

Some people you dislike instantly. Lewis Huntington was working hard at it. "Tell me about Hanna Kish?" I asked.

His arm lay along the back of Diana's chair, just touching her, as he sat on the arm. "Hanna is an excellent psychiatrist. Terrific credentials, even better performance. No one could have taken better care of Tony."

Diana disagreed with a "Phtt!"

"If he was sick before," I said, "he's well now."

Carefully modulated interest lifted both of Huntington's eyebrows. "Really? Don't you think he was? Before?"

"Do you?"

He finally rose from his awkward position and stood over me. "His story, as Tony told it to me," he said, "was pure bullshit. He couldn't have made it up."

The surprise should have knocked me over. Instead, it just made me choke on my drink.

"Lewis suggested I get a detective," Diana added.

"Why, Mr. Huntington?" I asked once I'd recovered. "No one else believes him."

Huntington sat down across from me. His smile made me nervous. "You do."

Diana's wide eyes swung over to me. "You do?"

The scrutiny of the two of them made me uneasy, but I had it with a healthy sip of my bourbon. "Why not? Hiller does. Or did."

"You are very observant, Mr. Carmichael. Very observant," Huntington congratulated me. "That is, of course, why they put him where they did. At least, it kept him out of jail."

"Poor Tony," Diana said mournfully. "Will he have to go to jail?"

"Mr. Carmichael?" Huntington asked, deferring, no doubt, to superior expertise.

"With the confession he will gladly give the police," I said, "yes, he will go to jail."

Drawing the words out, Huntington asked, "Suppose the son-of-a-bitch is innocent, what would explain what happened."

"Nothing," I replied.

He nodded unhappily. "That's my problem, too."

"Tony and Lewis are old friends," Diana said as if to explain.

"And rivals, Diana," Lewis added. "Once we fought over this delightful little prize. We were younger then."

I tossed out my own question to Diana. "Before or after your engagement?"

She flushed.

Her ex-fiancé smiled. Resigned, not pleased. "Oh, that. Before. Years before." He gave me a stern look. "That's all over now, Mr. Carmichael. I haven't bothered either of them for a long time."

"Self-exile," Diana called it.

"Where are you living now, Huntington?"

His gesture swept in the whole place. "Here."

"Permanently?"

He sucked in his drink and grinned. "No. I've taken up with a regional theater group in Buffalo for the time being," he said. "I'm not very stable, you see."

"You're an actor?" I asked. Another reason to dislike him, perhaps.

He allowed himself a shrug. "I tried to be. But, I wasn't very good. I handle business matters, stage design, make-up, lighting. Even the curtain in a pinch. And we usually are. It's a small company, Mr. Carmichael." His embarrassment made him more likable than I would have thought possible.

I tried to sound understanding. "Sounds rough."

"Oh, it is," he replied, enthusiasm coloring his voice. He backed it down. "But, for a guy like me, it's more rewarding than most things. It's the only thing I've ever really liked. Besides Diana, of course." He stroked her head.

"He ran away to join the circus," Diana retorted, shaking his hand away.

I let the bourbon influence me. "Maybe we all should, Miss Winter."

"Men," she commented. "You are all ridiculous."

Huntington didn't look at her, staring at me instead. "Perhaps we are at that," he said.

Chapter Five

I left Diana Winter and Lewis Huntington doing with one another whatever they were doing and drove to Franklin. It seemed like an excellent time to steal some ideas from the Venango County people who handled the Hiller case. One phone call to the Detective Bureau got me an appointment with Lindsay McGuiness, its Chief.

McGuiness' office in the county courthouse was unadorned and uncomfortable, as if he didn't want anyone to relax. It was small enough to remind me of my own place, so I didn't work on me.

"Carmichael?" he asked rhetorically. "Have you ever been up here before?"

"Once," I said. "For fishing."

The big teeth all showed. "What is it you're doing here now?"

"I'm getting paid."

That made him laugh. McGuiness put one foot up against his desk. "Listen, Mr. Carmichael," he said, "I know why you're here. I know all about you. My cousin Lewis checked it out with me first?"

All I needed was to fight across family lines. It's too damn easy to get all tangled up. "You're cousins?"

"Second cousins, yeah. But don't let that worry you," he assured me. "I can't stand Lewis. Nobody can."

His big head went back and forth. "I mean, in the family. And, I'd better keep it that way."

I shrugged.

He blew a gale of warm air out of his mouth and put his second size thirteen on the desk. "So, you want to help Hiller?"

"It's what I'm being paid for," I stated.

"Good," he responded. "Don't get too wrapped up in it. Some people did and it didn't help."

"Meaning?"

McGuiness took his time in answering. He wanted to know what I knew before he said anything.

I waited him out.

"Meaning me, I suppose," he admitted finally. "I believed Tony at first. I've known him a long time, Carmichael. Good solid kid, loyal to a fault..." He paused carefully and decided not to elaborate. "Never much of a problem for anyone. A pretty simple guy. Not like the rest of them over in Huntington." The Chief shook his head in disgust. "Corruption comes in a lot of ways, I guess."

His face was too big to be dishonest, too plain to hide a lie. The expression he wore indicated that the Hiller case disturbed him and that he wanted it out of his system.

"What changed your mind about Hiller, Chief?" I asked.

"Call me Lin, will you?" he asked. "I'm big enough, so it doesn't bother me." He stretched his thick arms behind his head. "Hiller went through three polygraph tests like a priest. There was no question. Then the stories started coming in." He stopped abruptly.

"Go Ahead."

The subject made him nervous. He countered the tendency by becoming more relaxed. His tie loosened, he continued. "First, the Party-Line business. That didn't appeal to me at the beginning. Too hokey, But when we looked over the books at Winter National I started to change my mind."

The point intrigued me. I know as much about money as I had in the bank. Embezzlement was a TV word to me, but I knew that one way or the other it was a key to Hiller's problem. "Tell me about that part."

"I'm no accountant or anything, Carmichael," McGuiness warned me. "But what I know is this. Someone had been fiddling with those books. The entries—debits credits, whatever—didn't square for about two dozen large, out-of-state accounts."

"Meaning?"

"About a hundred grand had evaporated," he explained. "We checked Tony's safe deposit box and found a key to another box registered in a false name. In that second box, we found about twenty-three thousand bucks in cash. That's twenty-two more G's than he should have had."

Any more would have been wasted on me. "What did Hiller say?"

"Denied it. Flat out. He said he didn't know what we were talking about. That was enough for me," McGuiness replied. "No one else could have done it. But the way he lied?" He shrugged.

"So when people started calling him nuts, you bought it?"

He gave me a queer look. "Yeah. But it doesn't feel right, Carmichael. You know what I mean?"

I did, but I didn't say so. "Tell me about this mysterious old stranger everyone's talking about."

He rubbed his chin and thought for a minute. "The little old, gray man."

"Right. Who was he? Where did he come from?"

He looked me straight in the eye. "We don't know."

"Not anything?"

"Oh, sure," he said. "Like, he's disappeared without a trace. Like, he appeared from out of nowhere."

I could visualize a ghost of a man carrying a sack of Winter National bank money. "Was he an accomplice?"

"On the embezzlement? Not likely. We do figure he could have been in on the Winter National robbery but since that was what screwed Hiller up, I don't see them working together." McGuiness was not at all satisfied. "I don't know."

"Who can give me more on the embezzlement bit?" I asked, trying to find a rabbit hole somewhere that would fit a little old man.

"Jack Pazinsky," he suggested. "Pazinsky helped me a lot. He's a smart guy, been with the Winter National a long time. He knows it inside out and back again. Only one problem."

"Really?"

"He hated Hiller's guts."

That reminded me of what Hiller had said. "What about the rest of the crew?"

McGuiness nodded his head. "Resentment is the word most often used. Hiller wasn't a bad guy. You couldn't really dislike him. But Winter moved him up so fast and—well, what would you think?"

My mind began to hum along nicely. "I'd hate his guts."

"Right,"

"Enough to set him up," I added flatly.

McGuiness jerked out of his chair. "What?"

"I'd love to make him look like a crook," I explained.

The Venango County Detective Chief said nothing as he paced around the room. Like most good cops he thought better on his feet than on his rear. He began to nod his head like a huge chicken as he walked. I waited.

"Yeah," he said. "A frame. It's possible."

"Not likely," I said. I hadn't even considered it before.

"No," he agreed, cheerfully. "But worth a look."

I waited for him to tell me to keep my nose out of the case, while he looked into it. Cops like to preserve their territory.

"Listen, Carmichael," he said, his voice suddenly lower. "I've got a proposition for you. You see, I'm supposed to be finished with this case. Winter's people in the DA's office didn't like my attitude in the first place. I can't reopen it now, or they'll howl. You do what you can and I'll help, on the sly, mind you. And I'll keep my people off your back. Not that their likely to bug you, but you never know."

My day was full of annoying surprises. Everyone insisted on acting contrary to expectations. The whole business was new to me, I suppose, and had me off balance. I began to yearn for a simple in-town adultery case. "You've got a deal, Lin."

"Just keep me informed on what you're up to," he asked.

"Okay," I agreed. "But don't tell your cousin." It came out involuntarily.

McGuiness seemed repelled by the thought. "Lewis? Christ, I can't stand to talk to him on the phone."

"I'll keep in touch," I said, heading for the door. I could decide later if I would.

~ ~ ~

The phone in the courthouse lobby got me Cath Mays. She sounded excited, in her way, so I knew that Janice Simmons had called. Cath kept the insults to two. She called me a jerk and she said I was lucky that she even would speak to me. The first I understood the second eluded me.

"Because," Cath declared, "you didn't tell me she was coming here."

I would have dropped the phone but it was my 85 cents. "Because... she wasn't."

"She was here half an hour ago." Cath was now shouting into the phone. "I looked terrible."

My brain worked for a reason. Not about Cath. She always looked the same. "As if."

Cath slammed the receiver down on my compliment. I didn't dare call back. I only had a dime left and the place had pretty much closed up. Cath never accepted my collect calls, not even when Fred told her to. And if she thought I was being sarcastic...

My wallet held Janice Simmon's number, so I tried that one.

After the operator did her bit, I heard someone yell into the background, "Hey, Sim, it's some clown called Carmichael! Collect."

No reply made it through the wire, but the voice returned and said, "Miss Simmons is tied up right now. May I take a message?"

I steamed for a minute and said, "Yes. Tell her that if she wants a key, she can reach me at City Hotel in Huntington."

The voice seemed skeptical. "Got it."

With my thanks the operator cut the line. Janice Simmons had no business at my office. I mean no interesting business. She could have the place rent free with everything in it, as far as I was concerned, but I wanted to be there so she wouldn't be bored. I didn't keep much in the way of records. If the IRS audits me, Fred says, I'm cooked.

It didn't matter. Besides, I still had my dime. I used it to call Diana Winter at home.

"Oh, Mr. Carmichael," she enthused, a little sloshed. "Are you coming over for dinner?"

I hadn't planned on it and I said so.

She let out a whimper. "Please come, Casey," she pleaded.

My first name had become a rarity in the past several years, especially from a woman. It unsettled me at first. "I've got to check in at the hotel, Miss Winter," I demurred, restoring formality.

Diana's voice became firmer when she spoke next. "Mr. Carmichael, please come here first. It is important. To me, at least."

"That's good enough," I said. "I'll be there as soon as I can."

She sounded pleased again. "Good. I'll wait dinner for you."

"Thanks." With that I put the phone back where it belonged and headed for the door. I didn't get far.

A tiny, unattractive man grabbed my arm from behind. "Mr. Carmichael?"

My quick spin wrung him loose and cost him his balance. I watched him reel for about thirty seconds before he regained it.

"Yes," I said, unfriendly.

Steadied by one of the marble benches, the guy squared his little shoulders. His face had the scars of a tough childhood and the eyes of a tougher adulthood. I put his age at 50 plus. "I'm from the DA's office," he explained. "My name is Collins."

"Glad to meet you, Collins," I lied,

It picked up his spirits all the same. "Same here. I have a message for you. From the DA."

"Really?" They'd already gotten around McGuiness. I was dismayed by the speed with which I had become a hot local ticket.

"The DA," he went on, "wants to welcome you to Venango County personally. Could you see him tomorrow around 10:00?"

The welcome made me laugh. "This is a friendly County. I'd be happy to return the favor."

He shook my hand and started to leave. As if he had just remembered something, he suddenly stopped and turned half way back. "Oh, by the way," he said, "just ask for Harlan Collins,"

"Okay, Harlan."

He grinned in a dirty way. "Oh, no, Mr. Carmichael. I'm Jim, You'll want the DA himself. Harlan Winter Collins." He chuckled and said good-bye.

Chapter Six

By the time I reached the Winter house, six o'clock was a memory. My stomach growled and not just from hunger. It was punishing me for hazarding out of its routine. Something gnawing in there told me that I belonged in my city, tailing a depressed husband or a suburbanite's weed-selling kid. Simple, straight-forward stuff. You sit in your car outside some run-down motel—maybe a nice one for that matter, I've done that—all night, waiting. It's but at least you know what you're waiting for.

From time to time, you end up behind a guy all the way to Miami. It's happened, but not often. I once tailed a truck driver into South Carolina before he met his boss' wife. At that place called "South of the Border." They took a room and didn't budge all night. At 5:30 he came out and threatened to break my head open.

It happens, but it doesn't happen very often.

This Huntington was another matter. Diana Winter hired me for a conscience-soothing look around. That was a bit odd, but okay. But since I had hit town, things had taken so many funny turns that my stomach and I had begun to lose track. We'd been wondering all the way from Franklin to Winter's front door, which is probably where it all started.

The girl was waiting for me in the foyer. She had perched herself on the bottom two steps of the staircase, her hand supporting a forlorn face. She looked up from under brows that hung like low clouds over her eyes.

"Hi, Mr. Carmichael," she said, her voice unnaturally low.

"Hello," I replied.

"I have been waiting forever. Everyone has left." She rose slowly from the steps, as if she didn't see the point in getting up. "Even rotten Lewis."

The house sounded empty, the way only big houses can. Voices become lost, footsteps sound hollow. The curse of a big place is that when you're alone in it, you are lonely. Diana was anyway.

"What would you like for dinner, Mr. Carmichael," she asked with very hard emphasis on the "Mr." "We have everything, but I can only cook hamburgers." Every word moped along as she said it.

"Hamburgers are all I eat, Miss Winter."

Her mouth drooped further and she started for the kitchen, her feet pouting their way along. She had changed to shorts and a light blue blouse. Unlike the rest of her, her legs were thin, too thin for that rest of her. The ankles were narrow and the feet small.

She sort of turned sideways when she walked, first one side then the other. That was not her normal walk, I'd seen that. Usually she walked from the hip. But at the moment, she had taken to walking like a little girl.

I followed her into the kitchen. It was a huge room, designed for three or four people to use at once, probably in uniforms. The amount of equipment was staggering. Out of all of it, Diana chose a cast iron frying pan, wiped it off and put it on the eight burner range.

After she had taken the meat from the giant refrigerator, she asked me politely, "Will you fix me another drink, Mr. Carmichael?"

I nodded instead of answering, to avoid calling her Diana, which is what she wanted. She stared at me as I walked toward the door. I stared back. It didn't do me any good, because I felt her "Be Sorry for Me" routine working.

The liquor cabinet in the dining room took my mind off of her mournful, brown eyes. It contained the finest selection of alcohol I'd ever seen. The best scotches, bourbons, gins and liqueurs. I judged the contents to be worth $1,000 in their half-drained state. The thought of a wine cellar shook me up.

In the kitchen I heard the crackling of frying ground beef. My stomach jumped into my throat to remind me how little I had eaten in the past 48 hours. My only meal in that time came when Harry forced me on Janice Simmons and I barely remember that there was food. I took a swig of Rebel Yell, smuggled in from south of the Mason-Dixon line, to mollify my stomach and headed into the kitchen.

Diana hung over the frying pan like a morning headache. One of her efforts had ended up in the sink and another across the room. The two in the pan were too red to have been there long. "God! Where have you been?"

"Someone needed drink. I Set down her drink. "And I got you one, too."

"Oh."

"Diana," I said, surrendering. "Are you all right?"

She stared down into the pan as if the question were not dumb. "Of course,"

I went over to the hamburger at the base of the wall. It wasn't burned.

"Can I call you Casey?" she asked as I flopped the burger in the sink.

Even though it's not a good idea to get on a first name basis with female clients—at least not for me—I knew it was hopeless. "Sure."

She smiled at the hamburgers. "You have to keep calling me Diana," she said, "or I'll hit you with one of these."

"It's a nice name."

"Good." The meat stuck to the pan as she worked to turn the patties over. "What is it with these thing?"

I figured she was paying me well and I couldn't do worse. I took the spatula from her shaking hand. It wasn't easy, but I convinced the things to warm their other side.

"I'm not worth much, Casey," she said.

"Depends on the standard. Cooking hamburgers isn't mine."

For the first time since I had re-entered the kitchen she looked at me. She had the kind of eyes that always made you give in. They were sad and hopeful at the same time, assuring me that only I had the answer to her problem.

"Lewis was mean to me after you left," she said. "I made him leave. He went back to Buffalo."

Our dinner was ready and I put the meat on two plates. I found everything else I wanted in the refrigerator: Ketchup, rolls, potato salad and even cole slaw. "Were you planning a picnic?" I asked amazed.

"In a way," she replied. "I can't cook much and I sent the cook and all on a vacation. No, I guess I fired them."

"Why? This is a pretty big house for just you."

Diana nodded. "I hate it here, Casey. But what can I do? I don't have any place else to live and my brother Bob won't let me sell it until everything is settled in the estate."

We went into the dining room where I took off my coat. As we took a couple of places at the long, mahogany table, Diana deliberately ground her plate into the finish.

She laughed. "I'm afraid to move to Pittsburgh, which is what I should do. Or New York. But I don't know anybody." The thought bothered her. "Actually, I don't really know anybody here, either. When I came back here, I thought, well, this is where I belong. My friends are here. I found out that isn't true."

"Without Tony..." She sighed and went still for a moment. It didn't keep. "I don't have a single friend. I had to beg Lewis to come back. That didn't work out so well, so I tried to hire one."

"Me."

"Well..." The flush of embarrassment came and went. "But, really, I had to. I failed Tony. I wouldn't have thought I could... I've thought so much about it... You probably don't believe me."

"I probably do."

That brought a relieved smile. "I was a mess. One night Lewis got so tired of my moaning, he told me to hire a detective and forget it."

"And so you did."

Silence was her answer. The hamburger, at least wouldn't make her cry. She chomped on it with a vengeance.

"A lot of people do, you know," I told her. "I get hired to do what is too hard or too painful for the client to do himself, or herself. That's natural."

She smiled more broadly. "Thanks."

My shrug said it was no big deal. "I can tell you a few interesting things I learned today, by the way. Not much, but interesting."

Except for the eyes she would have been all ears. "Really?"

"Have you met Lin McGuiness?"

"Linny? Sure. I've known him for years. He hates me."

"Maybe," I said, brushing by her statement. "But he seems to like Tony. He's all for my nosing around. McGuiness thinks something is screwy."

"That's ridiculous. He was after Tony from the beginning," she said, scornfully. "Once that bank stuff came up, he jumped all over him."

"What about before?"

"How should I know?" she snapped. The last word wasn't out before she put her hand to her head and began apologizing. "I'm sorry, Casey. Honest to God, I'm an idiot sometimes."

My hand found its way to hers for a pat. "Relax, Diana. I'm going to question you from time to time, and that can be kind of rough. If it upsets you, don't worry about it. It's my fault not yours." That was true enough.

"Did you call the hotel yet?" she asked quietly.

My head ducked as I recalled that I hadn't. "You were my last dime."

A small smile slowly flowered into a grin. "Good," she said. "Because I want you to stay here. With me."

Never, that's right, never, should a professional man take that kind of invitation. In my business, everyone is lonely. Only when feeling isolated will someone hire me in the first place. When they ask me to stay with them, and it has happened before, I find the door and say I'll call the next day.

"I'm sorry," I began.

"No, you're not," she declared, "Because you will not turn me down. You can't. I can't stay here alone anymore. I'm afraid and," she added shyly, "I'm lonely. It doesn't matter where you stay, just be in the house. It's a big house. It's huge. I won't bother you. I just want to know I'm not alone here."

The flood of words buried my reservations and revealed them for what they were—all wet. Every step I had taken in Venango County had been wrong so far and I didn't see the point in changing the pattern.

"I'll stay, but I have to make a call," I said.

She jumped out of the chair. "Call Paris, if you want. I'll go make up a bed for you. Do you like satin Sheets?"

"Sure," I said, not knowing what they felt like. I'm into Percale. "Anything."

In an instant she was gone. The dining room sat there stoically with me in it. I figured it couldn't be very pleased about that. Somehow, the whole house made me feel unwanted.

Been there. Speaking of which...

I placed a call to Cath Mays at Fred's office. She was uncommunicative but I could hear Fred singing in the background, so I understood. I had figured that the late hours weren't all business.

"Cath," I said, "tomorrow morning call WPPA and tell Miss Simmons that I will be at this number," adding the Winter number. "Unless you'd like to do me a favor and call her at home. number is in my address book."

"My ass." She snorted. "It's not even there."

My chin dropped so far it hurt. When I recovered, I covered. "Too much exercise."

After a pause, she asked, "Really?"

"Cath, ask Fred," I suggested, tossing my accountant toward the bus. "Are you sure about the address book?"

"I checked before I left," she explained. "For Winter's number. It's gone."

"Not a problem," I lied. Now I knew why my once-favorite reported had paid her visit. "Forget the call, I'll make it myself."

For that call, I would want to be alone. I called up to Diana that I had to dial Paris, in private. She giggled, suggested the study and gave detailed directions. Which I needed. I parked myself in a big leather chair behind a big desk with a pair of big phones on it. The steam in my head had to cool before I could chance the call.

Harry had warned me.

~ ~ ~

After five minutes of phone-staring and speculation, my anger cooled enough to become indignation. That emotion allowed me to up the receiver of the ordinary, black telephone on Winter's desk. It looked as if it had been in service for a hundred years. An experienced, old phone, it would help me say what had to be said.

Even before the receiver reached my ear, I heard voices coming from it. That put me off at first, but I listened anyway. A high pitched, rapid-fire conversation went on despite my interruption.

"He's staying at her house, you know?"

"So what?"

"You know how she is."

"Yes, and she is all alone out there. I feel sorry for her."

The drift of the conversation turned me around and brought out a chuckle. By the time I hung up, had lost the anger completely. Apparently, Diana and I were already the source of party line gossip. It made me feel, ridiculously, like a celebrity. Fame is intoxicating, especially to a teetotaler like me.

At least, I mused, I had stumbled upon the famous party-line that had cooked Tony Hiller. Winter had set it ajar while the confession rolled out of Hiller's cocky mouth and onto the public ways. Without that, Tony Hiller would be free and far away.

Experimenting with the receiver, I put my head down on the desk to try to hear the conversation about Diana's scandalous house guest, as I fiddled with the receiver. The phone was funny. With just one side tilted up, but not the other, the speaking came across clearly. Modern phones don't seem to work that way.

An old piece of equipment, the phone possessed a format similar to the current models. The answer was less in the design of the old phone, than in its condition. The cradle that held the receiver should have had two small black buttons that, when raised, activated the phone. Winter's had only one.

"Are you finished?" a voice asked from beyond the door.

My discovery made me anxious to talk about it. Janice went on the back burner for the moment, but only just. I intended to yank her front and center before the evening was over.

"Come on in, Diana."

The door swung open and Diana Winter stood in front of me in a loosely fitting, filmy dress. On a girl so short, it shouldn't have looked good. It did. "What do you think?" she asked.

The right side of my face compressed as I tried not to smile too much. "You could impress someone in the thing."

She floated over to the desk. "I certainly hope so."

"They are already talking about us," I advised, lifting the party-line receiver. Once it was back home, I added, "and we haven't even thought of anything yet."

"I liked the word 'yet.'"

That direction was all problems. "Then keep it in mind. Listen, Diana, I have a couple questions and then a couple of calls."

"Are they all for me?" she asked sweetly.

My head answered the question with a shake. "Only the first couple."

Diana shrugged and sat on the desk right next to me. With mock attentiveness, she leaned in very close. "Those are the most important ones."

I let my eyes bore into hers for a moment. Hers gave in and looked someplace else. My ethics took a breath. "Tell me about this phone."

Her back straightened and she looked at the ceiling with a laugh. "Oh, Casey," she cried, "this is my sexiest outfit."

"Probably not," I said, "but it'll do."

"Aren't you at all aroused?" she purred sarcastically.

"By this phone? Yes."

Her smile was one of temporary disappointment, nothing permanent. "Okay, you dirty, old neuter," she said. "It's an old phone. It's been in this office since I can remember. Father liked to listen to the gossip, if you must know. He and I would huddle in here listening, like watching a soap opera. I think it was his only entertainment."

"Or newspaper."

She looked at me, to find out what I meant. She gushed. "You mean he was a muckraker? Yes, I guess he was."

"Why is this button missing?"

Diana examined the cradle and its single button. "That's news to me. I've never noticed."

"When did you use it last?" I asked calmly.

"Not since father died."

"How about before?"

"I'm sorry, Casey, I can't remember that far back," she apologized. "Does it matter?"

My own smile lied. "Probably not." I had other ideas.

"You want to make your calls now?" she asked quietly, noting my reflection. "I'll go."

Something made me say, "Thanks. I won't be long," as if there could be something later.

With Diana and her tantalizing dress out of my way, I ran over the questions in my mind. Had the button been deliberately removed? By Winter? Did he intend the conversation to be heard? And Why? Of course, it could have broken, but I could find that out tomorrow. My real, daring questions were this: Did someone else remove the button? And if so, why?

The question of 'Why?' reminded me of Janice Simmons. She was the reason I had come into the study in the first place. Despite my curiosity about the phone, my mind suddenly filled with green eyes and a clever smile just hinting derision. I stalked into the dining room for my coat. When I returned, I seized the newer phone and dialed the number I had pulled from my wallet.

The ringing stopped and so did my breath. The click of an answer seemed to cut my nerve and, suddenly, I didn't know what to say to her.

"Hello." Her voice rang with confidence.

"Good evening, Miss Simmons," I said, stunning myself with the even tone. "This is Carmichael."

She didn't speak immediately. "Oh, Casey. How are you?" It sounded awkward, deliberate. "I mean... How are you doing?"

"Up here, I'm doing fine," I replied. "In Pittsburgh, I'm not so sure."

She didn't say anything and, for as long as I could, neither did I. Two tactics presented themselves to me: Confront her or force her to tell me the truth. I chose the latter.

"I was a little worried," I said, "that you weren't speaking to me. When I called earlier..."

She interrupted me. "I'm sorry, Casey. I was tied up. It didn't occur to me that I couldn't call you back. Where are you anyway?" Her voice had started to reflect concern, even petulance.

"I called to tell you," I lied. I had called to find out why the hell she'd been to my office. "And to tell you what I've found out."

She became more excited, if her higher pitch meant anything. "You did? Already?"

"Don't get excited," I cautioned. "I just wanted to check notes with you. I'm using you as my expert on Huntington, remember?"

"You mean you've found nothing new, then?" she asked, cool again.

More than anything, I wanted to drop the bomb on her as to what I had found out about her. Instead, I took the easy way out, pretending it was cleverer. "What was Detective Chief McGuiness reaction to all this when you were here?"

"McGuiness? The big guy in Franklin?" Her memory didn't take long. "When I first talked to him, he seemed skeptical that Hiller was guilty. After awhile, though he came around," she said. "I liked him. He threw a pass at me. Made me feel at home."

Her comment had an edge, but I ignored it. "What do you know about the DA?"

"Only that he wouldn't see me?"

"Why not?" I asked, only half curious. Every word she uttered twisted in me.

"I guess I'd gotten the reputation as a Hiller-ite, by then," she explained, archly. Her eyebrow had probably soared on that on. "The DA wanted me to leave his case alone. He sent his slimy older brother to tell me so."

When I said nothing, she continued, her voice beginning to show strain. "Jim Collins, I think his name was. He very politely suggested that I had gotten all of the information available and that the DA was very busy."

"Sounds fair," I said.

The conversation died at that point and the awkward telephone silence prompted her to sigh twice and ask, "Is something wrong, Casey?" T

The laugh that escaped must have hurt her ears. "I'll say. Everyone connected with this mess seems determined to cross me up. I'm getting nervous."

"Everyone," she said warily, "takes in a lot of people."

"It takes in what it says it takes in."

"Including me? Is that it?"

Answering wouldn't have helped, so I didn't. If she wanted me to tell her what she did, she was crazy. I gave her the chance to tell me, I liked her enough for that.

She sighed again, dramatically. "You mean my trip to your office?"

"You caught Cath without mascara."

"Come on, Casey! Be fair!" she cried. "I only wanted to know more about you. I talked to your friend, Fred, and that awful secretary." She laughed. "Besides, not I didn't."

"Didn't what?"

"Catch your Cath without her eye makeup. It looked very dark when she threw me out."

"She gets jealous easily," I snapped.

"Wow." Her voice sank an octave, to its TV level. "You're really mad at me, huh?"

Keep quiet! I told myself.

"Shit," she whispered. "I can explain, you know."

"Good. Does that mean I get my address book back?" I asked curtly.

Janice sounded stunned. "Address Book? What address book?"

The time had come to bear in on her. "Mine. From my desk. Top drawer. Check your purse. You'll recognize it right off," I said, heating up. "It's my only record of who I've worked for, when."

"I don't understand," she said innocently.

"It's gone. Right after your visit."

That cracked her and her voice, too. "Oh, Jesus, Casey! I didn't take it. Really! What would I want with it?"

"You tell me?" I didn't believe her.

Not much, anyway.

"Please, believe me. I didn't take it!" She sounded frantic. "I went to find out what you were like. How good you were. Damn it, this is my case, too!"

Her wounded anger impressed me and I relented. "Okay, Okay. Why didn't you just ask Harry?"

Janice Simmons fell silent again. When she spoke, her tone reflected the melancholy I'd seen in her beautiful face when she had Harry and me to her apartment. "He won't see me. Not for a long time. That dinner? It was a favor to you, Casey. He must think a lot of you, because it was terribly difficult for Harry. To be with me now."

My mouth grew cotton and my stomach wrenched sideways. "That's how he kept you in town." I had expected better of Harry Blair. He had more character than that. Or he had at one time.

"Don't do that!" she cried. "It wasn't like that! Damn it! He helped me when I needed it. My gratitude went haywire. So what?"

She took a second or two to calm down, before continuing. "I'm sorry. You're right about me, I suppose. But I hate this city. It's Okay for you and for Harry. You were born here. I'm an outsider here. I have been everyplace, for that matter. All I have is my work, don't you see that?" She didn't give me time to answer. "And when they pulled me off the Winter thing, the only good story I had covered in two years... Well, I must have fallen on my head."

"Yeah."

"Listen, Casey," she pleaded. "Don't begrudge me my one weakness, please?"

Her story had me going three ways at once and none of them led anywhere. "Never."

Contrition filled the voice on the other end. "Will you let me explain some time?"

"It's up to you, Janice. You don't owe me anything."

"Yes, I do. You're doubly important to me," she explained. "I need to be on this case. More than that..." She added just enough little feeling, "We can be more than that."

"We'll see."

"Thanks." Her voice had a cheerful note in it. "I have to go, Casey. Hope you find your notebook," she said. "Give me a call when you... want me."

We said goodnight. I hung up with the conviction that Janice Simmons had made inroads into my life that I didn't like very much. I also knew that she was not a perfect liar.

My address book, insignificant to me but missing all the same doubled as a client notebook. Janice knew that and she shouldn't have.

Damn. She had me, she really did.

And she still my had address book.

~ ~ ~

I was still glaring at the phone, when the doorbell rang. Diana's barefoot padding to the door sounded funny juxtaposed with my last view of her. So did her girlish yelp after she opened the front door.

"Tommy!" she cried,

"Tut, tut, Diana," I heard someone say. The voice had a trace of an English accent.

"I'm so glad you're home," Diana bubbled. "Hi, Jack."

The second new voice was older, a little disappointed. "Hello, Diana. You were out when Thomas called from Pittsburgh, so I went to get him." It was a favor and Jack, whoever he was, made it obvious.

The door to the study was thick enough to cover the ensuing conversation, but I heard Diana say, as if a warning, "Oh, Tommy, I have someone I want you to meet."

That had to be me, since I was alone with her in the house.

Sure enough, the girl burst into the room pulling a tall, hefty young man after her. On second look, he was as old as I was, or almost, but he did look younger.

"Tommy," Diana said, "This is Casey Carmichael. Casey, this is my brother, Tom."

His eyes were big and brown, like Diana's, but less the puppy dog's. His scowl intensified my unwanted feeling. "Carmichael? You're the detective?"

Detectives, like lepers, seem to repel normal folk. Unlike lepers, however, detectives inspire no sympathy or alms. Tom Winter knew me and what my disease was and he didn't risk his large, well manicured hand on either.

"Be nice, Thomas," Diana scolded.

He put his curved nose in the air so that he could look down at at me. He looked incredibly like Diana, though his features were bigger and rougher. His skin lacked the creamy texture and fine peach fuzz that so softened hers. His forehead creased in several places when he spoke.

"I hardly expected this cozy scene from you, Diana," he said coldly, looking at me. "Jack told me that you had brought this fellow around, but he didn't say that you kept him here.

He made me sound like a zoological specimen. Ordinarily, that kind of talk makes me mad, but his language had such a strange accent that I laughed instead. "They wouldn't take me at the hotel," I explained lightly. "No pets."

"I begged him to stay here," she snapped. "Nobody else would keep me company."

Thomas Winter flinched. A flicker of guilt passed over his face. "I suppose."

I looked at the second man, named Jack. "My name is Carmichael, as you obviously know. You may as well tell me yours."

"Or you'll ask." Jack walked over to me, wearing a tight little smile, the kind disgruntled underlings wear when ignoring their superior's disapproval. "Pazinsky," he said. "Jack Pazinsky."

"You're the wizard at the Bank," I enthused. He seemed ripe enough for flattery. He had already stepped beyond Thomas Winter's approach. I thought I could pry him away completely. "I have heard about you."

Pazinsky looked at Diana, and then smiled back at me. "Thank you, Mr. Carmichael. I'm flattered."

Diana bounced over to Pazinsky and put her arms around the little man. "He really is a genius, Casey. He does everything."

Her brother seemed put off by the spectacle that Diana was making of herself. "Diana, please calm down," he demanded.

With her eyes suddenly widened in something like a mixture of fear and shame, Diana released Pazinsky and stepped back toward the wall. "I'm sorry, Tom."

Stern as he was, Winter smiled at her movement. "No, darling, I'm the one who's sorry. It's not my place to bark at you." He shot me an it's-your-God-damned-fault look and took her hand. The two of them went out, beginning to chat about what had happened in the time since they'd last seen each other.

That left me with Pazinsky, whose eyes followed the duo out of the room. He was only about 5' 6", but solidly put together, with graying hair. His huge blue eyes, set in a broad face, made an immediate impression. His eyebrows bounced and he turned to me. "It's about time he came home," he stated.

"Where's he been?" I asked, propping myself up on the desk. The day had been long and tiring, and Thomas Winter's arrival gave me the sense of another unwelcome complication.

Pazinsky rolled those intelligent eyes. "He lives in London. I think he's a writer or some such."

"I'll bet he's a snob," I opened, to test Pazinsky's sense of the wind direction.

He glanced my way for an instant. Did he need so little time to assess my meaning? "Aren't we all, Mr. Carmichael?"

Defeated, I changed the game. "Who runs Winterbank now, anyway?"

He gave me a longer study this time, but remained inscrutable. "Right now, Mr. Carmichael? No one." He chuckled. "At least not the way it had been run."

I'd need a kayak with this guy. "How do you mean?"

"For years, Mr. Carmichael," Pazinsky proceeded carefully, "Winter National was run by Harold Winter with the proverbial iron hand. Then the idea of statewide banking began to affect the legislature. Sensing a trend, Winter ignored the Bank proper and set up a holding company, Winterbank. He spent most of his time after that entertaining state senators and lining up acquisitions all over the state. Bank operations were delegated to a nice, young fellow who could not handle them."

"Tony Hiller."

He cocked his head to one side. "Tony understood that he was not prepared to run an organization the size of Winter National, but that didn't help. It was a bad decision. A mistake that cost Hal Winter his life and may cost Tony his. It was Hal's error, it's a shame that Tony had to suffer."

"What about Diana?" I wondered out loud.

A cryptic smile crossed his lips. "Mr. Carmichael, Diana can balance her checkbook. But does not. She has no sense at all of banking. Which is just as well, for it can be a dry and debilitating profession for one of her spirit."

Well. "She had two brothers as I recall," I said. "Why don't they pitch in?"

"Hard driving men," he theorized, "have a way of encouraging their children to expand their talents to other pursuits." A quick smile told me the conversation was over.

Trailing Pazinsky's footsteps, I found the Winter's at the end of the path. Thomas Winter had an enormous glass of scotch in one hand and a plate of potato salad in the other. He was talking, or holding forth, on the sights of the villages of Wales when we entered the dining room. Diana leaned forward on the table rapt, those big browns glued to big browns.

"Paz," Winter said interrupting himself, "fix Carmichael a drink. He probably needs one."

The older man went to the bar and asked in a suggestive voice, "Scotch, Mr. Carmichael Mccallan 12?"

"The prepubescent?" There was a hint in the lilt Pazinsky used.

"Jack, it's potato salad," Tom Winter said.

"I leave scotch to the ladies, Jack." I took Jack's cue. "Pour me a Rebel Yell, straight up."

"Diana, you've had the guest serving drinks," Pazinsky chided.

"I'm trying not to be a guest here," I said, taking the glass from Pazinsky.

"Oh?" Winter's eyes tried to melt me.

One thing was clearer than Tom's weak stomach: Pazinsky's dislike for Diana's long lost, older brother. Clearer still was Tom's growing hatred for one Casey Carmichael. The silence had a seething quality, until Diana soothed it.

"Tommy, don't go away so soon, this time," she pleaded in a little sister voice. "I'm so lonely in this house."

"It's not that lonely," he remarked glaring at me. "But I'll stay as long as necessary."

I tried to make ground with Tom. "Then I should probably get back to the hotel and see if they have a room."

Diana frowned, but said nothing.

Pazinsky offered his note, with a sly smile for me. "Hasn't a room freed up here, recently?"

I dreaded finding out how Lewis Huntington's stay would go over, but Pazinsky left it.

In a voice lowered by firmness, Diana ended the discussion. "Casey, you will stay nowhere but here."

"But surely, Diana, if he'd rather..." her brother objected.

"I want him to stay because he works for me," she said with surprising finality. "And because I asked him to. Besides I've made up a bed for him, and you know how I hate to do that. The least he can do is sleep in it."

Tom drained his glass. Half drunk, he simply caved. "All right, all right."

His sister kissed him hard on the cheek. "Now, I'11 go make one for you, Tommy. In your old room." Before Tom could stop her, she was gone.

Alone with me, Tom would have silent, but with Pazinsky present, he felt free to speak to the inhabitants of the room in general. "We should have sold this dinosaur."

The Bank vice-president asked, "And why didn't you, Tom? You fired all the servants and left poor Diana here all alone."

Tom Winter waved his hands about ineffectually. "Aw, bullshit, Jack. You know brother Bob made that call. What do I care?"

I kept my voice soft when I spoke. "Listen, Mr. Winter, it's none of my business, but that sister of yours is worth taking care of."

A long, scotch laden sigh filled the room. "I know. I know. But not by you."

Pazinsky added the kicker. "Bob, he's the boss now."

"What about the bank?" I asked.

Tom looked sheepish and looked into his glass as he admitted, "He wants to sell it."

Pazinsky blew his slick persona in flash. "He what?" Animated by something other than his cerebrum, the fellow was something to watch. He quick-stepped to Tom Winter and literally lifted him out of his chair. "That son of a bitch wants to do what?"

Little Jack Pazinsky shook the six and a quarter feet of Tom Winter's flaccid body before Winter could react. Winter stared down at the red-faced aggressor with terror in his eyes, his hands making big circles in the air.

"Come on, Jack. Take it easy," he managed to croak. "It's Bob."

"Down boy," I said unevenly, trimming some distance.

Jack Pazinsky did not take it easy. He tightened his grip and spoke in a voice quivering in passion. "You tell that worthless bastard of a brother of yours, that if he so much as steps foot in this town with those asshole ideas of his, I will make his life extremely unpleasant. And much shorter," he said, spitting each word in Tom's eye, as though the older Winter were his brother's effigy.

Once released from the madman's grasp, Tom collapsed back into his chair. Somewhere near his naval, his head swung back and forth.

Pazinsky sensed my movement and his head snapped ninety degrees to stop me. The color drained as I watched. His eyes had lurched forward in their sockets, but were receding. They were now a darker blue against the white skin. "Harold Winter," he stated, "produced two entirely worthless sons, Mr. Carmichael. In Tony Hiller he sought a third. They've all come to no good."

My Sears suit could not afford Jack Pazinsky's rage, but I took a chance. He'd never be so open again. "What about the girl?"

"Hal Winter was not completely barren of goodness," he declared. "His only daughter is also his only worthwhile contribution to the human race."

"Along with his bank," I agreed.

His nostrils nearly burst. Only tremendous will seemed to hold his mouth above his chin. "His bank?" he said sharply. "For years, he has made only one real contribution to his bank's welfare: Me! And goddamn it, that part of his work will not die with him!"

With his speech complete, Pazinsky took a deep breath and said, "Now that you have all of that to digest, Mr. Carmichael, I shall leave you to it. Good night."

The door didn't slam until after Pazinsky had called out an incongruously hearty good night to Diana. Tom Winter, his head back up again, looked at me stupidly.

"Christ! He's a madman."

I shook my head. "When all you've got is threatened by some long distance idiot, I can see it."

"Bob is not an idiot," he argued. "At least not completely."

"Are you Okay?"

He tried to laugh. "I suppose I'll get over it. "Care to split a bottle of Mccallan? The 18?"

I must have made a face that put the laugh over the top. "Forget the Bourbon, Carmichael. Trust me. They finish the aging it in bourbon casks. "

"That... is my kind of aging."

We spent a half an hour splitting the pricey scotch like old bar mates before Diana marched into the room ordering us to bed. She stood over us, shaking her head, like a little girl playing mother to her dolls. With effort she coaxed us out our chairs and kissed us both good night.

It was a funny day, but it ended right.

Chapter Seven

Morning brings unpleasantness to me in any case, but in league with Mccallan, she really laid on the retribution. My eyes saw a strange room wrapped around me, filled with furniture I couldn't afford. There was a sensation of sliding off green Teflon sheets.

I did not think of Janice Simmons...

Something small and fuzzy sat at the foot of my bed. "Get up, Mr. Carmichael," it said, in a soft, sweet voice. "Have your hangovers on your own time." The specter laughed breezily. "We're going out for breakfast."

Suddenly, I was alone in the room. Searching in vain for something familiar, I began to feel that anxiety of displacement. Had I been moved during the night? By whom and for what? The chilling wave slowly gave way to a familiar, hollow drop of isolation.

Detachment allowed me to recall what had put me in this place. I have to get my bearings and my feet on a piece of ground, before I can start thinking or getting dressed. Secure, finally, in my knowledge that I had awakened where I was supposed to have awakened—in the room of Robert Winter—I vaulted from the double bed.

My feet pounded the floor a little too hard, but I kept my balance. On a chair across the room, my clothes had been folded neatly, except my coat which hung in an empty closet.

Undoubtedly, the elfin apparition that had awakened me had also put me to bed.

She greeted me at the foot of the stairs, as well, hushing my good morning. "Tommy's still asleep," Diana whispered.

"The rooms are sound-proof," I said, my voice lowered.

Her smile substituted for sunrise and she stroked my head. "Either that, or this is."

"I heard a rumor about breakfast," I said. Less quickly than I should.

"We have to go out," she replied, sheepishly. "I can't cook well enough to take on eggs."

"I'd help, but I can't see that far."

"The hotel restaurant makes really good breakfasts before nine."

Diana and I took my rented Granada to substantiate her claim. We passed the Bank and stopped in front of what must have been the hub of Huntington at one time. The building, now somewhat rundown, rose elegantly three stories. Its fine stone front maintained a look of stability and propriety that belied its interior condition.

The lobby of the City Hotel had declined faster than the exterior. The carpets had thinned, the curtains had a tint of finely aged yellow. The front desk needed a coat of varnish or something to restore a luster left behind in the twenties or thirties.

Behind the desk, an old man stood with his back to us. While his back remained straight, his shoulders drooped with age. A wrinkled white shirt, its collar too narrow to hide the tie, had the look of wear.

"Hi, Neddy," Diana said cheerfully. "I have someone to meet you."

Neddy took a breath and turned to face us. His smile was for Diana, the frown for me. "Carmichael, the detective, eh?"

My undercover days were certainly over.

Diana confirmed his suspicion. "Yep."

The confirmation only served to crinkle his dry complexion. He extended, none the less, a reddened, swollen hand that initiated the shaking process without me. I took it on the up-sweep and held on. The grip was, unlike the hand, steady. He didn't try for more, the mark of a proud man, with an understanding of his own decline.

"How do you do, Mr. Cooper?" I asked, displaying my newspaper knowledge.

His expression indicated that he could complain. "Not bad, Carmichael," he lied. "Half expected to see you last night."

That really meant, "Half not," I surmised. The man was on top of things.

"I was persuaded," I said. "to save the lady some expenses."

A smile cracked through the cloudy eyes, but not the mouth. "She's a Winter, our Diana."

"Come off it, Ned," Diana said. "I'm going to make it up to you by making him eat in the restaurant."

He received the idea with mixed emotions. "I'll take Winter money any way it comes, young lady," he stated, winking at her. The wink probably fooled Diana, but he wasn't kidding.

We left him to his vigil and walked through the warped. wooden doors into a more modern world. The City Hotel Restaurant had spruced up nicely on its way to 1976, avoiding the usual plastic. Wood still dominated, but stainless steel shared the limelight and glistened in the morning.

Our table sat far from the hotel door and beyond the entrance from the street. The clean windows beside us presented a relaxing view of the street, though the lower half of them were blocked by crisp white curtains. The place was full.

From behind the highly polished bar, a plain-looking waitress approached us.

Her face reflected the fatigue of years of table service, her smile the exhaustion of a busy morning. "Good morning, Diana," she said, in a throaty, almost smoky, voice. "Good morning, Sir."

She, at least, had not gotten the news. Her eyes showed no hint of recognition. They didn't show much, neither emotion nor age. Her skin suggested early thirties, her mouth early forties. Because a short skirt showed me most of her legs, I could place her properly in her mid-twenties.

"Becky," Diana said, indicating me, "This is Casey Carmichael."

Her head nodded in starts and stops. "Oh." A faint tinge of disappointment colored her voice.

"We'll have the special Becky," Diana ordered.

The young waitress bobbed her head and left. Her walk lacked the springiness her young legs suggested. The feet barely cleared the parquet floor. She had a good, medium figure stretched over about five feet and eight inches. As she moved about, I detected an occasional resetting of her sloping shoulders and a correction of posture.

"That is Becky Stockly," Diana said sharply, interrupting my scrutiny. "Like her?"

I kept my eyes on the waitress. "Someone has taught her how to walk," I commented.

"Carmichael," she said, putting her hand on my arm to get my attention. Once she had it, she asked, "Don't you like to just look at people?"

"Sure."

"I mean just look at them, not study them," she said crossly. "When you looked me up and down the other day, I had the feeling..." She shrugged. "I don't know. I usually like it."

"Sorry," I apologized. "It's a bad habit. When you have to watch as many people as I do, sometimes it's hard to just look."

Diana looked out the window. "Okay."

I followed her eyes as they scanned the street toward Winter National. At the door of the Bank, Jack Pazinsky stood staring toward the restaurant. He stood like a watch dog, his arms folded across his deep chest. The three piece, striped suit looked out of place on him, after the night before.

"Jack got mad at Tommy last night, didn't he?" Diana asked distantly.

"Brother Bob wasn't there," I responded. "Is Pazinsky like that often."

Dreamily she swayed from side to side. "He's very possessive of things he should be his."

"Like Winter National bank?"

"Mm, hmm."

I wondered if my next question would get by. "And you?"

Diana's head jerked back toward me. Her eyebrows crushed down on her eyes. "Me?" she cried, startled by the idea. "What do you mean?"

I put one hand to deflect her response. "Sorry," I said. "I assumed..."

"Assumed? Assumed what?" she demanded.

"Pazinsky would eat a brick topped with mortar for you, Diana," I explained wondering if she could be so innocent as she seemed. "Unless I'm blind."

"He's like a..." she puzzled a moment mortified and said, "an uncle.

"Okay, Diana. That's Okay with me. That could explain it."

She lapsed into silence until Becky Stockly brought our meals. "Thanks, Becky" she said then.

The Stockly girl shot me a hostile look when setting my plate down. When she saw I'd caught her at it, she blushed.

Diana looked around the room, and its thinning crowd.

I followed her eyes. The clock said 9:10. Huntington must have had a busy morning on tap.

"Hey, Becky," Diana asked, "could you spare a couple minutes?"

Becky Stockly's eyes did the same routine, sweeping more quickly, before she sat down beside Diana. "What do you want?" she asked warily.

"Mr. Carmichael is a detective," Diana said.

"I know," the girl replied, disapprovingly. "He looks like a salesman."

"I sold vacuum cleaners once," I admitted. "In high school." Neither woman was impressed with my resume. Rightly so: I only sold two.

Diana ignored me. "You were close to Tony's. Will you let him ask you some questions?"

The waitress shrugged helplessly. A sigh that went with the shrug was deeper than Diana's past tense had implied, too deep to reflect merely her helplessness in avoiding me. "What's the use, Diana?"

Tony Hiller had at least one friend, I concluded. A small-town waitress, clearly drained of hope at twenty-five. If anyone would cooperate with a stranger, nosing around to help Hiller, she was the one.

"Let me decide that, Miss Stockly," I said.

Her look suggested a decided lack of confidence in my ability to do that. "It doesn't matter to me," she said with an air of complete resignation.

Diana prefaced my questioning with some background. "Becky has known Tony and all of us for years," she said. "We all sort of grew up together in Huntington. She can give you the best description of Tony of anyone in town." With blink of brown eyes, she added, "Besides me, that is."

A doubting smile on Becky's unadorned lips told me that she knew who could give a better description of Tony Hiller. "Tony. Poor Tony," she said mournfully. "He was so happy before your father got a hold of him. That, was your fault Diana." Her words were not accusatory, but factual.

The Winter girl beside her flushed. "It was not! And you know it. Daddy just gave Tony a chance."

Becky brushed the objection aside with a small wave of her long, chaffed hand. "Tony was a good guy, Mr. Carmichael. Really. Nobody believes that anymore, but he was."

"Was?"

She blew a lock of dirty brown hair off of her forehead. "He changed. Everybody does. You stick around this place long enough, you see it," she said, weary-wise."After he came back from college, Amherst? He wasn't too bad. Not until he got that promotion at the Bank." The work "Bank" came out like the four letter word it was. "I think he went nuts."

Hiller hadn't much support in the sanity department, if she thought he was nuts. "That's starting when?"

She glared at Diana. "When was he promoted?"

Diana bent away from the look. "July first."

"July first," Becky echoed. After a second or two she corrected herself. "Actually a month later."

"Go on," I said.

"Oh, I don't know," she cried, frustrated. "Why don't you leave him alone?" She composed herself during my non-answer. "He started to forget things. He came in here twice for dinner one night and ordered the same thing. When I laughed at him, he said I was crazy. That he hadn't been in at all."

The memory was painful for her, but she set her shoulders and continued. "Sometimes, he'd sit in the corner, back there. Sometimes, he'd sit up front. That wasn't like Tony. He liked to sit in the same place all the time, where you are now. And he got mad at me sometimes and slapped me once." She started to cry, not much, but enough to wet her cheeks and shake her voice.

Diana's mouth fell open. "He what?" she demanded. "You never told me that!"

"How could I?" Becky snapped. "Why should I?"

They looked at each other for a moment and then looked away, in opposite directions. Diana looked hurt and angry. Becky was still allowing tears to make their way down her cheeks without interference.

I offered Becky my handkerchief, but I knew she'd refuse my offer.

She did, stiffly, shaking her head. "I've got to go now," she said, rising. "But I want to tell you that I don't think it's fair for them to send Tony to jail. It wasn't his fault. None of it."

She hurried away from our table holding her hand over her face. Diana did not watch or comment. I decided to finish my eggs and hot cakes. The Winter case just kept making my stomach feel empty.

~ ~ ~

I dropped Diana and her mood of reflection at Winter National. My appointment with the Venango County District Attorney was drawing nigh, as we used to say in my college days.

No, I guess. We didn't.

Ten o'clock had passed by the time I entered the DA's suite of offices. A secretary gave me a quizzical look, the kind usually reserved for exotic birds, and escorted me into Collins office. The giant desk stood empty before me, but its size diminished my sense of importance. As, no doubt, intended.

A double door opened to my left and a man, unmistakably related to Tom Winter, strode into the room. With his hand out in front of his wide smile, he should have been running for governor. "Mr. Carmichael," he sang in a basso voice. "Welcome to Venango County."

That's what he said. My ears vibrated for several seconds while I tried to convince myself I heard him right. Beaming or not, he looked so unlike his diminutive brother that I wondered if they were full brothers. Harlan Collins had reached average height and, from the look on his face, average intelligence without mussing his thick blond hair.

Nice county," I congratulated him. "I used to fish up here."

Sitting behind the mesa-like desk, he grinned. "So did I," he said. "Until the people of this county needed a real DA."

"You don't look real," I suggested.

His grin grew into a laugh. "I know. It's a drawback in your neck of the woods. Up here, you get away with it."

My forehead began to itch and I scratched it. "What can I do for you?"

Harlan Winter Collins held up his index finger. "No, Mr. Carmichael," he objected. "What can I do for you?"

My shrug said it was simple. "Give me your file on Tony Hiller."

He reached into his desk and pulled out a manila folder. It slid across the desk, revealing an upside down name, Anthony Peters Hiller. "Take a look," he said generously.

A gift horse can bite, but so can one you buy. I looked. Inside the folder, I didn't see anything I didn't already know. "Pretty Dry, Mr. Collins."

"Call me Harley," he said,

"Okay. "

He looked me over. "Listen, Carmichael. I don't care much what you do. I've worked with lots of good, honest private detectives, when I was in private practice. I even asked a couple to go out and destroy a DA's case, in anyway they could. That's okay."

"I'm glad."

He waved his finger again. "But, to be honest with you, this case is different." Collins' voice contained no hint of malice. He was just informing me. "One of the reasons my file is so thin, is that my middle name is Winter. I'm not handling this case, though I'd love to be. I get a lot of static about that from my family, but I'm a lawyer not a head hunter."

My smile came and went quickly. "Is there any chink in this case?"

"Not one," he stated.

"Your friend, Chief McGuiness," I said, "doesn't like the feel of it."

The DA's ample lips worked in and out. He rubbed his index finger over the bottom one. "McGuiness? What doesn't feel right to him is seeing anyone who killed Harold Winter go to jail. The Huntington's feel the man deserved it twenty years ago," he explained. "He pulled them down not quite that far back."

Intertwining family histories seemed wrapped all the way around Venango County. And Hiller's neck. "I've heard."

With his chair tilted back, Collins went on. "A long time ago, the Huntington's ran everything in these parts. Money coming out of their nice pink ears. They were in on the first oil wells. They even put our family in business. It was their money that got the Bank going, kept it going."

"But," he added, "once the Winter's got too big, it was war. Natural, I suppose. Hard cash means hard feelings, my grandfather used to say. And Big money means big hard feelings. High emotions."

Recalling the newspaper accounts, I said, "Didn't it come to a head in the sixties?"

"1970, as a matter of fact," Collins remembered. "Old man Huntington had a stroke the year before. He put his money in an account, a management account, with Winter National."

"You're kidding?"

"Funny, isn't it? The old idiot put his money with the only real enemy he had," Collins related. "He kept most of the control, of course, so it wasn't Hal Winter's fault."

"That is the dumbest thing I have ever heard."

"After the crash of the glamors, the old bird had a second stroke That was the end of the Huntingtons' power and their money." Collins shrugged. "That clan would love to see Hiller get off for spite, wouldn't they just."

I looked him dead in the eye as I got up. "Look, Collins. I can see your point. I can even appreciate it. Your people have done their job. An easy one at that. Give me a chance to do mine. It's a hell of a lot tougher."

The DA got up and came around his desk, without his smile. "Carmichael," he said, "that's up to you. It's not my place to stop you. But I thought that you should know what's what. I didn't want you talking to that bastard McGuiness without seeing me too. Fair?"

It was too fair. "Yeah."

His smile, less certain perhaps, returned. "I know Diana, too. She is a favorite here, Winter or not. But she's fragile and as far as this goes, she's smack in the middle. Don't make it worse for her." Genuine concern had raised his voice half an octave.

That wholly unexpected plea made our parting hand-shake genuine. "I'm going to make it better, Collins. That's what she's paying for."

Harley Collins showed me out of the suite and sincerely wished me luck.

Surely someone, some local weight wanted to pin me to a passing bus, not compete with welcoming floats for me and my investigation.

What the hell? No one was cooperating.

~ ~ ~

Ed Hiller, Tony's elderly uncle, seemed glad to welcome me, too. I had stopped at Hiller's house in Huntington on the way back from Franklin to see the basement in which the cops found Hiller all trussed up for them. I hoped would hold some tangible clue as to the truth of Tony's delusion.

For an old man—he was eighty-three—Ed Hiller moved like he a dancer. On our way into the living room of the renovated house, he pirouetted, glided backwards and struck poses. He was a small, bald cherub. The texture of his skin was like that of a pretty young girl. Only the lines around his eyes suggested age.

"Diana told me you were coming."

The stomach again. "Apparently, Diana told everyone I was coming."

His eyes twinkled. "So she did. So she did."

"I hope you don't mind if I ask some tough questions," I said.

Ed Hiller motioned me to sit down. He kept moving. "Tough, Mr. Carmichael? Any question would be a treat."

The comment struck me as odd. "Haven't you had enough by this time?"

He sat down spoke and rose again before half finished. "Didn't dare ask me when they were here. Not McGuiness or Collins," he chirped. "Didn't want to hear what I had to say."

"That's why I'm here."

My words made him stop for a moment. "You're being paid to."

"I'm being paid to.

"By Diana," he stated. "Isn't she a wonderful child?"

It was becoming uncomfortable, watching him. "She's all grown up."

He ignored that. "Tony has always loved Diana," he offered. "Everyone has always loved Diana. She makes no real demands on a man, don't you agree, Mr. Carmichael?"

"She made one on me, Mr. Hiller," I said, sternly. "If you'll sit down, we can get to it."

The dancing stopped and Ed Hiller stared at me. Uncertainly, like a scolded brat, he took a seat. "Sorry."

Since I had him still, I went fast. "I'm trying to substantiate your nephew's story, Mr. Hiller. No one even begins to believe him. Diana doesn't, his doctor doesn't, the cops don't and I don't. What about you?"

Shame flooded his normally pink cheeks. "Of course I do," he affirmed.

"Good. Why?"

Ed Hiller backed down. "I don't know."

"Figure it out." Being tough with him seemed the only way to keep him on his ass. "The kid will be in court in a couple weeks, so figure fast."

He blurted it out. "Tony never lies! Never! He takes care of me when no one else will. He wouldn't do it!"

"What else?"

He started to get up.

"Sit down, damn it"

The old man started to cry. "The stranger. That stranger."

"What about him?" I had to know immediately or it might be gone.

"I saw him," he cried into his hands.

"Where?" I was on the edge of my seat, incredulous. "Here?"

"Yes. From my room."

"That night?"

"Yes!"

"What time, for Christ's sake?"

"Late." One syllable taxed him to the limit.

"Why now?" I asked. "Why didn't you say anything..."

"They didn't ask," he explained, looking up from his hands.

Part of Hiller's story had a basis then. The strange old man had come to see him. Before or after Hiller killed Winter? But it wouldn't matter if Hiller did the killing. "Jesus."

At that, he hid his head again. "He hit him."

The words froze me in my seat. "He what?"

His peered through the fingers.

"Come on," I barked. "Did the stranger hit Tony?"

He nodded.

"On the head?"

He nodded again.

"What then?"

He made motions with his hands, but couldn't talk. Then he started to sob uncontrollably.

Across the space between us, I hurled my words. "What happened then? God damn it it, tell me!"

"He took him away," he murmured. "I couldn't see."

"Show me the basement."

Ed Hiller sprung out of his seat and ran, like a rabbit. The old man ran like a bloody rabbit. I made my way after him as fast as I could. When I caught up with him he was at the top of a flight of stairs pointing .

The house was old and its renovations had left out a handy light switch at the top of the cellar stairs. I broke out my penlight and picked my way downstairs. The overhead bulb had a string attached to it and I gave it a pull. Nothing happened.

Without the light, the basement relied on two small windows near the ceiling and one in a door for light. That was enough to keep me from tripping over the chair still sitting in the middle of the room, but not much else. My penlight shed some light on the mystery, but not much.

There was a door which led to the back yard. I didn't expect it to be open and it wasn't. But outside, through the dirty glass in the door, I saw something that looked interesting. It looked like a black bullet, partly covered with a layer of dirt.

My feet carried me up the stairs and out the front door in an instant. I bolted around the house in an unseemly fashion for a gentleman in his late thirties. But fine for me.

In my haste, I missed the first wooden step and found myself staring at my clue from an inch away, my back throbbing.

Dusting myself off, I kept my eyes on the dull black object as if it would disappear in a blink. My fingernails got a little dirty, but once I held the thing in my hand, I was more than satisfied. I wasn't quite clear what it meant, but in my hand I rolled a common, black button from the cradle of a very old telephone.

Chapter Eight

The door to Winter's house hung open and I went through it without a knock. Voices drifted toward me from the living room, but I didn't stop to listen to them. Instead I slipped into Harold Winter's study. The party-line phone sat peacefully on the desk, content to wait another fifty years.

Breathing hard, I took the black object I had been carrying in my shirt pocket and lay it on the desk. They looked good together, the phone and the "bullet". Satisfaction allowed me time to sit and reflect, before ripping the phone apart.

The chair was comfortable enough, but I could not relax. My finding the button at Hiller's could only meant that someone had intentionally removed the device from the phone. For so strange an action there could have been only one motive: To make it possible to tip the party-line phone up, almost imperceptibly, into a position that gave eavesdroppers a bird's ear view of Hiller's confession.

I interrupted myself to make sure that my clue fit the crime. The phone cover was held by only two ordinary screws. My knife had a screwdriver blade that worked well enough. With the black cover freed, I compared my button to its counterpart on the other side of the cradle. The two were identical. Someone had indeed tampered with the phone, having broken a plastic stop designed to keep the button in place.

The question of "Who?" would have to wait. Partly because I couldn't begin to guess and partly because Tom Winter was staring at me through the half open door.

"Cute phone, don't you think?" he asked, looking like he'd had more to drink than I had the night before. His face was red and his eyes, though probably the same color, were too far closed to show anything.

"Quaint," I replied, trying to decide what to tell him—or anyone—about my discovery. It was my only clue, so I decided to keep it all for myself. "Keeps you up on the news."

Winter snorted and then rubbed his nose as if it had hurt. "News, Mr. Carmichael?" he asked. "The people in this town, in 1976, still consider a strange man in a young girl's house, alone, to be news." He laughed. "Isn't that funny?"

The bile had returned with his senses.

"A screamer."

He plopped down in a chair across from me. "What do you think of Pazinsky?" he asked, changing his tone completely.

I thought it best to remind him that I had helped him drown his fear of that man away. "He can drive a man to drink."

Winter's laugh came out shrill for so big a man. "Frankly, the man scares me to death. Less so when he's like he was last night," Winter said. "Normally, he's so damn cool outside that you can't guess what fire is raging inside."

"I got to see two of them surface last night," I responded, hoping to keep ingratiating myself.

"The bank for one," he recalled. "The second eludes me."

He had been too shaken apparently to see the look in Pazinsky's eye when the subject of Diana came up.

"Your sister is his five alarmer."

Stunned, he stood up so quickly he almost went down again. "Diana! That's ridiculous!"

"Okay," I agreed.

"Why, she wouldn't have anything to do with a man like Jack Pazinsky," he declared. "He's a nothing."

Snobs are all right in my book, but not dumb snobs. "He's a smart nothing, Mr. Winter. From what the papers say, he's kept this operation of your afloat for longer than even he thinks."

Flowing back into the chair, like Jell-O on a hot day, Winter concurred. "I guess its true. Father didn't trust Jack completely, but he let him run almost everything."

Insight flashed through my forehead. "Including the books?"

He shrugged. "Of course."

If Pazinsky had complete control of the Winter National books, how had the lesser banker, Tony Hiller, doctored them? "What do you know about Tony Hiller?"

"Shit," Tom Winter said.

"Yeah. What do you know about him?"

His face changed to amusement. "Tony was a lightweight," he said. "I haven't seen him in about ten years, but I knew him as a kid. He always tagged along with Lewis Huntington. And Diana. Didn't seem to bring much, though."

Everyone thought of Tony Hiller as a harmless, over-educated puppy. And now, somehow, they believed he was ruthless or insane enough to murder. "Could you see him killing your father?"

"He did, didn't he?" he asked rhetorically. "But I was surprised. No, shocked. It made sense to kill Father, considering what had happened before... But what happened before that surprised me, too." He grabbed a couple of quick breaths. He talked in large lumps, pausing in between to reload.

"Tony started with nothing," he continued. "Not even ambition. Somewhere along the line, he must have picked that up with everything else. It's too bad, in a way. He wasn't smart enough to run away from father's influence." That slip made him turn away.

Though hesitant to get into a touchy area and end the dialog, I took the chance to pry. "Pazinsky said last night that your father had taken Hiller on as a third son. Is that true?"

His back to me, Winter replied in a soft, distant voice. "Mr. Carmichael, my father was a fighter. A proud man and a traditional man. He wanted someone to carry on after him. Bob, my brother, and I got the hell out of this hole as soon as we graduated from college, or in my case a little earlier."

"I ran to Europe," he continued. "That is the right word. That's where I've been living off the legacy our mother left, trying to be something else. A writer. It's a joke, but bad writing is better than stellar banking, as far as I'm concerned." He spread his large hands out in front of him as if before a typewriter.

He gathered them into fists again, shoving them into his pockets. "Bob, on the other hand, defied the old man outright, refused, to his face, to stay here and bugged off to Med school. He's out in San Francisco making his own bundle at age thirty-three."

"What about the baby of the family?" I asked.

Winter felt safe enough to turnaround. He smiled but melancholia kept its grip on the eyes. "Ah, our Diana. The family jewel. That's how we've always treated our Diana," he said, sarcastically. "Yes, she was our baby, our girl. Mother raised her to be a woman, Father an eternal child. Bob and I served as her umbrella. So naturally she craves like a woman, fears like a child and can't recognize rain."

Writers, in my opinion, are full of shit. Most of them. Tom Winter confirmed my opinion bravely. "You all fucked her up in other words?"

"She can't do a thing," he admitted, half ashamed.

"She hired me," I reminded him.

He frowned, but not an angry one. He was confused. "So she did," he said. "I haven't been able to figure that out yet."

~ ~ ~

If I had Diana Winter pegged right, she had hired me after agonizing for months over her "betrayal" of Tony Hiller. She had offered her fiancée no real financial support: According to the press he was broke enough to need a public defender. Worse, she had not given him the kind of support he really needed, the psychological kind. In nine long, hard months she had not once gone to see him in his suite at the Venango County Hospital.

The background added by her otherwise useless brother deepened my conviction. She had allowed the pressure from her brothers, and probably the entire clan, to block her from doing what she had seen as her duty.

All of which, I mused waiting for Jack Pazinsky, took me nowhere.

The short Winter National Vice President thrust his head past the door. He did not look unfriendly, but I remembered his performance the night before and went into his office on my guard. Once he had seated himself behind his narrow desk, I felt better.

Stark white describes his small room best. A couple of prints had cracks in the walls, but the rest of the office was singularly unadorned. The man was the most important figure in a substantial banking combine and he rated a desk smaller than my own.

"Good afternoon, Mr. Carmichael," he greeted me with good cheer. The white of the walls made his eyes look a pale blue, kind of transparent.

"How's the banking business today?" I asked politely enough.

Waving his arm around the room, he said, "It's quiet. Usually, I have papers everywhere. Fortunately, Dr. Robert Winter has relieved me of much of my work load."

"How can he interfere if he is in California?" The tentacles of Bob Winter were remarkably tight for being so extended.

Pazinsky lifted one finger, and put it to his head. "Psychologically, Mr. Carmichael. He has people in this bank in dread of him beyond his real powers. And I allow him as much room as I can."

The man knew his place: He was irreplaceable only in fact, not as far as Bob Winter was concerned. He knew that he had to behave or he would have to look for another job and the bank for another Pazinsky He shrugged and offered me a cigar.

"If you don't like him, you can quit," I told him declining. "From what they say about you, you could catch on any- where."

Peacefully, the light blue eyes wandered around the room. "Perhaps your life has been a good one, Mr. Carmichael," he said dreamily. "Perhaps you have many friends, a wife, chil- dren. A house with it own lawn. For all I know you have writ- ten books about your most difficult cases."

I laughed. "My most difficult case is the first hour of this one. Before that it was following a drunken locksmith to Erie by way of Memphis."

"Yes," Pazinsky said. "Then at least you have traveled." His eyes came down to mine. "I have this bank. I am forty-three years old and I have worked in this bank for thirty-one of those years. I literally started by sweeping the place." He smiled with satisfaction. "Do you see?"

My head nodded, more in wonder than agreement.

"And Bob may find the bank harder to run—or even sell—than he thinks." Pazinsky kept smiling. "What can I do for you?"

"Right now" I said, settling for the mundane after his inti- mate speech, "all I want from you is a description of the rob- bery and the related events. From the bank's point of view."

The banker nodded and picked up his phone. "Marjorie, bring me the book." Once he had hung up, he began his story.

"July of 1975 was a month of turmoil. On the first of the month, Tony took over as operating head of the Winter Na- tional Bank and Trust Company, that is, the bank proper. We have twenty-eight branches some bigger than this one. In fact, most are bigger than this one is now. Harold Winter as- cended to the new position of Chief Executive Officer of Win- terbank, Inc., the holding company. His idea, of course, was to prepare to take advantage of the proposed statewide banking law, which," he added scornfully, "has yet to materialize."

"In any case, Tony took over here. I remained, as always, second in command of Winter National. It was a ridiculous promotion, Tony over me," Pazinsky noted. "He still had to depend on me for almost everything."

"After a couple weeks, things returned to normal patters," he continued, "except that Tony began to come in late occasionally. That was unusual, because Tony did not really like to work evenings. Then one night, we had a bizarre conversation about the quarterly audit. I went into his office where he was sitting with the overhead light off. He said the florescent lights hurt his eyes, so he was using only a tiny desk lamp. He wanted to confirm the order he had given earlier in mid-July."

Only half interested I asked, "What order?" to show I was listening.

"Tony had wanted to delay the audit for one month, until September 15th," Pazinsky replied.

"Why? "

"He said the early date made it look as if Hal Winter didn't trust him," the doubtful banker explained. "He didn't seem to understand that everyone knew it was a routine thing. I let him have his way."

It seemed curious that Pazinsky, the slighted veteran had not tried to make an issue of Hiller's lapse, so I asked, "Why, if he was wrong?"

"He deserved the chance to make his own mistakes. We all do, Mr. Carmichael," Pazinsky said calmly. "That was all well and good as far as I was concerned. It was not vital at the time. But on that particular evening, about two weeks later, Tony became incoherent when I mentioned that the delay had been finalized."

"For almost five minutes, he chewed me out for changing a routine procedure," Pazinsky went on. "When I reminded him that I was only following his direct order, he backed off."

"What do you mean, 'backed off?'"

Gesturing with his hands, the small man said, "Oh, he apologized, profusely. Said he had forgotten, that he was having some problems. Vague things like that. I think I smelled alcohol on his breath, but I shrugged it off until a couple days later, when I reminded Tony of the episode. He sat smiling in the same chair and he denied even being in the bank that night."

My mind wandered back to the City Hotel Restaurant and Becky Stockly's complaints about Hiller's strange behavior in the August heat. "Was it the pressure of taking over such a big job?"

"How does one know, Mr. Carmichael?" Pazinsky wondered. "Certainly, there was an enormous amount of pressure, not only from his promotion but from employee resentment. None of them liked the idea much of a young man—a young Huntington man—taking over."

"Huntington man?"

Jack Pazinsky smiled at my incredulity. "Oh, yes, Mr. Carmichael. Make no mistake about that. To most of us, Tony Hiller was a Huntington creature, just as his parents had been. I recognize that may bean irrational idea, but we all had it."

"Were there any other signs of a problem on Hiller's part, Mr. Pazinsky?" I asked, leaving the old feud aside for the moment.

His sigh told me that he had a wealth of examples of Hiller's deterioration. "Little things mostly, I suppose. He would say good evening twice to the same people as if just meeting them. He did that often, greeting the same people twice. Occasionally he gave orders to have something done and then denied ever ordering anything at all. And," he added with emphasis, "he began spending a certain amount of time in the evening with the books. And the books were something he had successfully avoided from the start."

"Was he any good with the books?"

"Passable," Pazinsky replied. "He was competent at many things, but not really good at any one thing in particular."

"He was not a banker, not really," Pazinsky went on. "He worked in a gas station when he was young. He also worked here as a substitute teller during vacations. Then one day, Hal Winter walked down the street to the gas station and offered him a package that included a job, college and, presumably, Diana."

"And he took it," I stated, remembering how tempting some packages can be.

His eyes twinkling, he said, "A week later, the gas station suddenly closed and its owner, a fellow named Kowalski, headed for warmer climate."

"I see," was my comment, not sure I really did. Winter gone to extraordinary lengths to "adopt" the bottom rung of Huntington society.

"Anyway, Tony went to Amherst and CMU's business school. When he came back he was made senior Trust Executive."

"Pretty good for a raw kid," I said, still bewildered.

"Very good, indeed," Pazinsky agreed sarcastically. "And one of his first big accounts was an old man named Huntington."

"Fresh out of school, Hiller handled the Huntington account?"

Pleased with his little coup, Pazinsky confirmed his statement. "All the way through its complete collapse.

"Christ!"

"Don't get misunderstand, Mr. Carmichael," he said sternly. "Willard Huntington liked Tony and Tony did not make many investment decision alone. We have accounts like that, bona fide trust accounts. Willard Huntington, the last of the great Huntington's, could approve every move. And Hal Winter did the recommending. Mr. Huntington approved the investment in the high-fliers. The portfolio was a blue print for financial disaster. LTV, Litton, even Penn Central. Huntington had seen his money growing at a much slower pace than the market during the sixties, so he plunged."

"Fatally."

"Correct." Pazinsky laughed. "Conservatism turned around is wildly reckless. Willard Huntington was ridiculously leveraged. I don't know why, but he borrowed on everything, intending to make a quick glamor strike, perhaps. When the Conglomerates died, his collateral went down them, almost as though it was 1929 all over again. Until then, he owned half this town and three quarters of the county. Now, there's almost nothing."

I got the leverage part, the conglomerate part. I read the paper. I even own two shares of US Steel. But Huntington had put his money in Winter National. I had to ask, "Why Winter?"

Pazinsky grinned and shook his head. "You don't understand a small town, Mr. Carmichael. Willard Huntington didn't like Harold Winter very much. In fact, he hated him. But, for all that, he trusted him... more than he could an outsider. Especially with Tony there. You see, despite all that wealth, Huntington's mind was small town. He would be loath to give an outsider control of his assets. Both he and Harold Winter expected it. Neither was shocked or surprised," he explained. "None of us was."

Conceding the small town mentality—which escaped me entirely—I went back on topic. "What about the robbery?"

~ ~ ~

The robbery of Winter National's headquarters bank had been, according to Jack Pazinsky, a simple, even prosaic affair. A single man, with a stocking mask and a shotgun, stole into the bank just after high noon. Out of nowhere he appeared at the Bank manager's desk, ordered the doors locked and the vault opened. Ten minutes later, he crowded twenty people into the vault and walked out the front door.

"I was over at our Titusville branch at the time," Pazinsky said. "Part of my job is reviewing the operating status of each branch." For my purposes he added, "Following a pre-arranged schedule."

"That's the best kind," I responded. The Press had already told me that Pazinsky was between branches when the robbery took place.

"Would you like to talk to the manager. I got all of my facts from him," Pazinsky admitted.

I just shook my head. There were other things best answered by Pazinsky himself.

"The thief took the manager, the guard and three women with him into the vault, making it clear that he would kill them all if anyone left outside so much as tried the door," he continued. "He knew what he was doing, because he went very quickly from the cash drawers to the safe deposit box area. No hesitations. He went into both of those areas alone and came out with his bag full."

"Naturally, he didn't get anything from the safe-deposit boxes. Without the box holders' keys, the manager's key was useless," Pazinsky said. "All he got was about $23,000 in cash-on-hand and a few securities."

"No one used a phone?"

The smile he flashed wasn't for me so much as for the thief. "As a matter of fact, someone did try. The outside lines had been cut."

"What do you mean 'the outside lines?'"

"We have phone lines that connect with the outside world and inter-branch lines. The inter-branch lines carry inter-com and data-communications. They were not touched."

"Who would know about that?"

He shrugged. "Anyone who wanted to find out."

"And Hiller was at lunch."

"At the hotel restaurant, yes."

"Convenient?"

Jack Pazinsky shook his head. "Habitual. Tony did that every day, at the same time. He was a creature without creative impulse. Habit, routine, those were his strengths. He liked neither planning nor improvising. That is why I think he botched this whole thing up."

"He came pretty close, didn't he?"

"To some extent," Pazinsky replied. "But the whole plan he came up with was simple-minded. Following the robbery, he knew that Harold Winter would check over the books. And even a cursory look would reveal his sloppy embezzlement. At least, he didn't fool himself on that score. He had a very modest ego, Mr. Carmichael."

"I've seen how modest it is now.

Pursing his lips in appreciation, Pazinsky went on. "Once Hal took the books home with him, Tony knew he had to do something. So, he concocted, too quickly, his scheme to kill Hal Winter. The rest of it is less than a stroke of genius."

Conceding his point by changing the subject, I asked, "Who did it? The robbery, I mean,"

He scratched at his left temple. "That is still a mystery. The descriptions of the thief are vague. He could have been any-one."

"He came through your window?"

Pinching his eyes and mouth, Pazinsky glared at me. "Yes. So it seems," he acknowledged. "I do not recall leaving the window unlocked, if that is your next question."

It had been, so I had to think up another one. "What about the stranger? The 'old gray man' of the story. Did the police check him out?"

His smile was a gentle curve against the rough background of his. "That was Diana's term," he said quietly. "The name he used at the hotel was Samuel Weil. He was considered everything from a harmless tramp to a conspirator in the robbery to a ghost of Christmas past."

"He was an old fellow," Pazinsky said. "Probably not so old as he looked. He has a pronounced stoop and a slight limp. Most of the time, the limp was not noticeable. Occasionally, however, he seemed to have difficulty. His hair was gray, his clothes were tattered gray and skin had a gray cast to it; hence, Diana's popularized description of him as 'the little old, gray man.' After a while, the papers didn't even bother with his name."

"How long had he been in town?"

"Several weeks. He stayed at the City Hotel and ate there, too. Only dinner and an occasional breakfast. I didn't see him much during the day, or even at night. He seemed very bothered by the heat wave we were having that August. So were we all."

August of '75 had been a blistering month, I recalled. I had spent most of it sitting in a Buick with a broken air-conditioner, waiting to catch a building contractor at home to serve him papers. He never did show up and I ruined two shirts on the job. Mid-August brought some relief, but that didn't last long.

"His car was air-conditioned," Pazinsky suddenly remembered.

"I thought it an extravagance for a man with so little money. It was rented, a Pinto. His leg must have bothered him more in the heat, because he would drive anywhere in town whenever it was hot."

McGuiness' men must have traced the rented car and come up empty. I would have to ask him about it.

Pazinsky had seen that far away look in my eye, because he asked, "Is that all?"

His question reminded me of one more. "How had Hiller embezzled the hundred grand?"

Looking around his desk, he became angry. "I told that God-damned secretary to bring the account book in here," he snapped, rising. "Our friend Bob Winter fired Muriel, my right hand of twenty years."

"Forget the books," I said. "They wouldn't make any sense of them anyway. Just tell me."

He settled back into his chair, his face returning immediately to its normal color. "'Disingenuous' is the only word for it. We have many out-of-state accounts, checking, savings, trust. He creamed those. Particularly, the trust and management accounts, those he knew best," he explained. "It was flagrant. But only the routine audit or a reconciliation of the receipts book and the accounts book would turn that up."

"Ant Tony denies it?"

"Not anymore. But initially he did." Pazinsky laughed nastily at the artlessness of it all. "He should be ashamed of himself."

As I left, I figured that Tony Hiller was, at the very least, ashamed of himself.

Chapter Nine

There were plenty of lawyers and accountants in Franklin but my was car nosed toward Pittsburgh. My city was close enough and I figured Fred Tindale would tell me as much as anyone else could. I had a couple questions for Pete Kline as well and there was the hint of family feud dominating the whole county a complication best viewed for. Those two men would bring me an outsider's perspective, one that I was quickly losing myself.

And, incidentally, Janice Simmons was in Pittsburgh.

Since Diana was paying for the trip, I decided to do her business first, which took me to the Lawyers Building not far from Pittsburgh's City-County Building. Kline was on the sixth floor.

The receptionist hustled me into an empty office. Her apologetic grin told me that clients were about to come through the usual waiting area and wouldn't like my polyester appearance anymore than I did. All things considered the woman dripped charm and offered me coffee, which I took. I had enough experiences to expect a long wait.

Kline entered thirty seconds later, however and pumped my hand gently. Thin and wan, he looked tired and nodded when I mentioned it.

"We are bogged down," he said, grimly. "How are you?"

"Okay," I allowed, following him to his corner office. "I need some information, though."

His office, so neat the few times I had seen it before, was littered with papers, all of them legal-sized.

It was still a comfortable setting and Kline's harried expression seemed out of place.

Still he managed a weary smile once he was seated. "Okay, Carmichael." He called me that in private, Mr. Carmichael in front of clients. "What can I do for you?"

"How did you get this Winter business?" I asked bluntly.

He sighed, indicating that the Winter estate contributed to his problems. "I wish I knew."

"You don't?" Lawyers always knew where their clients came from.

"It was a referral, I suppose," he said. "A firm in Franklin is handling most of the straight probate, of course. But they did not send Diana to us."

"Diana?" I asked. That was mighty informal for Pete Kline.

He turned red, trying to rub it off his forehead with one hand, "Miss Winter," he corrected himself. "She is the kind of girl who elicits informality," he explained.

My chuckle put his at ease. "You don't have to tell me. I ended up her house guest yesterday."

The thin face brightened. "So was I at one point." Kline pursed his lips slightly. "My wife almost killed me."

We both laughed. "But you don't know who referred her to you?"

Kline motioned me to wait and went through a file drawer in his desk. It was head-marked "Winter Estate W-4587." He leafed through the papers, finally pulling out a long yellow sheet covered with small careful writing.

"She mentioned some individuals," Kline said reading the notes. "Several people we had represented in the past and a Lewis Huntington—the Lewis Huntington, I suppose—but we've never done anything for him." His face became reflective. "Lewis Huntington was the one who actually sent her to us," he said finally.

Curiosity cut through the confusion. "And you've never anything for him?" After he had nodded, I asked, "Then why would he, or anyone else, send Diana to you?"

Pete Kline smiled at my own easy use of her first name. He also shrugged. "It's not unusual in a way. But for a man of Lewis Huntington's position, even if his money is gone, it is very strange. I know of at least three firms in town, larger and, frankly, more experienced, than ours, with whom his family has dealings. One of them called me the other day, trying to find out why they had been left out."

"How did they know?"

The question had not occurred to Kline before. His narrow fingers played with his chin. "I don't know. She didn't say."

"She?"

"A secretary to one of the associates," Kline said almost to himself. "I didn't recognize the lawyers name actually, but her voice was familiar."

"You spoke only to her?" I asked, driven by the strange look on his face.

He shrugged again. "It's not unusual. And we deal with that particular firm quite a bit." He was explaining to himself, not me. "Since I recognized her voice, I assumed that she had been transferred from someone I had dealt with before."

He was losing me. "Hey, Pete," I said. "Remember me?"

Shaking his head he looked at me. His expression told me that he knew he had made a mistake.

Pete Kline hated making mistakes, even little ones. "Well, I called the firm back, several days later and asked for the same associate," he said. "And I got a different secretary. One who had no knowledge of the call."

"What about the lawyer?"

"He was a second year man," Kline went on. "He said he didn't have anyone call about it. He said it didn't make any difference to him. Then I talked to my senior contact there. He said it might have been a mistake. It seemed unlikely that they would get any of the Winter business after their ties with the Huntington's for so many years. He wished me luck."

"Are you saying that the call was a phony?" I demanded.

Kline shook his head and shoulders up and down. He fixed his eyes on a question he saw somewhere behind me. "Why did I recognize the voice?"

I didn't even have to think of the likely, beautiful reason, so I just made suggestions. "Maybe it was faked."

He worked his hollow cheeks in and out. "Could be. It had a deep studied quality to it. Her voice cracked a bit on the low notes," he said. "But why? What possible difference could it make?"

The question, like too many others piling up in the back and the front of my mind, did not have a ready answer. I let it slide and asked Kline for a list of beneficial interests in Winter's estate. We sat and drank coffee while the Xerox machine worked on the file. Neither one of us said anything. We didn't have anything to say.

~ ~ ~

Janice Simmons was out on a story, I was told. She wouldn't be back at the station until about 4:00. When I left my name the woman on the other end of the phone took a breath, a short sharp breath and said, "Yes, Mr. Carmichael."

That gave me an hour for Fred, so I headed back to my office. The uneasiness I had felt in Huntington disappeared on my walk from the Lawyer's Building to my landlord's Haller Building. A layer of smog I might not have noticed before protected me from April's cheerful sunshine as my feet trod the familiar asphalt path. To the people brushing past me, I was a stranger but not the curiosity I seemed in Huntington. Still, the crowded street felt oppressive.

The ancient elevator of the Haller Building greeted me with its usual creaky ride to the third floor. I crossed the old marble floor to my numberless office. Inside I found the room still in the artificially orderly state imposed by Diane's visit two days before.

When you've been a part of a something for a long time, you can tell when something is out of place. If they put a new manhole cover on a Fourth Avenue sidewalk, I can tell. And in my office, I could tell that the small, two-drawer file cabinet next to my desk had been disturbed.

No tangible evidence, mind you. Or rather, very little. Upon examination, however, I realized what was wrong. The cabinet is very old and dirty, as I can't spare the money to buy a new one or the energy to clean the old one. In any case, it smudges easily.

On the left side of the desk, however, it smudges usually on only one side. I open it facing the desk, being too lazy to turn the full ninety degrees required; consequently, I always open the drawer with my left hand, which leaves an attractive accumulation of smudges on the one side of the handle. To the opposite of the handle, I saw a couple prints, made by a right hand... with nice, thin fingers.

Janice Simmons had very nice, thin fingers.

And my address book.

I opened the top drawer. Again the appearance of the drawer told me that someone had carefully rummaged through it. The address book, of course, was gone from its usual place which was atop everything else. The other drawers had obviously been opened and searched as well, but nothing of value was missing. Nothing of value had ever been in there.

The file cabinet received my attention next. I hadn't spent much time in it lately, so I couldn't miss anything. All of the papers were old and useless, relics of another era in my life. I should have thrown all that stuff away after I got out of college, but the important stuff wasn't in any office in the city.

It occurred to me suddenly that Janice Simmons now knew more about my background than anyone, including my mother and Harry Blair. It didn't matter, but I hoped she wouldn't hold it against me.

That particular hope I had given up a while back.

Feeling a little deflated, I headed over to see Fred and Cath.

She was surprised to see me

"Christ, Carmichael. What the hell are you doing here?"

"I work here?"

She smiled the first real smile she'd ever given me. "Fred's going to leave his wife for me," she said. "How about that?" She held out her left hand, displaying the small emerald on her stubby ring finger. "We can't get a diamond, yet."

Cath Mays was always so dumb that I felt sorry for her, and for Fred, too, because he was so hooked on her. "Good for you, Cath." I meant it, because Fred's wife was a shrew and had never invited me for dinner in the entire five years I had known Fred and her.

"You can bring that Janice Simmons to the wedding," she said, with only slightly suppressed excitement. She probably figured it would make her wedding a social event.

"Sure, Cath," I said, wondering which was less likely, the wedding or my bringing Janice Simmons. "What did Miss Simmons say when she was here, Cath?"

Her broad, homely face took on a sly look. "She asked me about you," she said. "And Fred, too. Said you were working together and she might want to do a story on you."

And, of course, Cathy Mays had fallen for it. "Good," I lied. "She get to see my office?"

She nodded. "Sorry, but she wanted to. I didn't have time to fix up or anything."

"Is Fred in?" I asked, needing to get away from her.

"He's with a client," Cath said. "But I'll tell you what they talked about."

Undoubtedly, she had been listening in on Fred and Janice via her intercom, as she usually. It was probably just as well, because Fred had no memory at all for conversation.

"That's my girl."

She settled in her seat as though preparing to retell the plot of The Guiding Light. "She asked Freddie all about your past, where you came from, what you've done," and she added pointedly, "who your girls were."

I feigned dismay.

She giggled. "Don't worry, Freddie kept that quiet."

My life according to Fred Tindale was an open book to Janice Simmons. Fortunately, Fred knew almost nothing about me."

"She also asked if Fred recognized a mutual friend of yours who may have come to call," Cath said. "She asked me, too, of course. Neither of us had and she seemed disappointed."

Janice and I had one friend in common, Harry Blair. Cath and Fred knew Harry well. "Did she give a description?"

"Medium height, light brown hair, slender," she recalled, "intelligent looking. Whatever that means."

I laughed. "That could be anybody. Don't I have any friends like that?"

Disgustedly, Cath shook her head. "You don't have any friends at all, Casey. Except Fred and me." Then she added, suggestively, "And Janice Simmons," watching Fred's client leave.

"Who," I said with unfelt bravado, "I am seeing this afternoon." With that and an attempt at a wry smile, I left Cath to her telephone and soap magazines.

Fred sat behind his undersized desk bent over a sheath of papers, as usual. He had a pencil stuck behind each of his already too prominent ears and his sleeves rolled up about his skinny elbows. If I wanted to draw a cartoon of an accountant, I'd start with a photo of Fred Tindale at work.

"What's up, Freddie?" I boomed.

He dropped a third pencil on the floor. Momentarily shaken he said, "Oh, well. Casey."

Closing the door, I asked in a whisper, "What's this about you and Cath?"

A sheepish grin spread out over his narrow face. Before he started to talk, he put his intercom in his desk drawer. "I don't understand how she does that," he said. "I turn it off."

"She told me a fairy tale about marriage," I said lightly.

Poor Fred Tindale turned red. "I don't know what to say, Casey..."

"Did it have to be an emerald?"

He looked at me funny. "A diamond seemed like a bad idea…"

"Absolutely. It's just me."

"Last night, you know? I meant it. But how can I?"

"Start by dumping Sal, Fred," I instructed him, ever helpful.

Helplessly, Fred shrugged. "I suppose so.

Taking a seat in a hard wooden chair in front of the desk, I said, "I have a couple of questions for you." After he nodded, I went on. "I hear Janice Simmons came calling the other day?"

The accountant's dull eyes glowed. "Jeez!" he exclaimed. "She is beautiful! Is she really one of your…" He looked at me funny again. "Oh, I get it."

Fred had terrible difficulties discussing anything connected with women, especially the ones I knew. From some paperbacks, he had decided that the mysterious females tramping through my life had exotic wares to offer. I didn't tell him that most had only cheating husbands to peddle.

Fred surprised me. I'll bet he remembered what she was wearing, too.

He smiled, swallowing his own images of me whole. "She was very interested in you, Casey. She asked me a lot of questions. Mostly about your reputation. And your past."

About which Fred knew zero. "Anything specific?"

"She wanted to know where you came by the experience to get your license. I told her I didn't know." Then he wracked his benumbed brain for more. "Oh, yes. She wanted to know how you reacted to women, especially clients."

"And… how do I?"

He just laughed. "She seemed satisfied to find out that you are a 'tough nut with girls.'"

Holding in my reaction to Fred's Airport-book-rack vocabulary, I went on to my more important question. "Fred, how easy it is to doctor the books of a major bank?"

A scratch of his head reminded Fred that he had a pencil over his left ear. He took it down and looked at it, as if it were his lost puppy. Then he became serious. "Casey, I'm not a bank man, you know that. I just do small companies, individuals, that kind of thing. A bank is pretty complicated."

"Don't be so modest, Fred," I told him. "You started out in a bank."

He shrugged resignation. "OK, tell me what you want."

I related the story about the Winter embezzlement. As I went on, the furrows progressively deepened in Fred's short forehead. "It sounds to me like he didn't try to hide much. There are a lot of ways to do the same thing, but much more discreetly. It wouldn't be picked up right away, mind you, but the very first audit, that would be it."

"Then, only a guy getting ready to skip would do it the way Hiller did it?" I asked disappointed.

"Unless he was really stupid," Fred replied, "he'd be on a plane before they opened the books."

Fred's analysis pointed to Hiller's guilt no matter how you looked at it. The embezzlement ran counter to everything else I had begun to sense, or maybe, wanted to believe. "Thanks, Fred," I said, getting up out of the chair.

He smiled and took the intercom out of the drawer. "Anytime, Casey."

I glanced out at Cath, giving me her dirty look, and then winked back at Fred. "Good Luck, Fred," I added as I went out.

~ ~ ~

As I walked through WPPA's studio, the place bustled with activity It was 4:30 and the staff was deep into preparing the evening news. Vainly searching the corridors for Janice Simmons, I found myself in everybody's way.

A voice, warm and mellow, said, "You'll get in people's way standing there."

Turning, I saw the rich dark brown hair first. Then those damned, questioning eyes, the straight nose, the cleverly smiling lips. She wore a simple dual purpose suit of a soft green that paid proper homage to her figure and lit up her eyes. Annoyingly effective.

"I saw you coming," she said softly. "Come on. I want you to see the real me."

She took my arm and led me into a room filled with TV monitors. On two of the screens, Janice was speaking to some union pickets. Her hair was pulled closer to her face, making it slightly too dominant. Her outfit was striped medium blue and made her look thinner than she was and toned down the greens. The effort to tone down her looks—some—actually worked.

Over the speakers, I heard her coolly discuss the ramifications of a wild-cat strike. Her voice, deep and rich, sounded forced, cracking on certain words.

"Like me?" she asked.

I laughed at that. "Always the tough questions. You do look very professional," I added, "if less green."

She smiled back at my silence. "I try to look more natural on the screen," she said seriously, looking up at herself. "I want people to remember me as a reporter."

My question had to be: "How do you get your voice so low?"

She showed me, her voice sinking half an octave. "I have to do that to come across on TV as, well, very professional," she explained, flashing a smile. "When I started out, my voice—which even you think is pretty nice in person—sounded so horribly girlish on the air. I guess TV does not add ten pounds to one's voice. It took quite a bit of work, Casey. That and my accent." No trace of small town New Hampshire remained.

As we walked out of the room, into the lobby, I refused to admire her profile. She had a high forehead, angular nose, firmly angled jaw. I would try, but doubted I could put anything over on her. Direct and to the point, I said, "As I said, it sounds professional. Pete Kline thought so."

Her eyebrow went up and her mouth curved, but she didn't turn. "If you'll buy me a drink," she said, "I'll cop to it."

~ ~ ~

The nearest bar served us a double bourbon each. We took the glasses to a cozy booth. Janice settled herself across from me, took a long drink and stared at me. "Yes," was all she had to say.

"Why?" I demanded, locked on her gaze.

She looked away, at her drink, watching her fingers play with the rim. "It's a long story, Casey."

"I'm on my own time now." I had given Diana a good eight-hour stint, with more to come.

"Ever been to Toledo?" she asked.

I had tailed a runaway through there once, so I nodded.

"It's not a bad place. I had a pretty good job there, like the one I have now. They said they were saving me for something. I quit. Or, I took this job when offered. I wasn't getting anywhere, Casey. You see, I don't have much, except this stupid career. When it stalls, I overreact. I just can't stand it. Do you understand?"

"Sure."

"All my life, people have been clawing me. 'Oh, Janice, you're so wonderful this.' 'Janice, you're so beautiful that.'" She grimaced.

"Most of us hate that, too."

She frowned at me. "I know it sounds egotistical."

"No, actually, it doesn't."

That brought a smile. "So, you see? I need more than that. So, I concentrate on my work. When I came here, to this place, I had real hopes. It's the Group W Stations headquarters, a place you can get noticed. I was pretty high for this job. But what did I get? Nothing. No stories worth a damn. I tried to be patient, not my strong suit. And then I got lucky." Her eyes brightened with enthusiasm.

"Harold Winter's death," she went on, "I though that would be the big one. It was so bizarre. and it was all mine! I scoured the countryside up there." She laughed, happily this time. "I got in everybody's way. They chased me out of town twice. I felt I was onto something. Then it ended. They put Hiller away and I was pulled. They didn't want me in it any deeper. I was too valuable, they said, to be squandered on some beyond-I-80 country murder. So..."

"I've heard this part," I said sharply. "Let's skip Harry."

Janice closed her eyes. "I know what you must think of me, Casey," she said, all regret. "But it was part of the whole thing. He was so good to me. And, yes, I used him. He was strong and I needed that." After a lip-nibble, she added, "At the time, I really needed that."

"What about Pete Kline?" My patience was evaporating. "That other stuff you can save for your book. It's not my business."

Straightening her shoulders, Janice switched on business-like. "Yes, I called Kline. I used the name of a lawyer I knew and faked the rest. So I lied. Investigative reporters lie, Casey. So what?"

"It's the more 'why,' Janice," I said, leveling my voice.

She clenched her teeth as though my words hurt. "For the same reason I burgled..." she snapped before lowering her voice, "...your fucking office." That out she glared across the table, green eyes simmering. "There you stupid son-of-a-bitch! I've admitted it!"

I felt something inside collapse. My head throbbed with a strange dull pain. I wouldn't breathe. "That should do it," I said with what I had left.

She glared at me a long time before saying anything. Fighting to keep her mouth from shaking, she said, "I'm sorry." She forced out a nervous laugh that actually rallied me. "As you can see, I'm not always the calm, poised person I appear to be on the news."

That said, she became calm and poised again. "I was just digging, Casey. That's all. Diana Winter, to me, is a very suspicious character," Janice stated, everything okay on her end. "All that innocence must be covering up something. Besides, she's two-faced as Janus."

Still rebounding, I paused. And asked, "Long 'A?'"

"Very funny." She smiled, barely this side of condescending. "Janus—long 'A'—was a Roman God. They named January after him because he looked at what was coming and what was past. Literally, he was two-faced. Diana is the same way. I simply don't trust her."

I didn't wonder that Janice Simmons could not understand Diana Winter. And yet, they seemed to have a lot in common. Both had the looks that had put them on pedestals and both felt alienated by that very attention. Even isolated. Diana approached the problem in her own way, Janice in hers.

"So. You made her a priority."

Janice took a long, slow sip of her bourbon. "If Tony Hiller is not entirely lying or playing mad, I think she had something to do with it."

Her lack of empathy put me off. "Okay Janice, you play the woman, here," I said, words clipped.

"That's nice...."

"I mean, not the reporter."

For two seconds she returned my look with hard green crystals. "No, you didn't."

"Do you think she loves Hiller?"

When I didn't flinch, she looked away. "You don't think I'd know, do you?"

"I'll take your best guess," I said.

"Wow." Waving at the waitress, Janice put off answering. Once the order for another round was in, she said, again, "Wow."

I waited. It was very hard to do.

"Okay. No. Diana does not love Tony Hiller."

My face must have fallen, because Janice said, "I'm sorry, Casey. I don't think she does."

"It's fine. I'm no expert. That's why I asked you."

Both hands went up to her forehead and swept the hair to either side. She looked cleaner, more honest, the way she did on the evening news. "Oh, Casey. I'm actually glad you want her to. "

"But you don't want her to."

She flinched. "No."

"Maybe she does."

"Maybe she does," she admitted reluctantly. "Like a pet or something. But not really. Not the way... she should."

Janice struggled with her every word, a forced confession of weaknesses. "I tried to be fair, Casey. Really. Everyone else was so crazy about her, you know. Of course, you know. What's not to like?"

"I'm not arguing."

"A little would be nice."

"Okay. She is a fragile, young girl." I said.

"Who needs protecting," she added, her head tilted slightly. Nailing it.

"What about Lewis Huntington?" I asked, returning to offense, it being the best defense.

The greens flared and I misread them.

"More your type?"

"Lewis Huntington," she repeated. "He's very handsome. Very clever. Elegant, but effete. I tagged him as bisexual the minute I met him." She laughed, cruelly. "He's a perfect match for Diana."

"Is it him, then? Diana, I mean," I pressed.

She bristled. "You shouldn't question me like this, Casey. We're together on this. I'm not a witness. Or a suspect. I want to help you, but you're going to make me mad again." At the end, her voice acquired a pleading note.

I could hear myself being hard on her. She had earned it, I thought. Some. To be honest, though, she was simply too good to believe. That was on me. "Listen, Janice," I said, conciliatory. "I know I've been a little abrupt with you, but... When we sit, like this? I just want to listen to your answers. I don't even care about the questions. Understand?"

"Wow." She lifted her eyebrows. "You can disguise a compliment."

"Diana? Lewis? Your take."

As the drinks arrived, she was smiling. "Okay. No. Acknowledging my limited experience, I say Diana Winter does not love Lewis Huntington," she said. "Maybe she'd like to, but I don't think she's really capable of it, Casey. Not for Lewis, not for Tony Hiller. She's too self-centered."

"Hmm."

"Yes. Like me."

The self-commentary got me. It was either true or not, and I couldn't tell—and didn't care—which. "Jack Pazinsky?"

Her expression changed to one of fascination. "You're really something."

"Come on, Janice, help me out a little."

"Jack Pazinsky," she began, looking me in the eye again, "He's highly intelligent, highly belligerent and very strong." Her second double went down fast. "He picked me up—physically—and moved me out of his way at one point. I shook for an hour."

My own anger flashed. I would have to ask Pazinsky about that. "And Diana?" What do you think he feels for her?"

"Passion."

"Passion?"

"Sure, Casey," she said, voice smoothed. "You must remember passion.

Searching, I said, "It's a fruit?"

Looking me over, Janice smiled just a little. "Your friends told me that you don't have a passionate bone in your, not-too-bad-looking body. Should I buy that?" She didn't let me answer. "There are a lot of women's names in that little address book of yours. One of them must be special."

"If they pay in advance, they're special enough," I told her. "The really special ones don't want to be in my book."

She replied, eyebrow raised. "My name is in there."

"I wouldn't know. I lost the book."

"Careless."

"I'm working on that."

"This is fun." She was so obviously playing with me. If she wanted information, she could always ask.

"You asked Fred and Cath if someone had come to see me. Who?"

"Damn. You are too 'tough a nut' for me anyway." She allowed herself a brief, unconvinced laugh and answered my question. "It was Lewis Huntington. He bothers me."

"Why?

"He's 'too too,' you know?" she explained. "He seems to be the one who sent Diana to Kline's law firm, for no good reason. He couldn't even have known it existed. And then he recommended that she get a detective. That bothers me."

I shrugged. "I thought it was a damned good idea. Maybe, it'll catch on."

She looked at me, her green eyes lightening. "I think it was a damned good idea, too," she said.

It was getting late, and I wanted to see Alma Purcil in Huntington, so I said, "It's time for me to get back up north, Janice."

"I like the way it sounds," she remarked, puzzled. "Every time you say it."

Standing while I could, I searched for my wallet. One look reminded me to ask Diana for an advance of expenses. I pulled my last ten out and put in on the table. Before I could return the wallet to my pocket, Janice reached for it.

"May I?" she asked. "I'm curious."

"No secrets from you."

"It's almost empty," she said inspecting it professionally. "No pictures, or notes. Just this license and six dollars." Her eyes narrowed as she asked earnestly, "Why Casey? Why does a man like you end up with that neglected little office and this equally sad excuse for a wallet?"

It's not the kind of thing you explain, so I didn't.

Besides, knowing Janice Simmons, I wouldn't have to.

Chapter Ten

"Alma?" Ned Cooper asked. "Well, she lives on the third floor."

The old man looked at me disapprovingly. Ned Cooper had managed the rundown City Hotel for forty years and did not like my treading on his carpets. He let me know it in a variety of ways, none of which required words.

"Follow me," he said, resigned. He perched a small sign atop the front desk and led me to the elevator. "She's an old woman, Mr. Carmichael. I suppose you have to talk to her?"

"Diana thinks so," I said, employing my ace.

He nodded.

The elevator moved so slowly, it took sixty seconds to reach the third floor. During that time Ned Cooper worked his dentures around silently. Once the cage opened, he said, "Diana. should have let it alone, Mr. Carmichael. There's nothing she can do. There wasn't before either."

He didn't let me wander off by myself. Instead, he led the way down the dark hallway himself to Alma Purcil's room. "Alma?" he called.

The door tapped against the molding several times, as three locks were undone on the inside. The door opened, revealing a tiny, frail woman over eighty years old. When she saw me she smiled broadly, wrinkling her surprisingly smooth face.

"Mr. Carmichael," she enthused in a high pitched voice that made me think of Janice Simmons. It was as high as Janice made hers low. "Come in I've been expecting you to drop by."

Ned Cooper let me go in and, to my surprise, followed me. Alma led the two of us into a room that doubled as her sleeping room and social room. It had an old davenport—as she called it—and two fine old, stuffed chairs. In the corner of the room a parrot called out a greeting, "Hellos to you both."

"That's Willard," she said. "I named him after Mr. Huntington."

"Sounds like a smart bird," I said. Parrots made me uneasy, with their peculiar way of interrupting conversations. Willard gave me a sidelong glance that warned me he lying in wait for my big questions.

She laughed at me. "Don't worry, Mr. Carmichael, Willard is very well behaved. So you mind yourself, Willard."

The bird walked to the corner to the cage and pouted. "Aw," he said.

Mrs. Purcil settled herself and looked at me with interest. "Shoot," she said, brightly.

"You know why I'm here," I said, giving her credit for being on top of things. "I want you to tell me what you remember about August 18th last year.

"The party-line confession," she started nodding firmly. "That's what she kept calling it."

"Who?" I asked.

"The pretty young lady from the TV station. From Pittsburgh."

"Janice Simmons?"

"She tried so hard to get me to remember that I started to forget." Mrs. Purcil did not hide her amusement. "Nice young lady anyway.. But," she announced, "I still remember most of it."

"Shoot," I said, to her delight. She imagined that detectives talked funny.

"Suzanna and I," she began. "Wycick. Suzanna Wycick and I were chatting away. Suzanna being a dreadful gossip," she allowed, winking at me. "We do that every night from 9:30 to 10:15. It is our entertainment, like television or radio for everyone else. It is very regular, Habit is our weapon against boredom, you see. So every night we talk away, like Willard here, when I give him a little gin."

Willard heard his name, or the word gin, and started saying "Willard wants a drink. Willard wants a drink. Make it a double," over and over until he was sternly shushed.

"Suzanna and I carry on just like that," she continued. "But that night, we were interrupted. That happens all the time, of course, even though everyone knows our schedule. People have something to tell us and break in. But that night after we heard the click, we didn't hear anyone talk into the phone. Wilma, Henry Wiggin and Mr. Winter were the others on our party-line. There used to be more, but people have been dropping off, getting their own."

"As I said, so, anyway, we heard the click. I was going to ask who it was, when I heard Hal Winter's voice. He was mad, or almost, I could tell. Then I heard, I'm sure now, I heard Tony Hiller talking. They were arguing about something, something about the bank. That was when Tony got mad. But Hal Winter said he knew about Tony's embezzlement. That was a shock, I'll tell you. I've known Tony for as long as he's been alive and I couldn't see him taking anything from anyone."

Alma Purcil sighed, as though dismayed over a world without rules. "Then came the strange part. Tony admitted that he had embezzled the money. Very brazen, But he said, 'I have a plan to hush it all up. Starting with you.' That's when Hal let out a gasp we could hear easily."

"The shotgun," Ned cooper offered.

The narrator shrugged. "Anyway, he became very quiet after that. Tony did all the talking. 'That bastard'—That's what he said—'screwed me up. I have it all figured out,' he said.

'You're the only one on to me. I know Jack isn't,' meaning Jack Pazinsky, over at the bank."

"'If you're out of the way, I'll have time to fix it up and leave the state,' he said. 'That old guy staying at the City Hotel will be my cover. I'll just say that he hit me and handcuffed me. Handcuffed to a chair in my basement.'"

"So, Hal congratulated him on his scheme and asked why," she continued, assuming different voices as needed. "'What do I have?' Tony asked. 'Nothing that isn't yours. Including Diana. I want something of my own. I figured to buy myself a chain of gas stations, maybe in New England, I liked it up there.' Tony always wanted something like that."

The old woman stopped, worn out by her efforts. "Tony, Tony," Willard cried, usurping the pause.

After a quick glance to quiet the bird, Alma shook her head. "Then we heard a boom, like an explosion, right near the phone. That was it until the police got there. The line was still open. One of the boys even said hello to me. Then they hung up."

"And you called the police?"

"Yes. I had to find a dime for the pay phone first. Suzanna stayed on while I was out the hall. Someone had to." She smiled. "It's so sad really. I knew them both, Hal and Tony. I didn't blame either one of them for what happened to Willard. Willard Huntington, that is."

My thank-you smile in place, I rose to go. "Mrs. Purcil, you've been a great help, thank you."

She shook my hand, with hers barely able to cross my palm. "Come back when you have time and I'll have Willard do some of his impressions for you. He's very good. Say good-bye Willard."

The bird said "so long sailor" and I returned the compliment.

Cooper and I walked back to the elevator. The whole story didn't sound remotely right. It was too silly. And yet if it hadn't been for the party-line, Tony Hiller would be as free as a bird.

~ ~ ~

"Of course, it's unfortunate," Ned Cooper said, as we descended. "I have always been fond of Tony. He was a close friend of Lewis'. If that's possible... for a poor boy to be friends with a rich one." He added a well worn "I don't know."

"If Tony was so close to a Huntington," I wondered, "why did Harold Winter make him his heir apparent?"

It was a dumb question, I suppose, At least the look of incredulity on Cooper's face said it was. "The answer is the question."

"You mean because?" I asked, dismayed at the perversity of the feud that so twisted the small town.

Ned took up his vigil behind the desk. I hadn't seen anyone the lobby either of the times I had been there myself, and so felt as if I were a private office.

"Tony used to live in this Hotel," he explained. "Tony's parents both worked for the Huntington's. She as a domestic, he as maintenance man here. No one this town was more a part of the Huntington's than Tony Hiller. Not even me."

"You've managed this place for forty years?"

"And owned it for five," he added. "This was the only piece of property that Mr. Huntington didn't mortgage, though Tony recommended it. So, after everything came apart, this was the only thing that Hal Winter couldn't seize. Lewis inherited it and gave it to me before he left town again."

"Gave it?"

"Yep."

My disbelief doubled when I thought of Lewis Huntington's somewhat arrogant and effete manner. Would a man like Lewis Huntington part with the only tangible part of his inheritance? "That's generous."

Cooper let the scorn flow with his words. "The Huntington's, Mr. Carmichael, were generous people. Willard Huntington made an enormous amount of money, but he didn't hoard it, or put out to people as loans. He gave it, to me, to

Tony's parents, to the people of this county. He didn't deserve what happened to him."

"What did happen, Mr. Cooper?" I asked. "I have a feeling I don't know."

"A stroke," he said. "A stroke. There wasn't anybody left to care for him, not really. His brothers all died the war, the first one, or in the flu that followed. His sisters married fools and went off. Two sons volunteered for war, the second one, and neither came back. No, actually Sam Huntington, Lewis' father, went off to Korea for some damn fool reason."

"The old man sent Lewis to college, to learn some business," Ned continued. "And he wouldn't so much as let me tell the boy about his stroke So what did he do? He put his money in Harold Winter's hands. I don't know if Tony's being there mattered. I don't blame anybody, mind you, I just feel it wasn't right. They convinced the old man that the future was garbage scows called Conglomerates. Comparing his fortune to that one Hal Winter had tripled, Mr. Huntington figured he wasn't leaving enough behind, so he swallowed the advice."

"They call it leverage, now," Cooper said disdainfully. "But we called it 'hocking' in my day. Or worse. Well, he borrowed from Winter National to buy more of the junk they recommended. Nobody expected the stock market to drop like it did, but Winter stood by his recommendations, didn't call the loans at first, then he panicked. The bank's money was going down the same drain, so they called in loans like markers in a poker game. People in the county lost everything. Including Willard Huntington."

The memory made him more mad than anything else. "It killed him."

"What happened to Lewis?"

"He came back from school to wind things up as best he could. He damn near thrashed Tony. When he left he vowed he'd never come back," Ned replied. "He dropped out of school and, after giving this place to me, we didn't hear from him until after all this."

We stood in silence for a moment. My own voice was subdued when I spoke. "Why did he come back?"

Ned Cooper looked at me hard, but not resentfully as he had before "She asked him to."

"Diana?"

"Who else?"

"Why?"

"You ask her. You work for her."

I took his answer for what it was worth and left the City Hotel. I left by way of the restaurant. Becky Stockly was still hard at work, getting things ready for dinner,

She glared at me as I took a seat at the counter. I could tell she didn't want to serve me, so I ordered out loud. "How about a cup of coffee?"

Becky didn't answer, but prepared the cup. It was black and hot, scalding my tongue as I gulped it. I didn't usually drink my coffee that way, but it didn't matter much at that point.

"You'll burn yourself that way, Casey," a sweet velvet voice said to me.

Diana sat down next to me, nodding to Becky who brought a second cup. "Hard day?"

"They're all hard for me," I replied lightly.

She seemed eager and fearful at once, not hearing what I had said. "What did you find out?"

I tried to dodge and be clever at the same time. "That it's nice to see a pretty face at the end of the day."

Weak as it came out, it did have some effect on Diana. She blushed first and then said, "Why thank you, Casey. That's earning your pay."

Laughing helped lift me out of the blues Ned Cooper had given me somehow. I let myself feel even better when she took my hand and led me to the back of the restaurant. It was dimly lit and "more romantic," as Diana put it.

"Since I can't fix you dinner," she announced, "I'll order it for you."

Any man who didn't take to Diana Winter was simply bone dry and I wasn't quite there, yet. Sharing a table with her seemed a fine, if temporary, fate. Her life and warmth made the three foot square table a world by itself.

But thoughts left over from the other world out there, the one she wanted me to turn inside out for her, came back with Becky Stockly's every entrance. Her brooding, disapproving face reminded me of Janice's take on Diana. It immediately dampened the glow Diana imparted.

~ ~ ~

Back in the shadows of the City Hotel Restaurant, Diana Winter and I had a pleasant dinner. My only complaint lay in the lighting. Once I swallowed a grasshopper during a late-night picnic on a college green and have always examined my food since. It was not all that dark in the restaurant, but I was skeptical as to the identity of my meat.

The ceiling fixtures were all relatively new and well dusted, but three of four bulbs over our table had called in sick. When I asked Becky Stockly about it as she poured our coffee, she glanced up in disgust.

"Ned told me not to bother," she said, "So I spend half my time apologizing for them."

"Don't apologize to me," I told her with a smile. "Never apologize for something that isn't your fault." It was my favorite and often reinforced lesson.

She gave me an odd look, not knowing what to make of my unexpected profundity. Becky had ignored Diana all night, saving the little attention she had left for me. Every time she had passed, I could feel her dark circled eyes measuring me.

"Okay," she said finally. "Then I'm sorry for this morning."

"This morning?" Diana demanded. "What happened this morning?"

Miss Stockly sighed over Diana's insensitivity. "I was very rude this morning," she explained. "I shouldn't have been."

The three of us were silent for a bit, studying each other. There was an anxiety about the waitress, a reticence that told me she wanted to talk to me, alone. Diana, however, looked like she wouldn't leave me alone and definitely not with Becky Stockly.

"There are a couple questions," I said, watching Becky's shoulders sag bit by bit, "that only you can answer. I'm afraid they are very personal questions."

Her thick eyebrows went as far up as they could go. "Oh?" She shot a troubled glance at Diana.

Petulantly, Diana resisted the trend of the conversation. Her eyes wondered what anyone could want to ask Becky private. The set of her little mouth said she intended to stay and find out.

My hint failing, I came right out. "Diana, I'd like you to go home and get a flashlight or two," I said, "Then, meet me in front of Tony's house. In twenty minutes. Would you do that?" I asked, striving for a tone of gentle command.

Her head bowed slightly, she looked up at me, her big brown eyes shimmering with hurt. "Yes, sir."

Diana rose, walked slowly out the door to Main Street. She used the walk I'd seen before, the step from the waist. It was her most adorable little pout.

Once Diana had passed from view, Becky sat down. She didn't seem worried that the restaurant was still half-full. "What did you want, Mr. Carmichael?" she asked, unsure.

Conjuring up a question, I asked, "Did you ever serve Mr. Weil?"

She looked confused. "Who?"

"Weil," I said, "the old vagrant I've heard so much about."

A grin found its way onto her mouth. It probably didn't happen much anymore. "I didn't know he had a name. Funny, isn't it?" The mouth drooped as she shook her head reflection. "Oh, I served him all right," she said. "I've served everybody this town, Mr. Carmichael. Their meals, at least."

Her deep-rooted unhappiness made me curious, but I had to put that off. "Tell me about him, Becky."

Her eyes lit up a little, as though she hadn't expected me to use her name. "He was an ordinary looking old man," she said, cooperative now. "This town has a lot of old people. It always has, as far as I remember. He was like the rest."

Searching her memory, she began a description of Samuel Weil. "He was less than six feet tall, about five foot-ten, maybe. He had started to gain weight, he told me once. But he wasn't fat, for his age. His hair was gray, going on white, and short. Most of the time he was unshaven and his beard was gray."

"His complexion changed with the weather. When it was hot, he looked better; I guess hot weather was better for him, because in cool weather—we had about three really cool days August—he looked terrible. His skin was all pasty and sort of gray"

She had a pretty good eye for detail. "What about his limp?"

She smiled in a kindly way. "He hid it. He was funny that way. When someone was watching him, he walked almost straight up with no real limp at all. But I saw him walk through the lobby when it was empty, plenty of times," she said, grimacing at the recollection of the sight. "He had a terrible sway to the—let's see—the left. It was so sad.

"Anything else?"

"I think he had false teeth, which may have been why he always ate back here."

"In this corner?" I asked, surprised. "In this light?"

She nodded. "He seemed to like it dark. He never ate anywhere else." She caught herself and corrected the statement. "There was one time. Someone else had taken this table. He became very upset. He had to sit at the counter. Only he decided not to stay. I think the stool was bad for his leg, the way it kind of dangled. I could see the special heel he had on the shoe. His leg must have been pretty bad, and he was uncomfortable."

She got up and demonstrated, leaning her left elbow on the counter. "It isn't even comfortable for my leg."

Her right leg swung, its firm slender lines making her short outfit look right. Only a long scar over her knee marred the look. She caught me looking at it, and stood up abruptly.

"Anyway," she continued, "he left without ordering. I tried to get him to let me bring something to his room, but he said not to bother."

"Room service? You must have felt sorry for him."

Her rounded shoulders came up a little. "I suppose," she allowed, as though guilty. "I don't know. Sometimes, the way he'd look at you, I could tell that there was so much life left in him, but..." she finished with the rest of her shrug.

"When did you see him last?"

A smile crept back on her lips. "The day of the robbery, actually. He came down for breakfast," she remembered. "He ate a big breakfast and chatted for a while about the weather. He said the cool weather was good for his leg. And he put a really big tip in my hand as he left." Her hand involuntarily closed on the memory. "He said I was the nicest person he'd met in twenty-seven years."

Becky Stockly had probably waited about that long for a real compliment. The look on her face told me she figured she'd have to wait the same period for the next.

~ ~ ~

When I showed up late in front of Hiller's house, Diana was mad at me. One elbow on each knee, she sat on Hiller's front stoop staring at the ground. Beside her lay three very powerful flashlights

"Good work," I said cheerfully.

Anger shone her eyes, bright enough to be obvious in the dimming light of evening. "Don't hurry on my account," she snapped.

Letting the comment, and hopefully the mood, dissipate itself in silence, I gathered up the lights, and Diana, and went to the door. Neither the bell nor strong raps on the door brought Ed Hiller downstairs.

"I have a key," Diana said, still cool, but warming. "Tony gave it to me. I thought we might need it."

Cheered at that break, I took the key, tried it and opened the door. Hugging her shoulder, I said, "That's my girl. Shall we?"

"Humph," she replied, accepting my invitation to precede me into the Hiller house.

Inside, the first floor lights were out. Upstairs, the hall light glowed, but too gently to throw much illumination on the path we followed to the basement. We used the flash-lights

"What are we doing, exactly?" she asked, curiosity over-coming her snit.

Opening the door to the basement, I told her. "We are in-vestigating. Unfortunately, I don't know what we're looking for."

"Great," she said. "Is this illegal?"

My shrug did not comfort her, but she followed my lead down the stairs. The cellar lay open before us, darker than I had expected. No light at all came through the windows, all of which were at the back of the room.

I fixed my light on the chair, still in the dead middle of the room. It was a sturdy wooden chair, straight back, with no arm rests On closer examination, it appeared unmarked by any serious scratches except in the back.

"Do you know how Tony was handcuffed here?" I asked in an unintentional whisper.

Diana nodded and sat down. She sat on the chair back-wards and tried sticking her arms through the back. "I can't really do it, my arms are too short."

I lifted her up by the shoulders and took her place. With my shoulders hunched over the back of the chair, I could put my hands through the top opening back to front, and then behind my waist. It was very awkward, but not too painful. "Like this?"

"That's what I was told."

My hands were free enough to fasten cuffs on myself, so Hiller could have done the same. Again, it would have hurt, but it could be done. Moreover, it would have been very difficult to try to lift the heavy wooden chair from that position. All of which told me zero.

Abandoning the chair, I swept the beam of the flashlight around the room. There was nothing unusual about the cellar, nothing to abet or hinder either Hiller or Weil. The door, I tried out of habit.

Surprisingly, it was unlocked. It had not been when I had visited earlier in the day. I opened it carefully, noting that it had scraped a layer of dirt away from the area where I had found the phone button.

With my light on the site of my discovery, I could see that someone else had been digging around in the fine silt. Nothing else was obvious upon my closer examination, so I filed the information away for later.

Before shutting the door, I noticed an unusual accumulation of grime on the wood not far from the door knob. It smeared when I ran my forefinger across it. I detected a slight oily smell from the residue on my finger. For the moment I had to shrug that off, too.

Diana and I returned to the first floor and went out the back door. Hiller's backyard was small, but surrounded with high shrubbery. If anything had happened, as Ed Hiller had said, only someone in the house or yard could have seen it.

The back of the house had three windows on the upper floor. Two were large enough to be bedroom windows, the third undoubtedly a bathroom window.

"Which is Ed Hiller's room?" I asked Diana

Without hesitation, she pointed to the leftmost room, the one commanding the best view of the backyard. From there, Ed Hiller could have easily seen almost anything that had happened in the yard on that 18th of August.

I traced what I thought the most likely path Weil might have taken, assuming that he had done what Ed Hiller had accused him of doing. With Tony unconscious, Weil could have dragged him to the top of the steps leading to the cellar. The wooden steps were steep, and, as I had learned earlier, treacherous even in daylight. With care, however, Weil could have dragged Hiller into the basement.

He would have done it very carefully, for Tony had no bruises other than his head injury when found. An old man would have had great difficulty, but could have done it if necessary. If Becky Stockly were right, Weil had something left in him after all the years. Once in the basement he could have cuffed Tony Hiller to the chair. But why?

~ ~ ~

Diana offered to drive me back to my car, sitting in front of the City Hotel. I accepted, if only because her tone of voice told me she wanted to talk.

"Okay, Casey," she said stiffly as we drove off. "Have you been chasing ghosts all day?"

"Maybe," I replied. Miscellaneous information was piling up, but I was still short on theories. "If we assume, as you want me to, that Tony Hiller's story had validity, we have to first assume that Tony did intend to meet Sam Weil, the old vagrant."

"Right," she agreed. "And that Weil hit him and put him in the basement."

"The question then becomes," I stated, thinking as I went, "if Tony was out of action, how could he have been with your father when Mrs. Purcil says he was?"

Diana looked at me suspiciously. "She's lying?"

Alma Purcil could have been a good liar, but I doubted it. "That is possible, but it is more likely that she just thought she heard Tony and your father. Perhaps she did not."

"But she is so adamant." Diana did not like the theory any more than I did. "And Alma should know both of them well enough."

Alma's Willard came into my head for a second, flashing his bright green wings and chuckling. "Someone could have faked Tony's voice," I said suddenly. It wouldn't have taken perfection, due to the vagaries of telephone connections.

Things started to make sense. "There is only one reason," I said, "for the removal of the party-line phone's button: Whoever removed it wanted it to be possible to tip the phone just enough so that eavesdroppers could hear the whole conversation." I berated myself for being so dense.

"But surely Father did that," Diana countered.

"No, that's just it, Diana," I said. "He could have, of course, but he did not remove the button."

She shook her head as we pulled up behind my car. "It was his phone."

"The point is this, though. Whoever took the button out of the phone also dropped it at Hiller's house."

"Then Tony…"

My mind raced through a series of conclusions. "Uh uh, not Tony. Tony is the only one who would not remove the phone's button, who would not want to be overheard. His confession wasn't intended for anyone but your father."

Diana became more puzzled as I went on. "I guess."

"Let's look at it step by step," I said, "First, there is Tony Hiller. He does not want to be overheard, so he would neither tip the phone. He certainly would not remove the button to make it easier. Second, we have your father. He might want to tip the phone and remove the button to make it easier, but he couldn't have dropped it at Tony's. And if Tony had discovered the button he wouldn't have tried lying the way he did."

"I see. I think."

"With both of them eliminated, we can believe that Tony may not have been lying or crazy," I concluded. The idea, however farfetched, began to grown on me. It made a perverse sense. "Assuming Weil clobbered Tony—and we have Ed Hiller's viewing for that—then Weil is our suspect. He's the man who dropped the phone button which he could have removed from your father's phone."

Becoming excited despite her confusion, Diana asked, "Why?"

My smile was inappropriate, but couldn't be helped. "Because Weil wanted to frame Tony," I replied. "It's perfect for a frame. No one sees Tony. They just hear him. Only they don't hear Tony, they hear Weil impersonating Tony."

"Oh, do you really think so!"

"I think," I said, all of a sudden cautious, "that we may have a theory to go on. I do not think that we can begin to prove it yet. "

Diana's face became serious. "Casey," she said in a low, fearful voice, "How do you account for the fact that Father called the man 'Tony' several times? He didn't seem to have any doubts."

That quickly, my spirits deflated. "Well perhaps he couldn't see him," I tried valiantly.

"It is a difficult mistake to make," she insisted. "The study is never that dark when Father is working. The light over the desk was on."

"The theory needs work," I admitted, now feeling the length of the day. "But it is a direction. Backwards. Everything in this case is backwards That's just the way we have to think."

Since neither of us felt like continuing the conversation, I got out of Diana's car and headed for my own. For that short stretch, I had really felt the outline of the case taking a definable shape. Almost as quickly, the silhouette melted into shadows again.

My frustration distracted me enough that I didn't notice the bright red Porsche parked in front of my Granada, until I hit it gently in the nose. Slamming the door of the offending Ford, I got out again to inspect the damage

It seemed like a fitting climax to the day, my clubbing a twenty thousand dollar car. Fortunately, only the bumper showed signs of my negligence. That made me even more frustrated. I couldn't make a dent in anything. So I kicked the car in the license plate.

I succeeded only scraping my shoe on a plate guard that told me the Porsche had been purchased from a dealer Pittsburgh. Then it came to me: Janice Simmons was in Huntington.

Chapter Eleven

As usual, the City Hotel Lobby was empty. Except for Janice. Even Ned Cooper had disappeared, which gave the place more emptiness than usual. As for Janice, she sat in one of the ageless stuffed settees that dotted the lobby.

Her legs were crossed and gently angled, one foot dancing to an internal, nervous music. A tape recorder sat in her lap and she played with the microphone dangling from her right hand. The dirty nail on the index finger of her left hand dug into the hollow of her cheek as, she balanced her chin on her thumb. Her upper lip curled under while her teeth worked it over.

Janice looked very tired, nodding her head occasionally, then jerking erect. The dazzling greens were barely open.

"Tough to get a room this town," I said, sitting on the couch beside her.

She let her head slip off of her hand and looked at me bleary-eyed. "I've been waiting for you," she said thickly.

"Why?"

She chuckled. "I was lonely in Pittsburgh. I like the country better," she said, brushing imp hair from her cheek.

I looked her over closely. She looked as if she hadn't seen a bed in days, though she'd been fine just that afternoon. "You look dead, Janice." I said softly.

With my words, Janice's back became straighter, her eyes wider.

"I didn't mean anything by that, Janice. That wasn't meant as e slap."

A tiny smile overcame the frown of fatigue. "I know, Casey." She kissed me lightly on one cheek, her soft hand caressing the other. "I won't be so lonesome if you stay, but I don't suppose..."

"That would be a news flash around here that we do not need."

Leaning her heed beck, she sighed as though distressed, but her smile came beck when she lowered her eyes to mine. "You can take the car, if you'll meet me here for breakfast tomorrow at 8:00."

"Breakfast is not news."

"We could make it news, Casey," she warned me. "Goodnight."

Struggling against a dozen contrary impulses, I got to the door and into the air. Before I closed the door, she called me back.

"I was going to trade you some information," she said, leaving the other side of the bargain to my imagination. "But, if you can wait until morning for it, I can wait, too."

She had come all the way from wherever she had been to see me, to tell me something. It had to be important, or I had misjudged Janice Simmons. The funny thing about it, though, I didn't care whet she had to say. I also didn't care that her unpainted nails betrayed a fine layer of dirt. My curiosity, so active, so insistent all day, did not stir one bit. There was something else on my mind. "Am I supposed to think you're going easy on me?"

She tilted her head, her tired eyes showing only green half-crescents. "Maybe I am," she said. "Maybe because I'm on vacation."

Pointing to the tape machine I said, "From what?"

Her gaze traveled lazily to the cassette recorder and slowly back to mine. "From Pittsburgh," she told me. "I was in Cleveland, Buffalo and Elmira, since I talked to you last."

She sighed, putting her hand on my arm. "I mean, since you chewed me thoroughly out."

I didn't want to forget whatever anger, suspicions, or reservations about her. I resisted the gentle weight of her hand as she leaned close. Finally, she let herself collapse against my shoulder.

With Janice's hand now tightly grasping my arm and her thick hair spilling over my shoulders, I felt those feelings built up over twenty-four hours vanish without a trace. There was nothing I wouldn't do for her, including believe her.

"Casey?" she asked dreamily.

My "yes" came out a little weak.

"Will you drive me to my motel? I already paid for the night," she said, breathing deeply and snuggling closer.

I nodded.

She laughed softly. "Was that a nod or a shake?"

All my head could do, it seemed, was nod.

She put her hand gently on my face to make sure what I was doing. "My, aren't we taciturn," Janice said, struggling to sit up. She shivered as she shook off the fatigue.

The recorder sat demurely in her lap. "Interviewing you would be frustrating, Casey, you know that? How would I ever transcribe your half of our conversation?"

Helping her to her feet, I said, "I never say anything worth remembering. It's a trick I learned a long time ago."

Janice put her arm in mine and started for the door. I found she still had to lean on me to make it to her car. "I'll bet," she retorted. "I'll just bet, Carmichael, that you could say something worth remembering if you wanted to. Care to try?"

Without answering I shoved her into the passenger seat of her expensive German car. I couldn't take my eyes off of her, through the windshield, as I walked around. Inside, she shifted about the seat until she was nestled in, her face even more appealing for the fatigue. Whatever made her face look hard and sometimes, I guessed, unforgiving, was gone then.

After crooning out the directions, Janice said nothing until I cranked the hand brake in front of her motel room. "Are we there?"

"Yes," I replied. With mixed emotions I prepared to help her out of the low seat. I didn't want to leave her until she was securely in bed, and yet, I knew that I had better.

Once the door was unlocked, I made a move to go. She did not hold herself up, however, and began to slump to the carpet. My reflexes working better than usual, I caught her and sat her firmly on the bed.

I followed her motions to a bottle of scotch in the bathroom. Two glasses had been unwrapped and were waiting with melted ice in them. Restoring the ice, I poured a little for both of us.

With a shot of scotch in her, Janice could open her eyes a little. With her hand on my arm again, she made me sit next to her on the foot of the bed. "I was waiting for you so long," she said, forlornly, "Where were you?"

Her question, the first in minutes, reminded me of my own hard day. "Poking around."

"I saw your car," she said, letting her eyes close again. "So I figured you had to be upstairs or something. At the Hotel."

I just nodded.

"You aren't mad I came, are you?" she asked hesitantly.

"Should I be?"

Janice took my glass and drank my Scotch too. Her chest heaved as the alcohol warmed her throat. "What do I have to trade you for some four word sentences, Casey Carmichael?"

Avoid those leading questions, I told myself,

She rose, with a sigh, to replenish the glasses. "Look how the ice has melted in here!" she exclaimed. She came out carrying the plastic ice bucket in one hand and the glasses in the other. "See?"

I took my glass and shrugged. "So, I kept you waiting," I said. "If I'd known there was ice involved..."

"The ice has melted," she said again. "Why don't you?"

The glass slipped my hand, but it didn't go far. I was becoming accustomed to the unexpected. Nothing was more unexpected than a proposition from Janice Simmons. If that is what it was. "You'd need a bigger bucket."

My first Scotch went down in a hurry. I nabbed her glass and evened the score.

Her disapproving look became a smile and then an airy laugh. "You're funny, Casey," she said, "I can't help but like you."

"Thanks, for trying, anyway," I said. "I like you, too, even if you aren't always so funny."

Her tired eyes opened all the way. It could have been surprise but I guessed that she was mistakenly insulted,

"What I meant, Janice," I explained, "is that you are not a lightweight. You are way out of my division."

With that assurance her eyes became slits again. "Uh uh, Casey Carmichael," she said. "I know better. You went to college, three of them, and you did okay. As well as I did... better."

She had access to my college records, which bothered me a little. That part of my life belonged where it was, off a past not worth the trip back.

"Then you started doing this," she added. "Why, Casey? If you didn't have to."

Some questions don't deserve an answer. Over the last decade, "why" had become one of those questions. "Do you want anymore?" I asked.

She tried to understand me through eyelashes that covered the narrow openings of her eyes. She gave up, shaking her head slightly from side to side. "Yes," she said, "but I can see I won't get it."

"Can you get into bed by yourself," I asked, "or do you need help?" It was a bad question.

She kept me from standing, her hand on my wrist. "I can always get into bed by myself," she said quietly, "despite what you may think of me."

~ ~ ~

Thinking. Getting into bed.

Trying sleep. I did. Try.

Giving up, I exchanged Janice's Porsche for my rented Ford and I drove around the area a while. The clear spring night made it easier to think. Unlike a clear sky Pittsburgh, the Venango County heavens did not dim their stars with city lights.

Having always lived a city of some sort—except for a brief spell in the fifties, when I didn't look up anyway—I was unaccustomed to the splendor of a brilliantly clear night sky and it must have whisked my mind away. By two o'clock the morning, I realized that I had nothing to show for the hours of staring straight up.

Technically, that is not true, of course. The image of Janice Simmons occasionally blocked out even the blackness above me. Something inside me told me that coincidence and Janice Simmons were incompatible. The purposefulness of her expressions, of her voice and, above all, her mind suggested to me that she felt we had not stumbled upon each other.

Our mutual connection with Harry Blair had brought us together, a bit small-world for me. That and my involvement in the Hiller case. That had to be coincidence. Clearly, I had not sought her out and just as obviously, Janice had not wasted her youth looking for me. That she had gone to considerable lengths to investigate me after our introduction indicated that she had known little or nothing about me prior to the Press Club drinks. Something had forced us together.

The arrangement preoccupied me, to the point that I didn't check I checked my watch until it read 2:00 AM. A sense of frustration had crept into me by that hour, the result of unexplained fortune and its irresistible inertia. Coupled with my understanding of Casey Carmichael, Janice's interest me as either a detective or as a man defied any logic I could find with my feet on the ground.

So, I assumed that the stars had something to do with it. Obsession and futility.

Like everything else, Janice would pass from the scene and things would return to normal. But things had a ways to go to get back to normal. I hoped it would take forever.

Chapter Twelve

The following morning, after spending the balance of the night counting the starts in Bob Winter's ceiling, I woke up to find myself stuck on zero. And I was running late. If I were to meet Janice at 8:00, a shave would have to wait.

Diana did not approve of either my stubble or my early engagement. She stopped me at the door to question both. Pert and pretty, a shiny pink robe, she asked, "Who would meet you looking like that at this hour?" Wrinkling her nose suspicion, she added another question. "Not Becky?"

The name had an odd reverberation, as if I had heard it before, but not for a long time. I shook my head in response to both the feeling and her question.

"Who then?" she asked, persistent her curiosity,

Quickly, I had to decide what to tell her. There was no reason not to let her know, but I had the nagging feeling that she would object. I let the latter rule. "An old friend just in from Elmira," I said, truthfully "who has some information."

Her sidelong glance indicated distrust. "The same old friend you were out with until 2:30?"

Why did Diana keep such a close watch on me? Surely she had more important things to do. "No," I said, decreasing to half truth. "I had to keep myself company last night."

My comment made Diana issue a "humph," and walk away, that strangely petulant walk of hers.

Because of Diana's interrogation, I didn't even get into my car until after 8:00. Driving 75 miles per hour did not turn the clock back, but did get me to Janice's first floor motel room before 8:20.

Parking my car in front of her window, I peered over the air conditioner and through a slim crack in the drapes. The room was dark, with no indication of life. A couple of sharp knocks confirmed that the room was empty.

In the lobby of the small motel, the front desk was similarly unoccupied. I could tell on my own that Janice's room key was the slot. With the key there was a piece of paper. To get a closer look, I may have slipped behind the desk.

The note was concise and not very helpful. "Punctuality is desirable, especially in the most sought after people," it ran. "If you can get to Elmira before 11:00, you won't have missed anything." The hand was tight and small for a woman. The "Janice" showed signs of a lot of practice.

My disappointment blending with anticipation, I put in a call to the Winter house. Tom Winter answered.

"This is Carmichael," I told him.

He sounded groggy, the kind with rum in it. "Being your problem."

"Would you tell Diana that I have to run up to Elmira," I said, before thinking better of it. "No, make that Buffalo. I'll be gone most of the day."

He laughed. "Funny. She went to Buffalo herself this morning. Just left, as a matter of fact."

The news jarred me, but I just said, "Then she won't miss me."

"I'm sure she won't," he chuckled. "After last night, she decided to talk Good Old Lewis into coming back."

Hanging up without much of a good-bye, I cursed Lewis Huntington and his bizarre hold on Diana. Of all of the people I had met in the name of Tony Hiller, Lewis was the one I liked least. He seemed deliberately ineffectual. Deliberate. That was the word.

Once on the road to Elmira, I acknowledged that I had developed an attachment for my client uncommon for me. If I had one at all, my reputation pegged me as uninvolved and not inclined to become involved. I didn't cultivate it, it was just there. Considering the fact that half of the people I dealt with are desperate, lonely women (the other half being desperate, lonely men) that particular trait came in handy.

With the Hiller case, however, I found that I had fallen into the trap that had caught too many of my colleagues—if I can use that word—too often. It had always been the least of my problems, but my guard had fallen.

Diana's attraction, unlike Janice's, contained nothing to warn the unsuspecting. I couldn't analyze what it was, but it reminded me of girls we would fall for in college. The mixture of maturing femininity and lingering innocence. Perhaps that combination had a new appeal, a different but strong pull.

I had to force my thoughts to where they belonged, the road to Elmira, New York. Janice had given me no hint as to why I was on my way to the small border city directly north of Harrisburg. She had traveled there just the day before, but she hadn't said where and certainly not why. She had left me stewing in my own intuition.

It wouldn't help that there was no way to make Elmira in less than three hours. Whatever I wouldn't miss by being there before 11:00, I was going to miss. But Janice knew that. She knew that I would miss it, even if I made an 8:00 breakfast.

The tone of her note was goading, challenging. Pure Janice. Still, there had to be something of real interest Elmira at 11:00, something central to the case Janice so graciously shared with me.

Following the Allegheny-River on Route 62, I put my head to work on narrowing the field. Janice had been to Cleveland and Buffalo before Elmira. If she had information for me, she had gone all three places in search of it. Had she finally found it in Elmira?

More likely, Janice had back—tracked rather than followed. The trail had ended Cleveland, run through Buffalo and begun in Elmira. Not until I hit Port Allegheny, did I grab an idea. As my car filled up, I called Chief McGuiness back Franklin.

McGuiness came on the line quickly, so quickly that my question was halting. "Sam Weil. He rented a car. Where?"

McGuiness snorted. "Is that all the farther along you are?"

"As far as Cleveland."

Clearing his throat, the chief of Venango County's detective bureau replied, "Yes. At a local auto dealer, Pinze Ford, I believe."

With a crisp "Thank You", I left him to figure out how I had found that nugget without asking him. McGuiness' impression of me would no doubt improve on the basis of the call, since I left out the attribution.

Janice Simmons had put me on the track of one Samuel Weil, the "little, old gray" man who, I knew now, had assumed the center position in Tony Hiller's delusion.

~ ~ ~

The route to Elmira, fortunately, was wide open and I managed a reputable, if completely illegal, speed on it. By the time I saw a small road sign announcing that Elmira was only five miles off, the clock had passed 12:00.

I had begun to worry at that point, because I still didn't know where to look for Sam Weil or what name he would be using. There was little time to think about that problem with only a cemetery and a tiny church between me and the city.

In the cemetery, I saw a police car, and several others, black flags on the right front fenders. "You're never late for a funeral," I said aloud to an attentive audience of one.

The cemetery. The only conspicuous landmark I was sure to pass on the way into town. Punctuality.

Knowing that I had missed the funeral, and probably the burial, I turned my car into the graveyard and parked beside the police cruiser. The mourners were returning to their cars. Only the police officer and a woman remained at the grave site.

I waited until they, too, turned to leave. Walking directly up to the policeman, I introduced myself.

His eyebrows went up. "How do you do, Mr. Carmichael?" he asked politely. "Could you wait a minute? I'd like to take my wife to the car."

I apologized for the intrusion and walked back with them in silence. Once his tearful, young wife had settled into the back seat, he and I moved toward my car.

"I hate to interrupt you like this," I said. "But I assumed that you were here in an official capacity."

The young cop looked up toward the grave. "Oh, no," he replied "Will Stalls was my wife's uncle. Or great uncle." He smiled sadly. "Actually, he was her mother's uncle. Yes, that is it."

"This will probably sound strange," I warned him, "but did Mr. Stalls have a limp."

He nodded his head in resignation. "Are you with that girl who was here yesterday?"

"She suggested I come here, yes."

A frown came and deepened on his face as he spoke. "Well, I'd appreciate it if you would tell her that she really upset my wife. She asked some pretty persistent questions."

"She is like that."

"You are, too, I suppose," he said.

"Sometimes."

"Okay," he said grimacing. "I can tell you right off that I have never heard him use the name Samuel Weil and I never heard of him going to Franklin, PA, or thereabouts. In fact, as Carol could not tell your friend, Will was in Minnesota last August."

Janice's bubble would not be so frail as to burst with that pinprick.

"Could you describe him for me?"

His eyes rolling up, he said, "About 5'9", a little more. Grey hair, almost white. He had started putting on weight the last few years He was over 70 but still pretty active."

"What about the limp?"

With an involuntary look at his own legs, the policeman replied, "It was from an accident a long time ago. Sometimes it was not too bad. other times, it was. I don't know. We didn't see much of him, really. I think that's why Carol is so broken up."

"He lived here, in Elmira?"

"In an old building not a mile from our house." He shook his head. "Ridiculous, really."

"How did he die? And when?" I persisted, hoping to avoid any more psychology of his wife's grief.

He gave me an angry look. "She asked that, too," he snapped. "How do you think? It was cancer. He's had it for four years. Outlived the last set of predictions by six months."

I pressed on with my questions, leaving the impact on Hiller's story for later. "You say he went to Minnesota?"

"Right. Last August. From the second to September first."

"How did he go?"

He laughed out loud. Not a pleasant laugh, but one filled with resentment. "Allegheny with a change in Buffalo. His sister lives Rochester. Minnesota, that is. And no, I haven't checked with her. I don't intend to. She is a very sick woman and can do without your questions, too, Mr. Carmichael." His stance had the look of firm finality, but he threw out one last remark. "He did send us postcards. And they didn't come from Pennsylvania."

"Thanks," I said, inviting him to tell me his name.

He wanted no part of that. "Good-bye, Mr. Carmichael. It was nice talking to you... this once." Having finished with me, the officer went back to his car, got in and roared off, as if to punctuate his last few words.

I followed his example, heading for Elmira's airport. Once there, I checked with the auto rental agencies. I got cooperation only after flashing my license. I was told that a Mister

William Stalls arranged to rent a car in Buffalo to be turned in the downtown Cleveland Office.

The attendant also confirmed that Mr. Stalls had consummated his transaction on August third at 11:00 by dropping the car off. As to whatever happened to him after that, the agent confessed ignorance.

My call to Pinze Ford took less than a minute. They had their records very handy.

"Yes, Mr. Carmichael," the manager of the rental department said, "we have it right here. A young lady said you might give us a call on it in the next couple of days."

Terrific, I cursed under my breath, Damn it. "Could you tell me the time it was actually rented out, please?"

"Of course," he replied helpfully. "Mr. Weil picked it up at 1:30 on August third. He had reserved it at, let's see, in person at 11:15 AM. For sixteen days, until the nineteenth."

"How did he pay?"

I could hear papers being shifted. "His deposit was in cash, Mr. Carmichael. The balance was paid in advance by check."

"Drawn on what bank, if I might ask?"

"It's called Winter National Bank," he said. "In Huntington, Pennsylvania. That's near Erie, I think."

"It's close enough," I said. "Is it in his name?"

"Of course," he replied, sounding surprised. "And we called to check the balance since both he and the check were out-of-state."

Weil had had an account at Winter National. That threw me. "Who did you talk to?"

The professional, even voice answered, "Mr. Weil directed us to a Miss Winter there. She said it was all right."

"She did?" Diana had cleared Sam Weil's check over the phone? My head buzzed. "Thank you very much."

"Quite all right," he said cheerfully. "I'd be happy to help, anytime."

One more small question came to me. "By the way," I said, "I was wondering if Mr. Weil returned the car in good shape?"

"According to the shop report on it, the car was fine," the manager said. "Mr. Weil had it here early on the 19th of August."

My inquiry complete, I rang off. Sam Weil had tried to cover his path. From Elmira, he fled into Buffalo where he rented a car under his real name, Will Stalls. After driving that car to Cleveland, he dropped it off and rented a second one from Pinze Ford under his alias, Sam Weil. How Janice had cracked that Cleveland connection, I wouldn't ask.

From Cleveland, he had probably gone on to Minnesota. before returning to Elmira by way of Buffalo. How nice that Buffalo was where he had to start his twisting path to Huntington. Buffalo had another attribute. It provided Lewis Huntington with his current address.

~ ~ ~

I didn't get to Buffalo until a shade before six o'clock.

It was just as well, because I knew where to find Lewis Huntington at that hour. At the Buffalo New City Theater. He was standing on stage looking up at the curtain.

My walk became a wobbly jog as I came down the steep aisle of the small theater. The hours of driving, though unnoticeable in passing, were now taking their toll on my legs.

"Mr. Huntington?" I called.

He lowered his eyes from the curtain to me, before allowing himself a smile. "Mr. Carmichael. I had expected to see you sooner or later. Diana has already left, by the way."

"All the better. It's just you and me."

"She's a wonderful little thing, don't you think?" he asked ignoring me. "Not mature enough for a man like you to appreciate perhaps, but a charmer all the same." He took a seat on the edge of the stage. "I finally had to send her home."

"Really?"

Joining his hands and putting them between his legs, he said, "Really. I felt I couldn't go back with her and I certainly couldn't let her stay. Not here. Not with me."

It seemed that Lewis Huntington had a good idea of his real worth. I had a new respect for him. He wasn't worth a damn, but at least he knew it.

"But," he said suddenly. "You want to talk to me about Tony and all that, right?"

I nodded. "You knew Tony Hiller pretty well, I'm told."

"Yes, I did." Lewis leaned back on his hands. "In a town as small as Huntington—and I was forced to grow up there—well, you take friends where you can find them. That accounts for my relationship with Diana, too. We were from opposite sides of a family feud and, yet, it was considered natural for us to spend our time together. And Tony, he was my closest friend when I was young."

He sighed. "We actually had a foursome. Diana and I, Tony and Becky Stockly. You must have met her by this time."

"The waitress."

His smile became sarcastic. "The waitress," he repeated. "I suppose she is 'the' waitress in Huntington. She has always worked there. Since her parents died a long time ago, Ned Cooper has taken care of her."

"And you have taken care of Ned Cooper," I stated.

Lewis Huntington wiped his eyes with his hands. "You mean the City Hotel?" He shrugged. "Why not? It was his by right, not mine. I didn't put anything into it. I haven't put anything into anything in my life, Mr. Carmichael, not until this place. Since I now have nothing, I feel much less guilty about being a Huntington."

"What about Tony?" I asked.

He indicated that he didn't like my manners, but he answered. "Tony was a good guy. In the real sense. A sane, simple, slightly greedy kid. He had some nice little ambitions but none of them involved running a bank. That shit-head Hal Winter dangled some baubles before him, but that didn't work. Not at first. Then, old Hal bought off Tony's pal at the gas station to push Tony his way. That finally did it. My grandfather was appalled, of course. He had considered Tony something of a vassal, I suppose, a true Huntington man. For several years after that he called Tony a traitor. But he got over it, because he realized that Harold Winter had just maneuvered the kid. He was good at that."

Lewis had a soft, mild voice that never tired. It was facile and full of expression. He was handsome without being striking or out of the ordinary. He should have made a good actor. I remembered from his movements at Diana's house, that he had a dancer's control over his thin body. Too much.

"Do you think that he was capable of killing Hal Winter?"

"There are some of very fine people who regret not having gotten their licks first."

"Including you?"

"Why not?" Lewis admitted. "If only for his misuse of that wonderful daughter of his. To him she was something to use. He tried to barter her for a third son. When a man sees only his own advantage people then the man isn't worth much, Mr. Carmichael."

"What do you know of Sam Weil?" I asked suddenly.

He blinked his eyes. "Who?"

"Sam Weil," I repeated.

"Weil? Who is he?" he asked innocently. Then he added with a smile, "Is that a stage name or a real name?"

"A stage name," I said. "His real name is William Stalls."

"Sorry."

"He was the 'gray man' in Huntington when Winter was shot," I informed him. "I found him in Elmira New York."

He jumped off the stage. "Good for you!" His face had the look of excited surprise. He even clapped his hands together lightly.

"Unfortunately," I told him, "He's dead."

His face fell. His hand rubbed over his lips as he pondered my news. "What does it mean to Tony? Does this help?"

"I don't know, yet. It might." Huntington had shown no signs of knowing anything about Weil. Despite Weil's stop Buffalo, it was a long shot to think Lewis would have any connection with a broken down old man from a small up-state New York city. I decided to get back to what he did know.

"What else might Hiller have against Winter?" I asked.

He laughed again. "Christ, any number of things. But I wouldn't know specifically. Tony and I haven't been close for years. We took separate paths to school and all. I assume, though, that Tony began to resent the way Harold Winter manipulated everyone including Diana and him. Tony didn't have an intricate or subtle mind but he apparently figured out what was up after so many years. Nobody likes being a puppet, Mr. Carmichael." He clicked his tongue, as people in costumes began to filter onto the stage. "Not even actors."

"There are only a few strings to break," I retorted. "You don't have to kill the puppeteer."

"Ah, but you beg the question, Mr. Carmichael," Lewis responded seriously. "I'm not talking about strings. Not those thin nearly invisible threads you're talking about. I'm talking about something closer to rope, a thick hemp twine. The kind of thing that chafes and burns, Carmichael. The kind that does not break."

He leaped up onto the stage and shook the hand of one made-up actor. "As you can see, I've got to work. Have a pleasant trip back to Huntington. Diana expects you back tonight, my friend. You left her alone last night. She doesn't like that."

"Yeah," I said. "Thanks for the help."

He shook my hand from the stage. "I'm no help, Mr. Carmichael," he wryly declared. "You'll understand that before too long."

I watched him head for the wings before taking my own exit. Stopping in the mens' room to wipe a film of grease paint from my hands left from his handshake, I tried to sift through what he had said. The man was as helpful as the dead Will Stall would be.

Chapter Thirteen

The trip back to Huntington from Buffalo had the advantage of good roads and little traffic. I passed by Erie before realizing it and pulled into Huntington early enough to ask a couple of questions about Janice and her Porsche.

Ned Cooper, aroused from the room he slept in behind the City Hotel desk, was not at all happy to see me. "You must get paid by the hour, Mr. Carmichael," he growled.

He didn't flinch at the name Simmons. "Hard not to remember her," he said. "She was even more of a nuisance than you are."

"Did she pick up that red Porsche this morning?" I asked, trying to sound friendly.

Ned Cooper blew some of the sleepiness from his lungs and thought about my question. "The red Porsche. I remember it from last night," he said. "But I didn't see it at all when I go up this morning."

I made myself seem flustered. "Damn! What time did you get up? Maybe it was gone by then."

"Late," he said, more cooperative. "Usually get up at 7:30, but today it was closer to 8:30."

"Thanks, Mr. Cooper, she'd have been gone by that time," I told him, dismay cracking my voice.

He took a moment to study me, trying to decide whether I deserved help or not. I must have come across all right because he said, "Why don't you ask Becky, Mr. Carmichael? She would have been here."

With that advice, I thanked the old man again and took the elevator to Becky's room.

Ned promised to warn her that I was coming, somehow. The rise to the second floor took a lifetime, but eventually, I stood before her door.

After my knock, I could hear faint, deliberate footsteps coming towards the door. Becky Stockly opened the slightly warped door and motioned me in. She was dressed a faded blue cotton robe with matching slippers. Her hair was piled up on her head in a way that made her look taller, almost graceful.

I could feel her shadowed eyes watching me as I took the seat on the couch as offered. I did turn down her offer of coffee. "I'm sorry to bother you at this hour. I'm not even sure the question I have for you makes any difference."

She lowered herself into a chair with a weary sigh and half a smile. "It's no bother, Mr. Carmichael," she allowed. "I wasn't asleep or even tired. Besides, it's nice to have company sometimes. Even very late company."

A warmth replaced the edge of bitterness that had colored her voice in our previous conversations. Apparently, she welcomed intrusion and wanted me to know it.

"You deserve better company."

Becky shrugged her shoulders, so square when she had answered the door, but now gently sloping. "'Deserve' is a funny word, Mr. Carmichael," she said. "It means something like a right, doesn't it? Well, I know better than to believe that."

She lit a cigarette without wasted motion. She took just one puff and then held it. "What can I do for you at such a late hour? Aside from blemish my reputation." Her laugh had the touch of irony that seemed part of her.

To keep her company, I took a cigarette, too.

She lit it for me, and then blushed, "Sorry, it is habit."

Her manner made me regret that all of my questions dealt with Janice Simmons. I felt that I should be asking Becky Stockly questions about herself. "I came here to ask you about a car," I said apologetically, watching her smile and nod. "But it occurs to me that I should probably know more about you, too."

Becky let her eyes widen slightly. "Me? Why?"

I looked at her hard, interested. "You're part of this case. A bit of an unknown. To me." I added an encouraging smile to the statement. "Just tell me about yourself, then I'll ask my questions.

Before beginning, she took a drag on the cigarette, her last one. "Okay," she said, not expecting much interest. "Do you believe that I'm only twenty-five?"

"Yes," I said. "A more mature twenty-five. Than some."

The smile that had been playing on her lips since I had gotten there, in various configurations, deepened. "That's nice. I like that," she said, nodding. "Well, I have lived Huntington for all of those years. My parents died in a car accident a long time ago. A man hit our car head-on one day and that was that. The scar you saw on my leg the other day is from the accident."

"I'm sorry," I said automatically and it sounded it, so I added, "That's awfully tough."

She reached out with her hand but didn't touch me before retracting the gesture. "That's all right," she said, embarrassed. "It was so long ago, I don't really remember it. I think my memories of it are from what people have told me, you know?"

"Sure."

"The driver of the other car got out of it with only a little more than I did. At the time I thought that was unfair—about my parents—but he and I were probably the unlucky ones."

She meant it. "I came back from the Hospital and Ned took care of me. I've been in the hotel ever since, working down in the restaurant, at one thing or another, almost every day for nineteen years. It took a while to get over my leg, and I hurt my back, but actually Ned and Lewis—Huntington—they taught me to walk better than before."

"That was very good of them," I said. "Tell me about Lewis."

"He and I were friends after that," she recalled. "He was like my big brother. He was two years older than I was, but he let me join in with him and the others. Tony and Diana mostly. Things went on that way for a long time. By the time we had finished High School, we had fallen into pairings. Tony, he was the oldest, and me, the youngest, and Lewis and Diana." She shrugged. "Only it didn't work out very well."

"What happened with Tony?" I asked. "Why didn't it work?"

Becky rubbed her forehead and then swept her hand over her hair. "Pretty simple. He loved Diana," she stated. "I can't say I blame him. Diana has a quality that everybody likes. Me, too, in fact. I can't begin to measure up to that."

"And then Tony went away, to school," she continued. "They all did, actually. Lewis, Tony and Diana. I stayed here. One of these days, I'm going to leave. For somewhere."

"And when Tony came back?" I asked.

She had to swallow hard before answering. If she went on too long she'd break down. "He came back and went to work at Winter National," she said, her voice starting to tremble. "He told me that Mr. Winter had told him that the day would come when Diana and he would get married."

"What about Lewis?"

"What about him?"

"Wouldn't he object?"

That made her laugh. "Lewis? I suppose. But he never seemed to think that he was good enough for her. Or anything else for that matter."

Pulling herself out of the chair she went to the window. "Besides, not too long after that, Willard Huntington died and Lewis disappeared," she said sadly, "For a long time."

"You missed him?" I demanded, wondering if her relationship had evolved.

She turned to glare at me, sensitive to suggestion my voice. "Oh, you bet I did. Not the way I missed Tony, maybe, but I missed him all right."

It seemed like time for me to go. I had made her mad with my last question, with the implied doubt about her relationship with Lewis and Tony. I shifted gears.

"Okay, Becky," I said. "Now, I'll ask my original question Did you notice that red Porsche outside this morning?"

With her hands clasped over her face, she threw her head back. When she took them away, her face had dropped its anger to become sullen and melancholy again. "Yes."

"When was it picked up?"

"By that reporter, you mean?" she demanded, disgust her voice. "She came by at about 7:30 for breakfast and left at a little before eight."

In the pit of my stomach, something splashed into the churning acid churning. Maybe it was my expectations. Of Janice and me.

Becky's expression became one of concern and she started to approach me. "Are you all right?"

The honest emotion in Becky Stockly's voice riled me all the more. It was wrong that Janice should have so many advantages, while Becky had so little. What really made me mad, though, was that the two faces of Janice Simmons looked so much alike—and so damned good—that I could not tell them apart. Not in the cold light of day or the dim glow of night.

Janice had intentionally made a fool of me. For no reason, she had lied to and misled me. She really was playing me and I didn't even know what the game was.

"Are you sure?" I asked, as a matter of form.

Becky looked apprehensive, not wanting to confirm the truth. But she did anyway. "Yes."

I rose from my seat and said, "Thanks, Miss Stockly. I know what I need to know."

She followed me closely to the door. "Is it bad?"

"Oh, it'll do," I replied, unable to blunt the edge.

Her hand finally touched my shoulder and fought her impulse to withdraw it. "I'm sorry," she said. "For you, I mean."

Her sympathy soothed me unexpectedly and tempered my disappointment. I looked at her, finally understanding that her sorrowful eyes reflected more than the experience of one person. Becky Stockly had the unique quality that made her suffer for other people, as well as for herself.

Other people.

No wonder she was so old at twenty-five.

~ ~ ~

Tom Winter let me in when I dragged myself back to the house hidden away outside Huntington. His face had the puffy look that smoothed wrinkles and spoke of an aging drunk. Beneath the ruddy cheeks I found a big smile.

"Hello, hello, Carmichael," he enthused. "How was your Buffalo?"

I couldn't think of any clever bison comeback so I said, "Okay."

He led me into the living room where Diana sat, looking glum. When she saw me, however, her expression changed into one of relieved pleasure. "I was afraid you weren't coming back."

"I work here," I said. To Tom, I added, "I'll take whatever sissy drink you're having tonight."

Tom Winter nodded happily and waddled over to the bar. A man his size begins to waddle after about five ounces in an hour. He wasn't drunk, but he was prepared.

The girl patted the seat on the sofa next to her, but I ignored the suggestion. I didn't feel like playing her pet for the evening. At that moment I felt to old to play, period. After my talk with Becky Stockly, I wanted to feel older.

Diana frowned for a second and then said, "Well, if you're going to be standoffish, at least tell me what you did today." There was a springing exuberance to her every word. "Tell me about Buffalo."

Furrowing my brow, feigning reflection, I waited for Tom to bring me my share of good cheer. Once I had it, I played some catch-up. Then, warmed and calmer, I began to pace and talk.

"Today was an interesting day, Diana," I related. "With the help of that friend I told you about this morning, I located the whereabouts of Sam Weil."

"You did," she yelped.

Even Tom Winter was impressed. "Good work, Carmichael."

Pride no longer my weaknesses, I give full credit. "Not at all. I got the lead from that friend of mine, Janice Simmons of WPPA. She did the leg work. All of it."

Diana's nose curled up with distaste. "I don't like her."

"Who is she?" Tom asked.

His sister took care of the preliminary information. "She's a witch!"

I filled in the details. "She's a reporter for the top TV station in Pittsburgh. She's very smart, tough and even better looking."

Diana disagreed. "If you like that look."

Winter winked at me.

"She's been on this case from day one," I informed him. "This latest work she did on her own time."

Winter nodded his approval. "What about Weil?"

I stared hard at Diana, who was still simmering over the usefulness and looks of Janice Simmons. "I'm afraid he's dead. Cancer."

Diana's doe-like eyes widened instantly. "Oh, no!"

Confident that Weil's real name would mean nothing to them, I reserved that. "Yes. I got there just after they put him the ground. His relatives weren't overly cooperative, but they told me he was supposed to have been in Minnesota, last August. But he rented a series of cars one of which ended up here."

"That doesn't help Tony!" Diana wailed.

"No, it doesn't," I admitted, preparing myself. "But one thing I found out may: He contacted someone at Winter National before even coming down here."

"At the bank?" Tom Winter asked, amazed. "Whatever for?"

I didn't take my eyes off Diana as I spoke. So far she had shown no sign of recognition. "To get an okay on a check drawn on the bank."

She started and jerked her head up to look at me. Her mouth opened for a second and then closed. By the time it had shut, she was looking out the window.

My voice came down hard. "Do you remember Diana?"

Winter jumped to her defense. "And what is that supposed to mean?"

Without answering him, I continued to glare at his flustered sister. The soft skin became moist and her hand gripped her leg. She didn't look at either of us. When she spoke it was in a quiet, throbbing voice. "Yes, I guess I do. It didn't mean anything, Casey. Really. It was just an okay."

"When did you realize it was Weil?" I demanded.

She looked up at me forlornly. "Not until just now." Earnestly she added an "Honest" to assuage my obvious doubt.

"He had an account?"

"Yes," she said. "Now that I remember. But I'd never heard of him."

"Then why okay the check?"

Her mouth opened and then closed again.

"Come on, Diana," I snapped. "Tea time over."

She started to cry and sobbed into her hands. "He asked me to. He told me to."

Winter glided into the seat next to her like a sympathetic porpoise. He put his arm around her and held her head against his shoulder. "Who, Diana? You'd better tell us who it was," he instructed as though talking to a child.

The sniffling made it hard to understand the first two times she said his name. The third time. however, was clear enough. "Tony."

Chapter Fourteen

Like the loyal servant he was, Jack Pazinsky agreed to meet me at the bank in the middle of the night. My call had gotten him out of bed and on the front step of the Winter National five minutes before I could get there myself.

He looked tired, even the dark, but his voice was firm. "What's the matter, Carmichael?"

I watched him unlock the door before I spoke. "Did you know that Samuel Weil had an account at this bank?"

He shrugged and walked inside. "Could be. He was in town long enough."

Following him into the records-room, I replied, "Uh uh. I mean before he got here in August."

Pazinsky's stiffening betrayed his surprise. "Before?"

"He paid on his rented car with a check from this bank," I told him. "Before coming to town."

Peering into my eyes, he seemed to find nothing suspicious, so he nodded. "All right, Mr. Carmichael. Let's see."

Pulling off a silver vinyl cover from a micro-fiche reader, Pazinsky continued, "We have most of our permanent records on film after six months. If Weil had an account, he closed it out. That, I can assure you. I would have picked it up somewhere along the line."

He unlocked the safe and produced a micro-fiche file folder. Within seconds, he had the right cards. One by one he put them into the reader. Finally, the name Weil appeared the upper right hand corner of the card. "Here he is."

"What can you tell from this?"

"Quite a bit," he replied. Then he gasped. "Christ! This was opened under Tony's personal authorization mid-July of last year."

"Two weeks before Weil's arrival," I commented.

"Yes," Pazinsky concurred. "And take a look at this reference."

Following his eyes to the lower portion of Weil's record and saw the name which he had used as reference, the only name down there aside from Tony's. "What the hell would Ned Cooper have to do with this?"

Jack Pazinsky stared at the card. His head made several small shakes. "That, Mr. Carmichael, should be the first question you ask him tomorrow."

I grunted. "Like hell. I'm going over there right now."

He seized my arm with his strong hand. "Don't waste your time," he said. "He called me a few hours ago. He wanted me to lend him a teller to watch the hotel for the night and early morning."

"Shit!" I snapped. "Where'd he go?"

"He didn't say. Only that he'd be back by 9:00," Pazinsky said. "Do you think this means anything?"

"Weil didn't open this in person," I remarked. "He couldn't have. I'm willing to bet that someone opened it for him. And there are only two other names on that card. It had to be either Tony Hiller or Ned Cooper. I don't think that matters, but I do think that Ned Cooper knew about it. And he's going to tell me." I sounded too confident, so I eased back on determination a bit. "That is, if he ever comes back."

~ ~ ~

If Ned Cooper had left town, however temporarily, there was one person who might know where he had gone. In spite of the late hour, Becky Stockly greeted me with a gracious smile and, "Doesn't Diana ever let you sleep?"

Walking past her into the small apartment, I replied, "What's keeping me awake is Ned Cooper."

She didn't move, staying close to the door and staring at me. Her pale complexion became paler, and the smile disappeared. "Ned?"

"Where is he, Becky?"

Her shoulders sloping she said, "I don't know, quite honestly, Mr. Carmichael. He told me he had to go somewhere. I offered to drive him, but he said he had to go by himself."

"How soon after I left?"

Wandering over to the sofa, she answered, "Immediately."

Becky Stockly seemed unable to move. I took her by the shoulders and sat her on the couch. After pacing for a minute or so, I sat down next to her. "Listen, Becky," I began. "I want you to know exactly what I know. If there is anything that you want to tell me, about Ned in particular, then I want to listen Okay?"

She nodded.

"I have found Sam Weil. And I traced his car. He is dead, but he left us one connection," I explained. "He drew a check on Winter National. The account, in his name, gave Ned as a reference. I think Ned knows more about Sam Weil than anybody other than Weil—or rather, Stalls. That's his real name—other than Weil himself. And he is dead."

By the time I had finished, the girl had gone white. She held her hands slightly away from her body, as if involuntarily trying to repel on intrusion. Her eyes, always so tired and hurt, now added shock.

"Stalls?" she asked, her voice trembling over the one syllable.

"Do you know him?"

Becky ran both hands over her face, without erasing any expression. "Yes," she said. "Maybe. A man named William Stalls? He was the one who drove the car."

"In your accident?"

Heavily, her head went up and down.

"Good God." I was on my feet before I knew it. "Are you sure?"

"Oh, I'm sure, Casey," she replied without hesitation. "He lived Elmira."

My feet pounded the thread bare carpet, my head feeling each step. Sam Weil, alias Will Stalls or vice-versa, had a connection with the town of Huntington, a connection that went back almost twenty years. He was no stranger to the people in this town. At least, not to Ned Cooper and certainly not to Becky Stockly. He had come back to Huntington for a reason.

"Becky, tell me this: Did Harold Winter have anything to do with William Stalls at any time? As far as you know?"

Turning her eyes toward the ceiling, she dredged around in her memory. "Not that I know of," she said finally. "What does this all mean?"

"There is something I have to do," I told her. "And I'll have to ask you to help." Taking her hand, I led her to the door. "Do you have a key to his room, Becky?"

She did not respond, leading me downstairs in a troubled silence. After some hesitation, Becky unlocked Ned Cooper's room for me. To assuage her guilt, she came with me "to supervise."

The room had once been the manager's office and was located behind the front desk. Ned had converted it into his bedroom many years before. In the interim he had kept it spotlessly clean and remarkably uncluttered for a man of his age. There was no evidence of memorabilia or sentiment for that matter.

On his dresser, however, there was a small collection of pictures. One of Ned in front of the City Hotel the day he had been appointed manager. Another of Ned surrounded by four young children and three of Rebecca Stockly at various ages.

"I was such an ugly girl," Becky stated.

Preoccupied, I said nothing.

Watching me rummage through the drawers bothered her at first, but eventually Becky relaxed on the bed. "What are you looking for, Casey?"

Like most everyone else in the Hiller case, she had stopped calling me Mr. Carmichael. The informality sounded right. "I don't know."

Ned Cooper's clothes were ancient but sparkling clean and white Everything about the man was meticulously organized. The dresser held only clothes and toiletries. The closet only coats, jackets and shirts. That made the search of both tedious, but I had the feeling that if he had something to hide in his room, he would hide it totally out of place,

I tried to think as I talked. "We know that Ned knew Sam Weil. I think we can assume, then, that he knew Weil was really William Stalls. Why else would he vouch for him at Winter National?"

"Ned did try to get some money for my hospital bills from him," she told me. "A long time ago, of course."

"Any luck?"

A bitter smile presaged her answer. "The poor man had less than I did." She shook her head. "How could I take anything from someone worse off than I was?"

Ned Cooper must have known why Stalls had come, or was planning to come, to Huntington. He must have vouched for him advance and vouched for him as Sam Weil. Stalls had to have contacted Ned prior to July 16th when the bank account was opened. Ned had even put the man up his Hotel.

He must have realized that I had made some sort of connection. After my return, he took off for somewhere. He had also said he'd return and, if he meant it, that meant that he had gone somewhere for information. Now that the mysterious Sam Weil was dead, Ned Cooper became the man most likely to give credence to Tony Hiller's cock-eyed story. And since he had run, Cooper had to have something important to hide. People don't run for the exercise.

I began to doubt that he would come back. Stalls involvement with Becky and his presence Huntington the previous

August, could have been totally unrelated to Harold Winter's murder. But Ned's reaction and well-timed trip out of town suggested otherwise.

During the search of the last two drawers of the dresser, I started getting bored, stale, so I took a look at his desk. Oddly enough, he didn't have a private phone book, one of the items I'd wanted—It being open season on address books—There was no listing of addresses or scraps of paper in the desk. All in all, the desk was useless.

That done, I returned to the bottom two drawers of the dresser. Handkerchiefs and socks respectively. I ignored the handkerchiefs. Undoing all the pairs of socks, I felt each one for a hidden cache. In a pair of old argyle socks, I found one that made a crinkling sound.

Inside was a letter addressed to Mr. Edward Cooper. It was written in a sloppy long-hand and signed "W. Stalls." A rambling document, it contained two points of interest. The first was an admission that he had been the cause of much misery, despite his earlier denials, and that he wanted to "make it up to the little girl."

The second requested Ned to take the check enclosed and open an account in the name of Samuel Weil—"I'd like to remain unknown in this"— so that he could distribute money "as he got more of it." Stalls added that he would be arriving in Huntington August second and would like to reserve a room at the City Hotel, preferably on the third floor.

With the letter was a bank receipt for the deposit of $3,000.00 in an account under the name of S. Weil, signed by Tony Hiller. A notation on the receipt, in the upper corner, indicated a number at which Weil could be reached, "not his home."

I went to the phone and dialed the number. A recording said, "I'm sorry, but we cannot complete your call as dialed." Elmira information confirmed the recorded information.

Hanging up the phone, I noted that the sun had started to show itself and that Becky had fallen asleep. My watch told me that both were justified, even though my body disagreed.

Becky woke with a start when I touched her shoulder. She looked up at me from the bed and smiled dreamily. She took my hand and laughed softly, as she stood up. "I was dreaming about you, Mr. Carmichael," she said. "About you and me. Isn't that silly?"

"Not why you think," I said.

We left the room and she locked the door. We parted at the elevator with inappropriate "good nights." Once the cage had cleared the first floor, I shambled, exhausted suddenly, over to the settee backed against the front wall of the lobby. I didn't figure Ned Cooper would bother coming in the back way, if he bothered to come in at all.

Chapter Fifteen

"Wake up, Carmichael," I heard someone say.

The voice filtered through several layers of sleep before it got to me. When my eyes opened, they had to look back through the same layers to see Lewis Huntington bending over me. Behind him, the mist, was Ned Cooper.

Huntington smiled at my grogginess. "Ned wants to talk to you."

At Lewis' suggestion, the three of us, with me trailing the other two, went into the restaurant for coffee. Once planted at that table in the far, dark corner, we ordered a whole pot from Becky Stockly.

The young Huntington had a serious look on his face as he explained, "Ned came to me last night, Mr. Carmichael, for advice. He wasn't running. He simply didn't know what to do. I told him to tell you the truth about Sam Weil."

"So you knew too," I said thickly.

"No, he didn't, Mr. Carmichael," Ned interrupted. "I kept this to myself. I didn't think that it had anything to do with Tony's case. Or at least I convinced myself of that."

Lewis nodded knowingly. "I think the latter is the truer statement, Ned. You had to know that Becky was not involved."

Cooper looked despondent. "If Tony was..." he started to say. Then he sagged. "I couldn't be sure."

Holding his hand to his forehead, Lewis said, "That's ridiculous, Ned."

"I know, I know," Ned murmured response.

I cut them both off. "Listen, Cooper," I snapped. "You should have said something about this to the police, but since you didn't, you'd better tell me. I want to know everything you know about Sam Weil or Will Stalls. Everything."

The old man gathered himself together. "Yes, all right," he conceded. "I should at least tell you."

"No," Lewis interjected. "Not without a lawyer."

"Shut up!" I barked.

Ned put his hand on Lewis' shoulder. "I don't need a lawyer, Lewis. Not for this."

The younger man shrugged, deferring reluctantly to Ned's wish. He concentrated on drinking his coffee.

"Back in, oh, I guess it was 1957," Ned began, "the Stockly car collided with one driven by Will Stalls. Stalls had been driving like a maniac or something. He killed both Becky's parents and injured her. Thank God, she was in the back seat. Stalls was hurt too, but not critically. Unfortunately, the bills wiped him out. I wanted to sue him, for Becky—I was made her guardian—but Stalls didn't have enough to make it worthwhile."

"After about three years of trying, I gave up on him. Stalls was getting worse, not better, drinking all the time. I figured he'd never have any money again," Ned explained, each detail sapping him. "Then last summer, I got word from him, that he had some money. He sent me a check for three thousand, just like that!"

"Where'd he get it?" Lewis asked sharply.

"I don't know," Ned replied. "I was honestly afraid to ask. I was afraid it wouldn't be real."

I pulled the letter from my shirt pocket. "He also wanted a room here."

He nodded. "Yes."

"The third floor. Why?"

"He didn't say," Cooper responded, dismayed. "I opened the account, as he asked. In the name of Sam Weil. He said he wanted anonymity, which was just as well as far as I was concerned. Tony handled it for me personally. I guess he didn't think much about it. He did it as a favor to me."

"When Weil showed up early August," Ned continued, "I hardly recognized him, he had aged so. I took him to the room on the third floor, the one next to Alma, and he told me that he would be coming into some money soon and that he wanted to share it with Becky and me. And I said 'all right.'"

"Why had he come to Huntington?"

"He said he wanted to set things up right and that he was having someone meet him here with his money," Ned related. "When I left him, he was at the window, examining the view."

"Examining?"

"That's how it seemed, yes."

Lewis' voice was loud when he said, "The bank."

"That's what I was afraid of," Ned said. "And when it happened... well, I didn't want to say anything. What did I care if Hal Winter had lost some money? Especially if Becky got part of it."

"Noble sentiment," I said.

Ned turned on me with a snarl. "Noble, Mr. Carmichael? You want me to be noble? I've lived too long to be as noble as you are. I can't think of anything more fitting than to have Harold Winter pay a little of his money to Becky. If it hadn't been for him and the way he strangled this town, I would have had more to give her."

With a glance my direction, Lewis commented, "The aristocracy has robbed us of our nobility."

I just looked at him. To Ned, I asked, "What then?"

"Nothing," Ned replied. "Except that, for a little while Stalls sent me some money orders in the mail."

"How much?"

"Five thousand dollars."

The figure got me to my feet. "Five thousand? You idiot! You knew that had to come from the robbery!" I nearly shouted. "What the hell did you do with it?"

He looked at me his jaw fixed, his eyes angry. "The fuck if I'll tell you!"

I believed him, and decided to forgo the challenge. That was between Ned Cooper and the law. "Has anybody been in his room since then?"

"Cops."

"And me," Lewis added. "I stayed there before Diana invited me to the house."

Since I was still standing, I didn't have to get up. "Let's go."

The old man, powered by anger, marched out of the restaurant to the desk for the key and then to the elevator. Lewis and I followed impatiently. The ride to the third floor was interminable. It seemed like a lifetime before we were in the room once used by Wilma Stalls.

"You won't find anything if the police didn't," Ned growled. His mood had tuned ugly and I was there.

The room itself was similar to Alma Purcil's, except that there was very little furniture, no TV, phone or radio. There wasn't any rug on the wooden floor or sheets on the bed. The curtains had been washed out by sunlight, but little else lately. The dresser was empty, except for a couple spiders knitting silk.

It couldn't have taken the cops more than ten minutes to tire of the room, it was so barren. The closet had so little space, so few niches, that you couldn't hide a pin in it. The same was true of the tiny medicine cabinet.

"Who cleaned this place out after he left?" I asked.

Lewis looked sheepish. "I did, Mr. Carmichael. I volunteered, because Ned's short of help. And it wasn't anything I haven't gotten used to, believe me."

"Did you see anything?" I was reluctant to ask Lewis for information—I wouldn't believe him anyway—but he was a witness. Again.

He thought about it, posing. Everything about him seemed artificial, the way he talked, the way he gestured. "No, I didn't," he said, finally. "But I wasn't paying attention. I didn't do much. Changed the linen, cleaned the bathroom. Swept the floor."

My eyes ran over the floor automatically. It was old and warped in some places. The cracks between the planks were just big enough to swallow something under a broom. Crouching I began to run my hand over the surface. There wasn't that much of it so I examined the cracks while I was about it. The two men just stared at me.

A couple pieces of glass grazed my palm and then another sharp object, one that wasn't glass. I reached into my pocket for my knife. Digging the thin, minuscule object out of the floor took over a minute. And as it was, I cut it half. The two pieces were very small, shiny on one side, dull brown on the other.

Unless, I missed my guess, there would be some other scraps of the material around the room. At least, I hoped so, because of all the things I had come across, the phone button, bits of information, this tiny discovery would go the farthest in helping Tony Hiller.

"Well," Lewis finally asked. "What it is?"

Feeling successful and tired at the same time, I said, "I would say that this it Tony Hiller. Or perhaps, Harold Winter."

"Huh?"

"Or, at least, their voices."

Ned Cooper and Lewis Huntington exchanged astonished glances. "Their voices?" one of them repeated.

"Tape, my friends," I said. "Recording tape."

~ ~ ~

After scouring the floor of the room, the three of us produced no fewer than sixteen pieces of magnetic recording tape. No one of them was long enough to tell us what was on it, but a theory began to root.

"He must have recorded Tony and Winter," I explained to the other two. "And then edited the tape to get the conversation he wanted. Tony didn't have to be there at all. Neither did Winter. He may have been dead by then for all we know."

"Then," Lewis continued for me, "what Alma heard was a tape."

I shrugged. "In the meantime, Tony was out of action, sitting his cellar with his hands cuffed behind his back. In the confusion follows, Stalls takes off, meets his confederate, who had pulled the bank job and leaves Tony counting preserves and stuck with something he knows couldn't have happened."

"God," Ned said softly. "If only I had said something.

"It wouldn't have hurt," I said, without mercy. "It might not have helped much, but it wouldn't have cost you anything."

"Except the money," Lewis reminded me. "Anyway that's past. What about Tony's case?"

"I think we need a more than a few tape shards," I said. "I'm going back to Elmira today. I think we can turn something up there. Lewis, I'm going to ask you to go something for me."

"Sure."

"Go over to Diana's," I directed,. "and make a tape recording of yourself, Diana and Tom, if he can talk. Okay?"

"Why?"

"When I get back from Elmira today," I replied. "I want you to get on the party line, with the phone tipped so that we can hear and play that tape."

Lewis looked at me skeptically. "Who is the 'we?'"

My smile me away: I was sure that we were going to shred the case against Tony Hiller in one afternoon. "Alma and I, of course."

Young Huntington hesitated. "If you say so." Then he shrugged and left the room.

Ned Cooper collapsed on the stripped beg. "If only I had said something."

I went to the window to check the view. It gave me a nice panorama of the town, particularly, Winter National Bank. From his window, Stalls could have seen everyone entering and leaving the bank. He could also have signaled someone to go into it.

Turning my attention back to Cooper, I asked, "What did he bring in with him? Stalls, I mean."

"A big suitcase."

"Nothing else?"

"No." He sounded as beat. I figured the trip to Buffalo had caught up with him. Or maybe it was more than that.

My sigh sounded like an expression of sympathy and he looked up expectantly at me. "You made a mistake," I told him.

"I realize that now."

I nodded approval. "Then I have only one thing to add, Cooper," I said evenly. "She's worth at least one mistake."

Chapter Sixteen

To find the residence of William Stalls, who was not listed in the Elmira phone book under the names I knew, I went to the County Courthouse. A quick check of the death records told me what I needed to know.

First, I went to the home of Carol Burne and her police officer husband. She was Will Stalls' closest relative. A plain young woman opened the door and started. "You were at the funeral," she said incredulously.

"Yes, I was," I told her. "I talked to your husband."

She nodded, with a grateful smile. "He said you were an old friend of Uncle Will's. It was nice of you to come."

The kid cop had lied to her, which, I suppose, was nice. It also meant he didn't want me talking to his wife, a realization that made me very nervous. "Can you reach him? Your husband?"

Shaking her head, Carol Burne motioned me to sit down. "Not for half an hour. He's on duty 'til noon. Can you stay? I'd like to hear how you knew Uncle Will."

I had 30 minutes. My mind bounced around a little, trying to invent some connection. Looking at her red-ringed eyes and ruddy, plump face, I decided to wing it. "Well, it's a long story," I said. "Your husband knows the details. Quite frankly, I have come back for a couple things I loaned Will last summer. I hate to bother you, but something has come up and I need them."

Suddenly upset, she cried, "Last summer! How terrible of him? Will was always more considerate than that. He didn't like to take favors from anyone. Certainly not from me." She seemed to resent that.

"Oh, no," I explained. "It's not that. He offered to send them down to me, but I didn't need them then. Out of the blue, I do." Unsure of the life of baloney, I said, "After he got that money, he offered to send the tape recorder parcel post." I followed up with an easy laugh.

Carol Burne's resentment dissolved into surprise. "Money? Will didn't get any money. At least, nothing I knew of."

Disappointed, I lifted my shoulders. "He didn't say anything about coming into some money? That's funny. I thought a relative had left him something."

"His only living relative is his sister, Martha, in Rochester. Minnesota."

"Martha," I repeated and then fudged, "Martha Stalls. It doesn't sound like the one."

"Oh, no" Carol corrected me, "her married name is Taylor, but she isn't dead or anything. She's just sick."

I nodded. "Oh, yeah. She's in Mayo."

Sadly, Carol confirmed my guess. "She had a stroke two years ago." After a sigh, Carol changed the subject. "You say you want a tape recorder back?"

"Yes," I replied, filing Martha Taylor away. "I have some editing to do for a friend."

Her warm smile filled the round face with pleasure. "I have a key to his apartment," she said enthusiastically. "It's the least I can do, your coming all this way.

"Hey, I'd appreciate that." I felt that I sounded like a hack actor, delivering lines in a flat, awkward way.

Still, I don't argue with success, so I followed Carol Burne the short distance to Will Stall's apartment, chatting like a trouper about any manner of things unrelated to my supposed friendship with Will Stalls.

The dead man's room had the dingy look of the Huntington City Hotel room where he had stayed for nearly three weeks. It had, however, been organized after his death, the objects and clothes arranged in neat piles in the middle of the room.

There was just enough there to tell me that Will Stalls had died with very little. An old clock-radio, with a cracked case, and an early sixties TV set represented the bulk of the value. Canned goods and a well-used can opener suggested that he hadn't eaten well for a decade.

The tears in Carol Burne's eyes finished the picture of an aging, broken recluse, unattended by anyone, alone and friendless. Yet there was another face to Will Stalls, another name. That was the one I had come to Elmira to find.

My eyes roamed over the things I dared not touch. Nothing suggested a tape recorded or magnetic tape to go with it. "Is this all?" I asked. "I don't see my tape recorder."

She shrugged. "As far as I know. Bud did most of this, two days ago. I couldn't bring myself to."

Frustration forced me to look again, and hard, for something, anything to give me a clue. Looking would take too long, so I took the chance and started to rummage through the old man's effects. "Boy," I said by way of excuse. "Old Will never changed, did he?"

She started to cry, which was good for me. "No."

In the pocket of a ragged coat, I felt what I had hoped for: It was a cassette tape. My heart started beating fast, as I pulled it out to examine it. The wheels had run half way, an even amount of the tiny tape on each. The label said only, "Phone."

Through the middle of one of the tape spools was tied a dirty pink ribbon which ran to a small brass key. Tiny precise lettering on a strip of adhesive tape on the key said more than I could believe. The letters were faded from use of they key, but I could make out three of them easily. "S.W_i_." That was plenty.

I checked Carol Burne, who was still wiping her eyes, and put the cassette and the key into my shirt pocket. Feeling lucky, I asked her, "Did he have any notebook or something that would tell me what he had done with it?"

She shook her head, unable to stop crying long enough to speak.

"How about a pawn shop?" I asked as a last chance. "I know he used to use one."

Through her tears she managed to laugh. "I'll say he did. It's called Milt's Jewelry, just down the block. We gave him a color TV last last Christmas and he took it right down to Milt's." That memory changed her. "Christ."

Her went bitter and the tears stopped. "I tried, we both did," she said. "He didn't want us. Or anyone. He got mad when we did anything for him and when we didn't. Ever since those people hit his car, he's been impossible to understand. I'm only thirty-one and I've lived through twenty years of misery because of him." She wasn't done.

"I'm glad he's dead."

Before things got worse, I walked her back toward her house. I cut my walk and my thanks short. A patrol car sat in front of mine, ominous but empty. Before Bud Burne let his wife in, I was on my way to Milt's Jewelry.

~ ~ ~

The obligatory bell ever the door brought Milt himself to my service. He was six four and leaner than a customer's wallet. If he had wandered to the morgue by mistake, he'd still be there. "Can I help you, sir?" he asked with smooth civility.

"You knew Will Stalls?" I asked directly, figuring he could spot a lie.

"That was my singular displeasure, yes sir," he replied, meaning it. "The man did more business with me than with the bar next door, if that helps."

I let my eyebrows raise themselves to show I was impressed. A foot lower, I held my license. "Mind if I ask a couple questions?"

His mouth spread out into a condescending smile. "Of course not."

"Has Stalls ever brought in a tape recorder? Or maybe a box of some sort?" I asked as professionally as I could without crossing over to tough guy. This guy would have eaten me up if I had come on like Bogart.

The tall man's eyebrow twitched and his voice had some respect in it. "As a matter of fact, Mr. Carmichael he did. Some time ago, last fall I believe."

"Do you still have it?"

He laughed. "Heavens no," he replied. "When Will's loan is due, I sell the collateral immediately. There is no point in waiting. That one went quickly."

"Could you tell me anything about it, that you could remember?" I asked, letting him feel that it was important, if not critical, to me. "I realize it was a long time ago."

Milt held up a long elegant hand. "A great deal of merchandise goes through here, Mr. Carmichael, situated as I am between a tavern and a flop house. I rarely bother to remember anything," he said. "But this was a peculiar case. I have been handling Will Stalls for ages. Around Christmas time or his birthday, in March, he might bring in some nice things, presents, of course. Last January, a very nice little television set."

"But last fall, October, I believe," he continued, "He brought in two very nice pieces. He said a fellow had given them to him. He was lying and I made him tell me the truth—Will was a terrible liar—He finally told me that a man had asked him to hold them for him for a while and hadn't returned for them."

"Was he lying then, too?"

A slight expression of appreciation stole onto Milt's face. "I would assume so, Mr. Carmichael. No one would entrust valuable machines to Will Stalls. But, it was not an obvious lie and I did have my eye on the collateral, so I let it go."

"Could you tell my what it was?"

He nodded and pulled a small composition book from behind his register, "I use this for notes on special transaction. If any one is interested—like you—I have it handy." He paged back through the book and then looked up. "A compact, but very good reel-to-reel tape recorder, a Sony, and a cassette recorder with telephone hook-up, voice-activated, also a Sony. By the way, neither was purchased in Elmira," he let me know. "I checked, just in case he had stolen them or taken them on credit down the street."

"Did he ever come back for them?"

Milt looked at me with disappointment. "Come back, yes, he did, but not for collateral." He just shook his head. "No, Mr. Carmichael, Will had no intention of coming back for them. He said that if the fellow who gave them to him had need of them, he might come get them. The way he said it, I was confident that the gentleman, a Mr. Weil, would not have that need. As it turned out, I was right."

Stall's use of Weil's name caused me to hesitate a hair. Not enough for Milt to see. Pulling the cassette and key out of my pocket, I asked, "Do you recognize this key?"

Milt took the key and examined it carefully. "Sorry, Mr, Carmichael. But I have a suggestion for you. The bar next door served Will Stalls as a home. You might try his 'family' there."

Leaving my thanks behind in the form of a twenty, I headed for the bar in the rundown building next to Milt's Jewelry.

Why would Stalls mention his alias to Milt? It seemed a completely useless ruse. Of course, he was a drunk.

Which brought me through the door of the bar. Even this early, the stools were half-filled with men already in the same condition. Not wanting to seem out of place, I ordered some bourbon.

When the bartender, a stocky young man with a beard, returned with my drink, I showed him Will Stalls' key. "Did you ever see Will Stalls with this key?"

His sharp eyes studied the key quickly even in the darkness of the tavern. "Yeah," he said. "If that's the one that was attached to the cassette."

I hid my satisfaction and pursued the point. "He kept it attached to this cassette?"

The bushy-faced young man nodded. "He said it was his lucky charm."

After showing him my license, I asked, "Can you tell me anything else?"

Suspicious, he looked me over. "What's up?"

With a couple theatrical glances around, I drew close and whispered, "Could be money."

His grin said he understood, but didn't expect a slice. "Sure," he whispered in return. Then he stood back up and spoke conversationally. "Last fall, I guess it was, he come in here flashing a bundle of bills around. For him the size of the wad was something. He lived on social security and pawn money usually. He said he got some of it from Milton's next door, but most of it some guy gave him."

"He told you that? About the money?"

"It's funny what these guys volunteer, you know?"

"No secrets between us friends."

"Yeah. That's it. Anyway, after about half an hour of drinking, he took out the pawn tickets and tore them up. But he said he'd hang onto the key, the one you've got there, because it was lucky."

"Why?" This path was leading somewhere, I could feel it.

He pulled at his beard trying to recall the conversation. "Well, he was kind of sloshed at that point. Will said something strange like this guy told him to hang onto some machines for him—Will would have pawned those—and the key. For that the guy paid him $1000. I figured he stole it."

"Did he say anything else about the key?" I asked.

The bartender motioned me to stay put and went to the end of the bar. There he shook a slumped-over customer several times, rousing the man from an early drunken stupor. After a couple words from the bartender, the guy squinted my way and, then, with bar as support, slid over.

"You asking about Will'am?" His question came soaked in gin and an indeterminate accent.

"Stalls, yeah," I replied.

He flopped down on the stool next to me. "We were... associates," he said.

I shot a glance at the bartender who nodded, so I asked, "How about a drink?"

"Tryin' to quit, sir" he managed to say. "What can I tell you?"

Turning the key and the cassette over to him, I sat back and hoped for results. Dealing with a drunk is difficult. You have to let them have their way in most cases. If they want to talk, they can't help themselves. If they don't, they pass out under pressure. All I could do was wait.

His eyes narrowed to the point that they were actually closed. In fact, from the motion of his head, I assumed he had lost consciousness. Suddenly, he opened his eyes and mouth together. "These are his lucky talismans," he said with effort. "Had them with him all the time."

"What are they?" I asked politely.

Holding up the cassette, he replied, "Don't know." Raising the key in its turn, he said, "Key to box."

Curiosity churned inside me. "Where?" I demanded, sounding impatient.

The snap of my voice made the old man start. He glared at me his eyes glassy. He was seconds from passing out. I grabbed his shoulders and shook him hard to keep him conscious enough to answer me.

His head wobbled around, like a fuzzy ball on a spring. The words came out throbbing with the motion. "Post office." When I let him go, his head fell hard to the bar.

The whiskered bartender stared at me in a mixture of fear and amazement. He stepped back as I went for my pocket.

The slapping noise my hand and the twenty made on the bar caused him to jump.

"Thanks," I said and bolted for the door and the post office.

~ ~ ~

The Post Office down the street from Milt's was intimate and empty. I had hoped for a good crowd, because what I was about to do was probably illegal. The wanted posters decorating the cork board beside the attendant window didn't help.

The man who came up to take care of me looked disgruntled and about 240. When I asked for the box number of my uncle Will Stalls, he shook his balding head. "Sorry."

"About what?" I asked nicely.

"Nobody here by that name."

The way he leaned forward on the counter worried me, so I pulled out the key. "Son-of-a-bitch," I said. "What do I do now?"

Sticking to the uncooperative, he shrugged. "Maybe you got the wrong branch."

My despair was complete, but I took a shot. "For all I know he used his stage name, Weil."

The attendant's face curled up in curiosity. He was staring out behind me. I stopped turning when my eye caught the posters again. "Wait a second," he said.

The second he referred to stretched into minutes. My hands were getting wet and my throat dry. Though I felt like a crowd had gathered around me, I was still alone when he came back.

He didn't stop at the window, but continued to a door that put him beside me. "Here," he grumbled, "give me the key."

His bulk obscured my view of the wall of post boxes. He tried the key. "Yeah." Shaking his head he turned to give me a look at the box. "I thought the guy'd never come back."

My hand shot into the small hole. "Yeah," I said. "He moved in with his sister in Minnesota."

"Too fucking cold up there for me. I can live with the snow." With that he slammed the tiny door shut, and went back behind the counter. "Anything else?"

Defying my inclination toward a hasty exit, I nodded. "How about ten bucks worth of stamps?

My stamps in hand, I strolled out to my car to examine the contents of Will Stalls' P.O. Box. There were three plain envelopes, each one stamped with a blue ink stamp with the name "Samuel Weil" on it with the PO box address under it. A fourth had the name typed and was from the phone company serving Elmira.

I opened the first of the three envelopes in a near frenzy. Too near: Pieces of tape flew out into the car. Shiny, brown pieces of tape, cut at angles, Its postmark said "Huntington, PA," and was dated August 15, 1575.

The second envelope, postmarked the 18th, contained a reel of Scotch recording tape. It was a three inch-spool and the tape on it. As I could see from the first few feet, had been heavily edited. Scratched on the surface of the reel were the initials H.W. and T.H., separated by a long slice of a hyphen.

In the third blue-stamped envelope also mailed on the 18th of August, I found a key. This key was large and probably a room key of sort, or maybe a house key. On closer examination, I could make the etched numbers 203 on the face of the key.

Turning my attention to the bill from the phone company, I learned that Will Stalls had in July of 1975 a telephone installed.

The envelope contained not an original bill but a notice of termination of service for failure to pay past due amounts. I immediately recognized the phone number as the same one written by Ned Cooper on the receipt he had hidden, the receipt for the first deposit in the Weil Winter National account.

The address on the bill proved to be two blocks down the street from Milt's Jewelry.

Leaving my car, but not the new key and tape, I walked hurriedly to the building containing apartment number 203. An old building, it still had enough security to require a key to get in the front door. Mine worked smoothly.

The interior would have seemed like home to Will Stalls. It was, if anything, darker, more grimy than some other places where he had spent his life. The stairs, directly in front of the door, were dark and steep enough to frustrate a mountain goat.

The second floor was a copy of the first. Only one incandescent bulb served a hall forty feet long. Halfway down it,, I found the filthy number plate of room 203. Only a quick look at the lock told me it was newer than the key I had in my hand. I didn't even bother to try it. Instead I knocked.

"Huh?" came a muffled voice. It could have belonged to either a man or a woman, or anything else for that matter.

Avoiding explanations through wood—as I was once instructed by a vacuum cleaner salesman—I just knocked again.

"Shit, okay," the voice muttered, still neuter. "Christ, you can't leave shit alone, can ya?"

Banging against a chain, the door opened a crack. Through the opening, I could see a haggard face and dirty long hair surrounding small blue eyes. They could see me, too. The door closed and opened again, only this time all the way, like the invitation I half expected.

The woman could have been any age or none at all. She had all of her teeth, most of her hair and half of her clothes on. "Hi, handsome," she said, instinctively making up a compliment. "Come on in."

Hesitantly, I accepted the explicit part of the suggestion. "My name's Carmichael," I informed her.

"Good," she said, smiling broadly. "I like Irish guys. I'm half Irish myself. I don't really know which half." With that she laughed, a merry, unexpected laugh.

To forestall any further nonsense, I gave her a shot of my license.

The woman wrinkled her nose and made a clicking sound with her tongue. "I should have known, They wouldn't be likely to send me anyone like you, huh?"

She noted my scrutiny of the room, and misunderstood it, for she said, "Yeah, Not in this doghouse, huh?" She shrugged her very broad shoulders and offered me a cup of coffee. "I was making it for myself, but I always make a bit extra just in case, you know? I don't want to be caught short."

I gave her a knowing smile. "What's your name, kid?" I asked, figuring that the "kid" would flatter her.

It did. Her tiny blue eyes danced with pleasure. "Kathleen," she said proudly. "But everyone calls me Kat." Another shrug. "What can you do?"

Taking the coffee, I asked, "Listen, Kathleen, how long have you had this place?"

After savoring the sound of the name, she replied, "About six, seven months. Why? You looking for one that used to live here? Shit. Figures, huh?"

"No, it doesn't," I told her. "Neither do you, living here, if you know what I mean."

"Don't I know what you mean?" she responded. "Bad for business. I don't get many repeats if that's what you mean. How could I?" She blew out a sigh, making her thick dry lips shake. "Maybe I wouldn't anyway. Right? I'm not as young as you think, Carmichael. Hey, what's your real name? I mean your first, huh?"

"Casey. Everyone calls me 'Carmichael.'"

Gulping coffee, she nodded hungry approval. "Yeah? Too many syllables. For everyday use, you know."

"I have a couple of questions, Kathleen," I said, adding, "that is a beautiful name."

Her head wagged up and down, like the tail on a puppy when it's happy. "I don't hear it much anymore."

"Do you know who lived here before you did?"

Shaking her head so that the strands of hair whipped about in the air, she said, "Uh huh. The place was empty, you know? The guy had moved or gotten evicted, I guess. The landlady told me to change the lock. Just in case. Not that she'd pay for it."

"Good idea, though."

"Oh, yeah."

"Did she tell you anything about him?"

"Only that he was a drunk," Kathleen said with a shrug of her incredible shoulders. "She said he was never even here. Except at the beginning, and at the end. He probably couldn't stand to be here. Maybe he kept someone here. Must have been a cheap asshole, huh?"

Finishing my coffee, I asked one last question. "Was there a phone when you came in?"

"Disconnected, yeah. I had to get one anyway. They don't let you just go on, you know?" She stretched her arms and her legs, driving her slip up her thighs. When she caught me looking at her legs, she blushed and pulled the slip down. Then she laughed. "Stupid, huh? I should be embarrassed about showing anything?"

I stood up and smiled at her. "You shouldn't be embarrassed about showing anything. Not from what I've seen, Kathleen." With my hand gently on her shoulder, I added, "Except this excuse for an apartment." With that I pulled out my the last sixty dollars and put it in her chafing hand. "Thanks for your time, Kathleen."

She looked at the money and, then, at me. "Come any time, Casey."

The sixty bucks was Diana's money and she would hardly miss it.

~ ~ ~

I knew better than to con information out of a phone company on my own authority and without any more of Diana's money. I would have to let that wait until I could get McGuiness or Collins to wangle the records of Stall's phone out of AT&T.

Instead, I went back to Milt's Jewelry Shop. The bell and the angular cadaver of a proprietor greeted me simultaneously. "Back already, Mr. Carmichael?"

"Yeah," I said, "you headed me in the right direction, Milt."

Tentatively, he moved out from behind the counter. "I hardly expected the trail to lead you back to me, Mr. Carmichael."

"It didn't," I told him. "But you're the only guy I know in town who might let me use a tape recorder."

His laugh must have come from deep inside him, because it had a low hollow sound. "Is that all?"

"Yep."

Milt waved his hand at a shelf of machines. "Take your pick, Mr. Carmichael. No charge."

"Thanks." Since Kat had my last bills, I was grateful.

The tape machines varied in age, condition, value and type, I picked the best looking reel-to-reel I could find, hoping to get decent sound reproduction. I pulled it from the shelf and put it on the counter, which Milt had cleared for the purpose.

His eyebrows went up, when he saw the tape. "Have you made a find, Mr. Carmichael? Very good."

"Maybe," I allowed, putting the tape on the machine. It took a little while, as I took care not to pull the spliced tape apart.

With the Wollensak tape recorder humming away, the reel began to spin rapidly. Sounds sped by, totally unrecognizable. My host adjusted the speed control appropriately and the words began.

"Won't you sit down, Tony," a man's voice suggested. There was a touch of condescension in the voice. "We really should have a talk."

Though the voice sounded very conversational, I could detect an occasional jump in the rhythm of the speech. A couple words broke in half due to the editing.

The second voice shocked me for some reason. It was Hiller's voice but it sounded cold and hostile. "Talk," it said. "Not any more, Winter."

"Don't you think I deserve an explanation of your handiwork with the books, Tony?" Winter's chilled voice asked.

For the moment I had heard enough, enough to tell me what I had and what it meant. I pulled the reels from the machine and examined the length of tape. It had been edited to an incredible extent.

"What is it?" Milt asked.

He'd earned a a brief explanation of the case and I gave him one. Summing up, I told him. "This is what Hiller needs to get him out of jail."

Milt seemed skeptical. "Are you saying that poor, old Will Stalls, drunken, foolish, senile Will Stalls could have done that."

"Perhaps," I replied. "Perhaps, he had someone to help him."

"What about the cassette you had earlier?" he asked, his curiosity breaking through his icy, professional veneer. "What's on that?"

Turning to the shelf, I grabbed a cassette recorder and swung it to the counter. "You ask good damned questions, Milt."

Once he had plugged in the cassette player, I put in the cassette. As the tiny spools spun slowly, we heard the voice of Harold Winter.

"Hello, Harold Winter here," it said.

"This is Samuel Weil," another voice said, "I have an account at the bank,"

"Oh, yes," Winter responded on the tape. "Mr. Weil, what can I do for you?"

"I'd like to meet with you if I could," the other man said.

"Of course, of course. Won't you come over this afternoon. Perhaps Tony could direct you. Then you and I could sit down if you'd like. I'd like to get to know what you have in mind. We really should have a talk."

The same words, but from a different conversation, as on the reel-to-reel recording. I flicked off the machine and ejected the cassette. "What do you think?" I asked Milt.

The tall pawnbroker stared at me a long time before answering. "I think that you may have earned a nice bonus, Mr. Carmichael. A very nice bonus."

Chapter Seventeen

Milton loaned me his two tape recorders. He also promised to find out what kind of equipment Stalls had handed over to him in October after Harold Winter was murdered.

Returning to Huntington, I took advantage of the fact that the cassette player was battery driven and I listened to tape recorded conversations of Harold Winter and a couple of another voice, that of Tony Hiller. The cartridge didn't have enough on it—only about five minutes—to fabricate the "confession." Apparently, Stalls recorded a series of conversations on several cassettes, of which mine was only one.

With the raw material of conversation in his hands, Stalls had transferred the voices to a reel-to-reel system so that he could splice the tape and do the editing. The resulting conversation was undoubtedly smooth enough to fool Alma Purcil over the phone.

Hiller could then have been out of action in his own cellar while Stalls killed Winter, at his leisure, and played his ruse on the party-line. It was so easy, I felt slow for taking so long to figure it out.

Only the motive remained a question. Even assuming that Stalls had a partner who had robbed the bank, why would he want to kill Winter? To cover his own path? That was the only definite conclusion I reach, but I didn't like it.

Somewhere in the past there might have been a connection between Winter and Stalls that I didn't know about.

One, probably arising from the incident in the late fifties, the accident between Stalls' and the Stockly's cars. I would have to find that connection before it was all over.

The black button, from the party-line phone, suddenly came to mind. Stalls had dropped it at Hiller's house when had knocked Tony out and dragged him into the basement. But why did he have it? Why did he doctor the phone at all? He had the tape, so that he didn't need to jack up the phone, with no one noticing, in order to frame Tony. He could have killed, or knocked out, Winter first and then just played his tape into the phone.

But the button was unquestionably removed from the phone, and removed before the playing of the tape. It didn't fit into my new explanation of the murder.

Unless he had used the phone to record conversations! Of course. The cassette recorder had a phone hook-up. Stalls had gone into Winter's house and spoken to him in the house. With the voice activated recorder he had pawned at Milt's, he could have recorded the entire conversation by remote hook-up.

With the party-line phone "off the hook," thanks to the missing button, Stalls could pick up the conversation on any party-line phone. That also explained why he had wanted a room on the third floor, near Alma Purcil—to gain access to a second party-line phone. It was an elaborate scheme, but for Stalls, at least, it had worked.

The smoke-screen had kept him in the clear. Not that it had helped very much. Cancer had caught up with him long before I had. The real beneficiary was his accomplice, whoever that was. And Becky Stockly, it seemed. Stalls, as rotten as he had been, had shared his spoils with the girl he had robbed, of her parents, twenty years before. Maybe that helped him die more easily.

~ ~ ~

When I arrived back in Huntington, at the Winter's place, I found lots of people waiting for me: Lewis Huntington, Jack Pazinsky, Diana and Tom Winter. To my surprise, Harley Collins was also among them.

He greeted me in his affable, Republican manner and asked me to sit down. "Tom called me about this tape business," he said. "He should have, Carmichael. This comes mighty close to tampering with a witness."

"Relax, Harley," I told him, feeling calm myself. "I'm glad you're here, as a matter of fact. I want you to come with me to Alma Purcil's."

His grin was ironic. "Love to."

Near the corner of the hallway, Lewis Huntington called out to me. "I have that tape you wanted."

The twinkle of triumph must have been obvious in my eye, because Collins remarked, "It looks like you've got something in store for us, Carmichael."

Producing the spliced tape, I waved it in front of the company, "Lewis, I want you to play this tape instead of the one you made up."

"But..."

"Believe me this one will be much more interesting," I assured him. "Coming Harley?"

The district attorney shrugged indulgently and followed me out of the house.

Over my shoulder, I directed Lewis, "Play it at 8:15."

Young Huntington waved his agreement and Collins and I drove off toward the City Hotel. The DA studied me and the tape recorders in the back seat as we made our way down Main Street.

"You're not going to tell me, are you, Carmichael?" he asked, amused with my melodramatics.

Suppressing my smile, I replied, "I don't want to prejudice you, Harley," though really I wanted to see his face when I pulled my coup.

We got out of the car and hurried through the door. At the elevator, I heard Becky Stockly and Ned Cooper talking in Cooper's room. Motioning Collins to go on alone, I retreated to the doorway to Cooper's room.

Apparently, I had interrupted a serious conversation between the two. Becky sat straight, and square-shouldered, her lips pursed. Cooper sat slumped in a chair, haggard and pretty much used up.

"You told her?" I asked loudly enough to startle them.

Cooper nodded limply.

"Becky? How much?"

She snapped, "Enough!" Becky stood up and faced me. "He told me that you accused him of helping that man. He told me he didn't."

"How about afterwards, Cooper?" I demanded. "Did you tell her you deliberately didn't tell the cops a thing? Did you tell her that you obstructed the investigation? Did you also tell her that because of you, Tony Hiller has gone through a year of pointless hell? You happen to mention any of those things to her, Cooper?"

He said nothing, but he left no doubt that his tale had been somewhat incomplete, probably in just the particulars I recited.

The son-of-a-bitch was trying to make me his goat, at least in the girl's eyes. That had happened to me before, but I deserved it then. I wasn't about to let it happen to me this time. Not with Becky Stockly.

She was one person who deserved the truth. "Tell her, Cooper," I insisted.

Helplessly, Ned looked from one of us to the other. I glared back relentlessly, but Becky shied away, physically, from his pleading eyes.

"Now, Cooper."

"He's right," the old man finally blurted out. "But I did it for you, Becky. There was no other way for me to give you anything." Tears welled up as he spoke, "I didn't know. Not outright. I didn't actually do anything... to help him."

Becky closed her eyes and bent her head back. "My God, Ned," she cried. "What have you done? What have you done to yourself? To Tony?" She didn't mention herself, of course.

"Where's the money, Cooper?" I barked. "No more fun and games. If I'm going to get Hiller off for that murder, I need proof. I want that God damned money. I want to be able to dump it in Harley Collins lap when I tell him the rest. So where the hell is it?"

Wrecked by Becky's outburst, Cooper could barely talk. My slapping him should have helped. It took a second. Finally, he managed something, his voice shaking, "In the bank. I put it in the bank. In trust for her. Under my name."

"How much?"

"About $5,500.00"

The beneficiary of Cooper's tacit cooperation with Stalls, Becky ran her hands hard over her face. The color had gone out of it and her mouth could barely hold up under the weight of her words. "Can Tony use it? For his defense. The money, I mean."

"I don't know," I answered, pacing and looking at my watch. In five minutes, Lewis would be ready to go with the tape. "Your pal here may need it more, when the police hear about this."

She jumped up and grabbed my arms. "You mustn't tell. Please, Casey!" she cried. "Don't tell them!"

Her eyes shone with fear and her hands gripped me so hard I thought the blood would stop flowing. Becky was shaking herself and me as she lost control of her body. Having first debased her protector and main comfort in life, Ned Cooper, I threatened it with annihilation.

"Do you want to make the same stupid mistake?" I demanded harshly. "I can't give Collins half of the case, Becky, and get Tony off the hook. Cooper did what he did, that's all there is to it."

She shook me and her voice with fury. "Don't give me that crap, you bastard! You God damned bastard! It's not that easy! It can't be."

"Sorry," I said, as sympathetically as I could. "It's the same damn choice." Turning to Cooper, I asked him, "Isn't it, Cooper?"

The old man's silence answered the question. He couldn't look at Becky, who stared at him with a betrayed pain in her eyes. She began to nod, over and over again. Spitting out the words, she said, Okay, damn it! Do it your own God damned fucking way!" Then she tore the door open and ran from the room.

I had poured the gasping Cooper a drink before she passed the desk, a suitcase in hand, heading down the street. It occurred to me that there was a bus stop a couple of blocks from the City Hotel. I didn't know anything about the bus schedule, but that didn't matter.

Almost unconsciously, I ran out the door and down the street as fast as I could, which is not so fast as it used to be. Even in the cool of an April evening, I soaked my shirt through.

Just in front of what used to be a Mobil gas station, I caught her. Spinning her around so hard that she dropped her suitcase on the street, I said, "Don't be a fool!"

In the same motion as she whirled, Becky flung her hand toward my face. I could have dodged the blow, but I decided to take it full on the cheek. It stung, the way she intended it.

With that out of her system, Becky Stockly just stood and glared at me.

"Are you going to leave that poor son-of-a-bitch?" I demanded. "Not Cooper. He's gone. I mean Tony Hiller."

She literally snarled. "He has Diana."

"But you love him." The words sounded dumb, but I was desperate. "He's going to need that more than he needs Diana!"

Becky started to cry, suddenly and very hard. To hold herself up, she leaned into me. "I can't. Not any more," she whispered. "Let me go. Just let me go."

~ ~ ~

Though convinced it wasn't right to let Becky go, I did. I still had the paying job of persuading people that Tony Hiller was innocent, at least of murder.

Preoccupied, I passed Alma's door and entered the room next to hers. Only after standing in the middle of the empty room for a minute, did I realize that I had mistakenly wandered into Will Stalls former base of operations.

It was just as empty as before, and yet emptier. Glancing around, I could tell that something was missing. It had always been missing, hadn't noticed until that moment. There was no phone in Stalls' room, no way for him to connect his tape machine to the party-line. Unless, of course, he used Alma's phone.

The wall between Alma's apartment and the one I was in had a faded flowery wallpaper. It would have been difficult for me to spot any imperfections if I hadn't been looking in the right place. The hole was in the lower corner, just above the fine wood baseboard, where the common wall met the front wall.

The paper had been carefully peeled back and then reglued into position. Only a small wrinkle remained to indicate that Stalls had tampered with the surface. Under the flap, I found what I expected.

Ned Cooper's building was old and well built, but age wears down the best structures and the City Hotel was no exception. A variety of cracks were hidden behind the paper and a particularly deep one ran right down to the corner. Stalls had helped it along by boring a small hole through to Alma's room.

The hole was just large enough to accommodate a thin wire that could have run from Alma's phone to Stalls tape recorder. With that access to the party-line, Stalls would have been able to record conversations with Winter and Hiller over the phone when the opportunities presented themselves. The rest was simple editing.

With time running short, I joined Collins and Alma in the adjacent room. The DA was chatting amiably with Willard when I entered. He saw me, checked his watch and kept on talking with the bird.

Alma stood at the window near the wall she had shared with William Stalls. At her feet, the party-line phone's wire ran into a small metal connection box. Six inches away, there was a tiny hole in the wallpaper.

I moved over to the window, beside Alma. She didn't turn to look at me. Her gaze was fixed on a lonely, hunched figure sitting on a bench down the street. "She's finally going."

"Yeah."

Alma smiled. "It's better for her," she said flatly. "A young girl can lose everything staying here. It's best to go."

As she spoke, a bus pulled up in front of Becky, its door swinging open. The girl hesitated, making a show of preparing her bag, handing it to the driver and watching him stow it. Several times her eyes turned toward the building from which we watched her. The driver finally touched her shoulder and we saw her nod. Ten seconds later she was gone.

"Eight-fifteen, Alma," Collins announced.

Alma Purcil and I turned together. As we passed, I detected a pair of tears stealing down each of her soft skinned cheeks. She caught me looking but didn't say anything. Instead, she paused a moment, took a quick breath and hesitantly, picked up the phone.

As quickly as she had put the receiver to her ear, her mouth dropped open and her eyes widened with horror. "Oh, my God!" she exclaimed dropping the phone on the floor.

Collins picked up the receiver as I steadied the victimized woman. The DA's face ran through a series of expressions from incredulity to resignation. He turned to the woman and asked, "Well, Alma?"

"It's what I heard," she said, her voice weak. "It's horrible."

"Lewis," Collins called into the phone, "Shut it off." He listened for a second and then said, "I'll say it is. Very persuasive." With that comment he hung up the phone.

"You'd better tell me what else you found out, Carmichael," he said to me. "I've only heard part of your theory."

He whistled after I had related my findings in Elmira. "I'll check with the phone company for you," he agreed. A laugh shook the room. "I mean for me. Hell, I'm the DA."

"Do you know of anything that could connect Winter and Stalls?" I asked.

Collins shrugged. "Maybe there isn't one. Your first theory, the one about the smoke-screen, that sounds good enough to me."

"No, somehow it isn't," I came back. "Things don't quite jibe yet, Harley. All we need is that last link, damn it."

He clapped me on the back. "Well, one thing is for damn sure, Carmichael," he said grinning. "I'm going to take a lot of flak when I let Tony out tomorrow. Especially without a warm body to replace him."

"The embezzlement," I said.

"Pardon?"

"What about the embezzlement, Harley?" I asked, my sense of accomplishment dissipating. "We have to find an answer to that."

Collins looked at me as though I had worked too long. "Hey, Carmichael," he said, cheerfully. "You got him off on the big one, forget about the embezzlement. Christ, we'll probably let him go altogether after what he's been through."

"Yeah," I agreed, not totally convinced. Collins was right as far as it went. And yet, Tony had denied the embezzlement along with everything else. Why? Most people cop to lesser offenses to avoid murder.

"Harley, he couldn't have done it," I stated.

"What?" Collins asked, having obviously lost my train of thought.

Pacing off the room, I said, "Tony told a bizarre story. He denied that he had anything to do with Winter's murder. Well, he was right," I said. "He also denied anything like embezzlement. Why would he lie about that?"

The handsome DA sighed and plopped down into a chair. "He wouldn't," he concurred. "At least probably not."

Yes, I decided, here it was. "The connection between Winter's murder and the robbery is definite. Obviously, the embezzlement is part of the whole picture," I explained. "That is where the link between Stalls and Winter has to be. I'm sure of it!"

Collins jumped to his feet. "Why not? Maybe Stalls' account was intended for the embezzled funds."

"Someone was setting Tony up, all right from the beginning," I declared. "But it wasn't Stalls. At least, not alone."

"Who are you suggesting?" Collins demanded skeptically. "Certainly not Harold Winter."

~ ~ ~

Harold Winter was a possibility. But I had another in mind, one that made more sense to me.

At Winter National Bank three men had complete access to the books. Hal Winter, Tony Hiller and the disgruntled Jack Pazinsky. Of the three, Jack Pazinsky had the least to lose by fiddling with the books. He was obviously not going to take the reins of the bank, that plum had been stolen from him by Tony.

I explained my idea to Collins as we drove back to the Winter mansion. "Suppose, Pazinsky had it in for Tony Hiller," I said. "He could easily arrange the books to make Hiller look like a clumsy thief. Then comes August, when Pazinsky knew the routine audit was coming. He could have had it all set up for then, but Tony ordered a delay in the audit."

"Throwing Pazinsky's plan out the window," Collins went on for me. "Sounds good so far."

Things were coming together for me and I felt brilliant. "Assume then, that Pazinsky contacts William Stalls somehow, and arranges a small bank job with him—to force a review of the books in Mid-August. When it comes off, you remember, he was not in town."

"Are you suggesting Jack pulled the actual robbery?" Collins asked, incredulous.

"The thief knew the bank inside out," I said. "He came through Pazinsky's window. Because of the air-conditioning, that window was usually locked. Someone had to specifically unlock it. The thief knew about the telephone system. The layout of the vault, everything." I paused to breath. "Then let's assume that Winter, in looking things over, figures that it wasn't Hiller who played with the books after all."

The DA stared ahead of him, at the Winter house as it approached. "It looks so serene, Carmichael," he said. "Could all of this have happened here?"

Thinking aloud, I ignored his question. "Pazinsky and Stalls must have figured in advance that their scheme might be too obvious to fool a man like Winter. So, in advance, they planned to murder Harold Winter in the name of Tony Hiller."

"We can't begin to prove it," Collins objected. "No one, including you, has uncovered the slightest indication of Pazinsky's involvement. We need something pretty damning."

The car safely stowed away beside the house, Collins and I went in to confront Jack Pazinsky with our new speculations. That's all they were, of course, because Collins was right: We had nothing to connect Stalls with Pazinsky. We'd have to get it.

The four people we had left behind, Jack, Lewis, Tom and Diana, were all gathered in the study, playing the edited tape I had given Lewis. Huntington switched it off when we entered. "Great work Carmichael," he enthused.

Pazinsky skeptically demanded, "Is this real? Or some kind of mock up?"

Collins and I planted ourselves in front of the assembly. "It's real, Jack," Collins assured him. "Alma thought so anyway."

Diana flew at me from her chair. "Then you were right, Casey," she cried, hugging me impulsively.

When I didn't respond Diana retreated holding her arms close to her chest in surprise. She became frightened when she saw me staring hard at Pazinsky. "What's wrong?"

"Only one thing," I said. "We know that Tony didn't kill your father. But there is the matter of embezzlement and a bank robbery. We don't think that Tony had anything to do with either of them."

A wry smile creeping onto his face, Pazinsky asked, "Who would you suspect, then, Carmichael?" The question was intended to be rhetorical for he had drawn his conclusion for my expression. "It would have to be someone with access, opportunity and motive, if I recall the formula."

Lewis Huntington sounded shocked when he demanded, "You're not suggesting Jack here, are you?"

Returning my glare in kind, Pazinsky replied, "What's the motive? Resentment at being ignored, abused, passed over all my life?" He considered the idea with a frown of approval. "Could I have hated Harold Winter for sucking me dry and then handing my work over to an inexperienced simpleton? And my revenge against Tony would be well deserved, too. And ironic. Tony had stolen everything from me without conscious thought. How appropriate that he should be destroyed in a state of complete helplessness? I'm almost convinced myself."

Diana had staggered against the wall and suddenly began to cry. Tom Winter's mouth hung open, except when he had to gulp for air. The shaking head of Lewis Huntington conveyed his opinion.

"Pure bullshit!" Lewis snapped.

"We'd like to search your place, Jack," Collins stated.

Pazinsky chewed on the inside of his cheek, deciding what to do. He took his glimmering blue eyes away from me to stare at Collins, and then the others, one by one. His gaze finally settled on Diana, who could not return the compliment. Still looking at her, he lifted his muscular shoulders high and sighed. Resignation colored his voice.

"If you must," he said. "It's funny, but I am afraid. Honestly. For the first time in my life, I am genuinely afraid. I think you're going to find something."

~ ~ ~

Jack Pazinsky lived in a small apartment not far from the Winter National Bank. It was on the first floor of an old house north of Winter National, on a back street. For a man as organized as Jack Pazinsky, he had managed to neglect the outside of the place pretty well.

Inside, the few rooms were small and sparsely decorated. The man clearly did not indulge in nick-knacking or collection of anything. The living room, for example, contained one sofa, three chairs arranged in a geometric pattern around the couch, and two small tables. Five lamps made up for the lack of overhead lighting without doing anything about the lack of furnishings.

"This, my friends," he announced, "is the resting place of John R. Pazinsky." The way he said it told me that none of the others had ever been in it before. "If you have any trouble finding anything, I probably won't be much help." With that, he sat down on the sofa, his face calm, his back stiff. His left hand curled around the arm of the couch, tightening until the knuckles went white.

Collins headed off for the other rooms, while I rummaged about into the living room. The others, all of whom has accompanied us on what amounted to an expedition, each took one of the chairs.

"It's not cozy," I heard Pazinsky tell the others. "But it will seat the spectators."

"They won't find anything, Jack," Lewis said.

"Oh, please shut up, Lewis," Pazinsky suggested. "I have never been very fond of you and I am not likely to change just because I am in trouble."

The living room proper yielded me nothing. There was, however, a small writing desk around the corner in the tiny dining room. Concentrating on that, I examined bills and a few, very few, letters. An old diary was secreted in a bottom drawer but it excited only sympathy.

It's last entry was dated June 12, 1972. It read, "I am now too old to maintain a journal as trivial as this one. Only events of merit should be recorded and of those there are not enough to bother."

Closing the book, I spotted the familiar black and gray logo of GTE. Pazinsky had retained his telephone bills for the past four years. I didn't have to go back far to find what I had expected to find.

The July 1975 billings included three calls to a number in Elmira, New York, a number immediately recognizable as the one maintained by William Stalls. The calls had been made on three evenings in mid-to-late July. No one call took more than a couple of minutes.

Other than that, the desk and the rest of the room for that matter, was empty.

Collins was having no success in the bedroom. My find brought a discouraged look to his face. "Can he really be guilty Carmichael?" he asked in a whisper.

I shrugged and helped him through the rest of his search. Pazinsky had so few things, so small an apartment, that our labors embarrassingly short. Only the telephone bill supported our theory about Pazinsky.

"Is that all?" Pazinsky said, in mock astonishment.

Sternly, Collins asked, "Can you explain these calls?"

The small, graying man, shrugged, "No."

"Don't you recognize this number?" I demanded.

"I make many calls on my phone based exclusively on messages left for me at the bank," Pazinsky offered. "Anything I don't recognize, I submit to the bank for reimbursement. There is no check-mark or anything, so the request for reimbursement undoubtedly went through. That's all I can say."

He studied the bill a long time. "It's funny," he added, "this thing. So subtle."

As he stood holding the bill, Diana rose and went over to him. She placed her hands on his arms. "Is what they say true, Jack?"

Closing his eyes, Pazinsky grimaced, as though her words were small, delicate knives. He opened them again and the hurt was even obvious. "No, Diana," he stated, unevenly. "But if you don't believe me, I will understand."

She spun around to look to me for guidance at first. Her face was filled with a strange childish yearning. Did she want me to make this one work out right, too? Like Tony's guilt, she wanted Pazinsky's erased. But it was different. She had no obligation to Jack Pazinsky, not like the one she had to Tony Hiller, the fiancé abandoned. She didn't have to believe Pazinsky, she didn't have to save him, not way she had to for Hiller.

Her voice had a determined edge to it, unlike the uncertain innocence it usually projected. "You're wrong," she said to me, her soft, rounded jaw set.

It shook me, stung me even, to hear her say that. She had leaned on my every word before then, accepted my lead. I had gotten used to it from her. And, if the expression on her brother's face was any indication, so had he.

Lewis Huntington looked angry. When he caught me looking at him, he started. Flustered for a moment, he just glared at me. Finally, he said, "She's right, Carmichael."

A smile had come to the lips of Jack Pazinsky, or rather to his whole face. He was the kind of man who usually smiled only with his mouth, while his eyes conveyed something else, something grim. But not this time. Standing of the edge of disaster, the son-of-a-bitch actually seemed happy.

I didn't care if he was nuts. As far as I was concerned he was guilty, period. If he thought he'd get off just because gullible Diana and contrary Lewis believed him, he'd have an unpleasant surprise waiting for him.

Pazinsky acceded to Harley Collins reluctant request that the pair of them go to the station house in Franklin.

Strangely, no one objected at all. They accepted the fact that Jack Pazinsky would spend at least the night in jail.

It was a mighty weird group of people in Huntington, Pa., that I'd gotten myself tangled up in. But I had come out okay.

I was feeling more than satisfied with myself in the strained silence when Diana suddenly spoke.

She said firmly, finally, "We won't be needing you anymore, Casey."

Chapter Eighteen

Leaving Huntington as quickly as possible, I made it back to Pittsburgh in time to try for some decent sleep, the first time in days. For a long time, however, I couldn't get comfortable. Maybe satin had spoiled me. It wasn't until sun-up that I finally conked in the rough Percale.

Eight o'clock had rolled around by the time I woke up. In the evening. The dark room itself felt wrong and outside it was darker, damper and colder.

Disgruntled in general, and with telephones in particular, I made my way over to mine and called Cath Mays at home. Her voice was shaking when she asked, "Hello, Freddie?" When I told her it was only me, she hung up. I tried again and she apologized.

"That's all right, Cath," I lied. Nothing seemed all right. "I just want to know if anyone called."

She sniffled. "Janice Simmons called three times. A DA named Collins to tell you he'd had someone booked. Chief McGuiness to congratulate you. And a young guy named Bud something, threatening to kill you if he ever saw you again."

That would be Bud Burne, the Elmira cop. "Anything else, Cath?"

"Fred won't marry me, if that's what you mean?" she blurted out.

It wasn't, but I pretended it was. "Give him time, Cath." Everybody needed time. "Good-bye."

After finishing with Cath, I went out to a bar down the street. It wasn't a nice place, but the drinks were cheap enough and strong enough to make the evening go faster than it might have. Lingering in my mind, the Hiller case seemed bent on ruining the rest of my week.

Every time I turned around someone was talking on a phone and I had had enough of phones. I fumbled through my pockets more than once and pulled out the little black souvenir I had kept for myself. The innocuous phone button had really gotten me excited before and now it wouldn't leave me alone.

I got sufficiently drunk so that I could go back to sleep easily. In fact, I fell into unconsciousness on my beat-up old couch.

When I awoke around noon the next day, I panicked at the surroundings. It passed quickly as I recognized the place, my own cell-sized bedroom. Everything was back to normal. It was still raining. Normal.

The afternoon, I spent figuring the bill due from Diana. It was a goodly amount, especially the expenses, but it didn't seem like enough. Still, I resisted the urge to pad it. She hired me to do a job and I did it. She didn't really fire me, I was just done.

Repeat ten times and feel less betrayed. I stopped at five. I kind of liked the feeling.

Writing the address on the envelope reminded me that Janice had stolen my address book. I still didn't know why. So far as I could tell, it was a pointless exercise on her part. The only use the book had to anyone was to me, such as telling me Diana's zip code. Without the zip, it would take me forever to get my money.

Money, as it turned out, was in short supply. Trying to scrape up enough change for a stamp and a hamburger underscored that fact. The stamp was to get Diana her tab as quickly as possible; the hamburger to quiet the hunger I always felt when things went awry.

I skipped the hamburger in favor of a bourbon and sent the envelope on its way before returning to the apartment. It was done.

Only, it wasn't. There on the desk sat Diana's bill. The envelope had left without it.

Jesus. I slammed the paper on the stupid desk.

Yeah, the desk was stupid.

I was half tempted to dive into the mail box, dig out the envelope and put the bill in it before it left the neighborhood and exposed my poor desk to...

For reasons of his own, Sam Weil popped into my head at that instant. Ironically, if he had left his tape out of an envelope—and Pazinsky—would still be all innocence.

I wasn't the least bit sure, suddenly, that he hadn't. I could almost see him, posting an empty envelope to himself, to be filled later. This thought circled my mind like an endless loop of magnetic tape.

Obviously, I had to get Weil and Pazinsky and Diana and everyone else the hell out of my system. I had been through it before and knew one thing: I wouldn't be able to just forget them.

For that reason and to restore my telephone voice, I called McGuiness and Collins. Neither was much help. Tony Hiller had been released from the hospital and had returned home, his brain addled. Ned Cooper had been admitted to the same hospital with a well-deserved heart attack. Diana had flown to California to convince her brother, Robert, to bail out Jack Pazinsky. And failed. Everything was almost done. Almost.

It was almost a hollow triumph. I had to wonder what Tony Hiller thought about the whole mess. Almost one year of brain-washing, a year of learning that he was guilty of something he knew he hadn't done. Then, through the wonder of the efforts of one Casey Carmichael, he is free to return to a town which, without Diana, Becky or Ned and with Pazinsky in jail, must have seemed more desolate than his hospital room.

I had to put it out of my mind. It didn't help to think about that kind of thing, especially after being bounced unceremoniously. Which shouldn't have bothered me, because guys like me are designed to be loaded with everyone's problems and then chased out of the village scapegoat-like. It's part of the job.

For about an hour, I stared past the phone, out into the rain beating down on my living room's one lonely window. Dark, dreary weather never helps my moods and I was doubting that the May flowers would be worth my April.

A jangling of the phone disturbed my reflection and I couldn't stand the noise, so I answered.

"Casey?" a woman's voice said,

I gave her the bad news. "Yeah."

"This is Janice," she said as if she knew it should help. "I've been trying to reach you all day. Are you all right?"

Had she? Why?

"Casey?" she asked more loudly. "Are you still there?"

I nodded automatically, then I laughed. "Yeah, Janice. I'm here. What can I do for you?"

"Your answering service told me you had finished the Winter case." She sounded upset that she had had to hear that bit of information from Cath. "And so have all the papers in town."

"North of I-80 news."

"Except it's my case and I've been scooped!"

"Sorry." I was, too, because she deserved a fair share of the sour fruits of cracking the Winter case.

Her voice rose annoyed to promising. "I'll accept that if you'll take me to dinner. I'm an even hungrier reporter, now."

That was the least I could do for her. And probably the most I could do for myself. "You pick the spot, Janice. We can still charge it to Diana Winter," I said.

"There is a nice little place near where you live, Casey, "Adolpho's," she replied. "I'll meet you there at...how's 9:15?"

I said it was fine and we hung up.

Fine, my clock told me, but damned soon if I aspired to looking presentable. Shaving and showering were minimum requirements for being seen on the street again. More than that was recommended for being seen with Janice Simmons.

9:15 just slipped by me, but I entered Adolpho's as the hostess seated Janice. The scene reminded me of our aborted breakfast meeting. I suppressed a flare of indignation. Once the green eyes caught mine, I forgot all about it.

She smiled politely at me as I sat down next to her. "So, Mr. Carmichael," she said stiffly. "You are a hero."

My tongue rattled as the air blew over it. "Is that why I get to go out with the princess?"

Her manner changed abruptly and she laughed. She leaned close to me. "Yes, I guess it is."

"Then maybe being a hero isn't so bad."

Even in the dim light of Adolpho's, her face managed to glow when she smiled. "Actually, I was going to brow-beat you into a public apology for losing my story. But I should thank you," she admitted. "I have been vindicated, after all."

I thought of her comments on Diana. "In more ways than one," I agreed. "You did most of it. I just followed you around picking up some table scraps."

Her hair rippled when she shook her head. "You always so self-deprecating, Casey. Why is that?"

"I like to call it realism, Janice. And, yes, my nose still hurts."

"I admitted what I did, remember," she snapped so hard her hair rippled again.

Focusing, I asked, "What about Cleveland?"

Janice waved her hand. "Something someone said made me think of that. It wasn't very hard. It was an agency right across the street from the Ford place."

"No one else made that connection, Janice," I reminded her.

"I was going the wrong way the whole time, Casey. I was so sure that Diana and Lewis Huntington had something to do with it. You were the smart one." With a contrite nibble on her finely-drawn pink lip, she added, "I horribly under-estimated you."

The way she was talking, she must have thought I was an idiot before. Now, she had swung too far the other way. I let her stay there a bit longer. "I like to think you did."

Abashed, she lowered her eyes to watch her hands. "I have a confession or two to make, Casey." When she brought her eyes back to mine, they were almost mournful. "What I have done I did for a reason, but it seems pretty silly now,

"They usually do," I said. "Reasons, I mean."

Janice shrugged, seeming, all of a sudden, vulnerable. It was the way she had when she talked about Harry Blair that first night I met her. "In a way, I'm glad," she said. "I would never have found out anything about you. Nobody knows anything about you, did you know that?"

"An air of mystery, Janice. We have so much in common."

"Originally," she confessed, "I broke into your office to find out who you'd worked for in the past, looking for some connection between you and Lewis Huntington. That's why I took your address book. It was the only record I could find of people you'd worked for or with."

"That didn't help, of course," she continued uncertainly, "but I tried another tack. To find out about you, your past particularly, There's even less of a record of that."

Janice Simmons had her ways to penetrate any screen between past and present. I was certain she had in my case. That should have unnerved me, but instead, it made me laugh. "I'll bet there was just enough of one to get you started."

"Just barely enough," she suggested, shaking her head. "You had a license, I knew that. And to get one in this state you have to three years experience with the police or the FBI or something. Your file, it didn't say anything about it."

"No, it wouldn't."

She put her hand on my arm and squeezed gently. "You went to three colleges, I knew that, too. I checked the records at each. Oh, yes, I went to an awful lot of trouble. At first,

I didn't come up with anything other than a pretty fair performance for a guy who ended up in such a dumb business."

"One thing I've learned: If the facts aren't there, look for
'timing.' And that's what I did. First, I saw that you got your
license right out of NYU. Then, I found that you had transferred twice, shortly after major arrests of students by the
FBI."

So Janice knew and that was all right. Someone had to
know and it wasn't a crime, after all. It just wasn't popular,
then or now. Not with anyone.

"Twelve 'communist student organizers' in all," she said
using the official phrase. "They went to prison because of
you. Isn't that right, Casey?"

"Eleven," I said, in a hollow-sounding tone. "Hank Bissel
was guilty of something else, too."

She was close enough, then, to whisper in my ear, "I won't
tell anyone if you don't want me to."

Everything should have been fine. It was almost twenty
years ago that it happened. And it was perfectly all right
then. It paid my way through colleges I'd never have seen
any other way. It introduced me to people I ended up liking.
It got me a detective's license, no questions asked,

I hadn't made any decisions. I hadn't convicted anyone. I
just handed over the information of their activities, their
causes, their friends. It was twenty years ago, or almost. And
it didn't bother me at all any more. Not a bit.

~ ~ ~

Janice also coaxed the details of my work on the Hiller
case out of me. It was the least, she told me with a smile, that
I could do for her, since I had let her get "scooped."

Since my dinner was cold anyway, I told her everything I
could think of. I left out a few things, things, things that only
became evident as I spoke. My embarrassingly complicated
attachment to Diana, for example, would best remain my secret.

Having resisted the temptation to examine it earlier, I found my, strictly internal, revelation about Diana and myself dissipated my anger about my firing. My real problem with her at the end, I realized, was that she grew up so suddenly and abruptly rejected my ambiguously fueled intervention. Unfortunately, I had grown to like her dependence on me. Maybe I was too old for a Diana.

Maybe I had always been too old.

"You look more reflective than usual Casey," Janice said, settling into the sofa in my living room. She had looked the place over, disapprovingly, before deciding on a safe place to sit.

Curled up on my twenty year old sofa, surrounded by the limited elegance of my apartment, Janice Simmons looked like an emerald on a counter at K-Mart. And suddenly, she was all I could think about. I remembered thinking of her hair. That made me laugh.

The change must have surprised her, because she became upset. "What are you laughing about?"

Sitting beside her, admiring her flashing eyes, I put her at ease. "How did a woman like you end up in this place?"

Janice leaned against my shoulder, her arm inside mine. Her voice was mellow, low, but not forced. "I wish I understood you, Casey," she said. "I've known a lot of crazy guys—not for long, mind you—but you're the most curious. You should be all over me by this time—I know you like my hair, at least..."

Great.

"...but you're sitting there so stiff. And not in a good way."

I hadn't notice, until she mentioned it, just how taut my muscles were. The incongruity of the situation, of her and me, so like that of the Hiller case, it put me off. It wasn't right.

Pulling away from her, I agreed. "Something bothers me, about you. About me."

She ran her hand up and down my back, causing it to tighten all the more. "God, Casey, what is the matter with you?"

"Something I've been thinking about," I said, pushing up. "The feeling I have about all this, well, it is a sense that things aren't meshing."

"You mean you and me?" she asked from behind me. Her voice cracked, almost inaudible, afraid perhaps, but I didn't flatter myself. "It's not important, Casey."

Her comment echoed inside, but my mind brushed it aside. "We are too bound up in this, Janice," I declared, facing her. "This Hiller case. You and I, we can't separate ourselves from it."

Janice swayed forward and then collapsed back onto the arm of the couch. "We can. The case, the story. It's all over."

"It isn't."

"I know we started out that way—and I screwed up—but you know that doesn't matter, now."

"But it does," I said, sure I was right. "I'm not talking about all the stunts you pulled, the notebook, the breakfast..."

"Wow!" That was for her, not me. "I knew that would have to come up sooner or later," Janice admitted. "It was silly of me and I am very sorry."

"That was fine," I said, gently. "It pissed me off, sure. You did make me feel pretty slow, but it was your lead..."

"... our lead?" She suggested the finish. "It seemed like that to me, too."

"That's what I am talking about. The case is the sole basis of our relationship. It's your part in the Hiller case. The 'our' is only because of the case."

It hit me then, very hard. "That was why you wanted to find out who I was, and who had put Kline on the Winter estate. You knew there was only one guy Kline would recommend as a detective. I'm the only one they've ever used."

Janice buried her head in her hands. "Yes."

"You were kicking up a fuss in Huntington, Janice," I went on. "Everywhere I went, everyone talked about you. Always you. I wrote that off to your looks. I didn't even question beyond that."

She wasn't looking at me.

"But no one else questioned the case against Tony Hiller. No one. Just you. And you wouldn't let go. Right?"

"Yes." One small word. A whole confession.

"Then one day, some clown named Carmichael is hired by Diana Winter to look into the possibility that only you had accepted: That Tony Hiller wasn't either lying or crazy. That he was telling the truth."

For once I was thinking faster than I was talking.

It was like everything else in the case, Janice and me. She was smart, and tenacious, first class. I was none of those things. I was a small-timer. I'd never even sniffed a murder, but, suddenly, I chasing the case with her watching me. She was involved, stuck with me, with my investigation.

Janice Simmons, passive? Please.

She had dug into my past, into my present. She had helped me, and yet not cooperated with me. Prodded me, even tricking me. She kept her distance, as though I had to have her help, but would reject it outright. Look at it from the other side, I reminded myself, everything else was backwards.

"It's turned around, Janice," I explained. "Like you and me. Here you are, falling all over me. Christ, it's ridiculous."

"Don't think that way, Casey," she pleaded.

"This whole time," I said, "I have felt out of place. Felt. You knew."

"Yes." Her voice trembled as she spoke, "You are out of place, Casey. You shouldn't live like this, here. You are better than this."

A sincere compliment, maybe, but it was a dodge. Janice was apologizing for something. She was trying to make something up to me. The way she had acted at the start of the Hiller case? But there wasn't anything else between us then.

Was there?

Looking at myself, turned around, I saw what Janice had seen. A coincidence? Too much a coincidence. "You didn't like it, did you, Janice?" I asked, my voice edged. "That I should be in on this, when you were in on it too? The world isn't that small. People sharing a man like Harry Blair? They don't just happen to fall together on something like the Hiller case."

Shrinking into the corner, she cried, "Casey stop it" Please!"

"Stop it?" I asked, wanting to, but unable to, ease up. "How can I? Now, that I understand what you were up to? Now that I know what you thought of me?"

My laugh sounded bitter even to me. "No God damned wonder you were digging around. You figured that I was the sop being thrown your way. That I was the red herring Diana—and Lewis, too—a stooge they hired. To do what?"

She was shaking and wouldn't answer.

So I repeated my question, sharply, closing in on her. "To do what, Janice? What did you think?"

Her green eyes were so brilliant crystals, even in the dim light of my apartment. Janice buried them in my shoulder. "I was wrong, Casey" she cried. "I thought... I thought that they had hired you to convince me, everyone, but mostly me..."

"Some ego, huh?" She looked up. "But that's what I thought, that I was their target. They needed someone to convince me that Hiller was guilty."

"And, so, I concluded for her, "Patsy Carmichael would go there and purposely find nothing new."

She nodded her head back into hiding.

"And because Harry trusted me, they figured you would, too." I felt physically sick, now that it was all out. "You don't trust many people, do you, Janice?"

She pulled back and rearranged her shoulders, her defiance reasserted. "No, and usually I'm right." Her voice took on its TV gravity. "In your case, I was wrong. I admit it. And you have made it very obvious that I will regret it."

Brushing by me, she headed for the door. Before opening it, she added, "One thing, I want to make clear, Casey. I do regret it. And I am ashamed of myself for the way I treated you. Good-bye." With that, Janice Simmons opened the door and took the air out of the room with her.

~ ~ ~

Since I couldn't breathe, I decided I was hungry. My refrigerator was as empty as usual. The evening was pretty much done and my pockets were damned near as empty... Almost. Since there wasn't much else to do, I took that little black button I had saved and pitched it right through the window.

Chapter Nineteen

Weeks passed before I heard from either Janice or anyone connected with the Winter-Hiller—and I suppose Pazinsky—case. They weren't good weeks for me or for business. If I hadn't gotten such a good bonus from Diana Winter—for my "diligence and patience", she wrote—I might have lost weight.

So when Pete Kline called, I had to ditch my reluctance to talk to anyone who knew anyone in Huntington in favor of a chance to do something. As cool as usual, Pete said he had someone at his office who wanted to talk to me.

During the walk to the Lawyers building, I worried about who it would be. I couldn't be sure that it wasn't someone I wanted to avoid, because Pete usually said the same thing when he wanted me to serve a notice to a suit, or locate an absentee heir.

By the time I entered the offices of Kline and Company, I expected almost anybody.

I was relieved that it was a man I'd never seen before. He rose, to a height of maybe five-ten, when I came in, showing off an expensive pin-striped suit. The face was young, but not youthful, with an expression of solid, subdued confidence. His hair was already graying at the temples, though the rest of it remained dark brown, the color of his narrowed his eyes.

"Casey Carmichael, Dr. Robert Winter," Pete announced.

Dr. Winter shook my hand with a tired firmness. When he smiled, even that little bit he had for me, the skin around his eyes cracked. For a man of thirty-three, he looked ancient. "How do you do, Mr. Carmichael?" he asked pleasantly. "I was in town on some matters regarding my father's estate and thought you and I should meet."

Studying him intently for the first few seconds, I had forgotten that he was 'the' Bob Winter. Once I remembered, my stomach tightened. My smile felt more like a grimace. "How're things in Huntington, Dr. Winter?" I asked, striving for correctness.

A vague wave of his hand pretty much dismissed my question. "As always, Mr. Carmichael. You probably know Huntington as it stands now much better than I. I have purposely stayed away from it for a long time," he said. "Perhaps I shouldn't have."

"You missed the whole season," I told him.

Nodding slowly, he agreed, "So I did." He breathed in before taking up another subject. "Diana has spoken rather highly of you, Mr. Carmichael. Despite the fact that she believes you are wrong about Jack Pazinsky, Diana seems to think the world of you."

"Does that bother you?" I asked, skeptically.

He allowed himself a knowing smile. "Yes. I suppose that it does bother me. So does her over-developed attachment to Jack." Bob Winter paused, looking over to Pete Kline, as though trying to remember what the lawyer was doing in his own office. "She has always chosen her associates unwisely, Mr. Carmichael."

Measuring my own words, I offered, "At least she did better with her siblings."

Bending his eyebrows down at the corner, Bob Winter said, "You should reserve your judgment of me, Mr. Carmichael. I suggest that your qualifications do not extend to evaluating a man on first sight."

He was right and I conceded with a shrug. There was something to him that helped me understand why people talked about him as they did.

"In any case," he said, his tone more gentle, "I wanted to meet you and to thank you for whatever help you might have given Diana in a what was a very difficult period for her."

"Everybody needs someone to dump their shit on," I said, irked at the way he was talking. He didn't sound like a real person and didn't deserve my best manners. "That's what I'm paid for."

Not a line in his expression changed position. "Getting paid must make it even more demeaning," he said, revealing an edge of bitterness that cut us both. "I understand that Diana's friend Lewis Huntington suggested you," he added. "Have you any idea why?"

My mind ran back and fetched Janice Simmon's suspicions. I felt for an instant like waving them in front of Bob Winter, but I held off. The age in his face reminded me too much of someone else, maybe of Becky Stockly. "He didn't. Pete here did."

Bob Winter disliked being misinformed and his face showed it, from the white lips to the working of the cheeks. "I see. Then, as usual, Lewis claimed too much for his own efforts, in taking the blame for what you did."

Huntington taking blame for me?

"Diana," he explained, before I could ask, "has thrown herself over to Jack Pazinsky. Tony Hiller was quite bad enough, but this has torn our family apart, Mr. Carmichael. The damage it has done to Diana may be irreparable."

"What the hell do I have to do with it?" I demanded, getting out of my chair. He was referring, no doubt, to the argument over Jack Pazinsky's bond. "Diana's old enough to make her own stupid choices. I didn't have to help her!" My piece said, I nodded to Pete and went on my way.

Nothing miffed me more than a pompous clown like Bob Winter—not to mention a queer like Lewis—blaming me for kicking someone out of adolescence. If Diana wanted to make an ass of her brother, good for her!

I hit the street feeling pretty righteous. I wanted to stick my fist into anyone in a striped suit. The traffic cooled my bravado, a delivery truck nudging me half onto the sidewalk while the crowd kept me half in the street. I must have walked for a block that way, one foot in the gutter, one on the sidewalk. It reminded me of Stalls, or Weil, or whoever the hell he was. It reminded me of something else, too. Something that Becky Stockly had shown me and something that Janice had told me.

The Winter case had had me running all over Up-State New York and Ohio looking for the clues to Stall's identity. And I could have cooled my heels in the City Hotel chatting with Becky Stockly instead and been better off.

Everything was backwards. Every goddamn step. But I knew one thing: Everything has two sides, two faces, like Janus. Like Janice. A right and a left. Back and front.

And suddenly I knew, that Sam Weil had it backwards.

Chapter Twenty

At first, Janice refused to see me. She was putting the finishing touches on a story for the evening news. My barging into the room where she sat with the tape editor changed her mind.

She jumped to her feet, eyes flashing green with anger. She ordered me out. "I don't ever want to see you again," she added, helpfully.

I just laughed and grabbed her by the shoulders. "You were right about me!"

Shaking me off forcefully, Janice hissed each of four words: "Get away from me!"

The harsh reception daunted me for an instant. I was willing to be reasonable to get her attention. "What if I told you that you weren't scooped?" I asked politely.

That made her turn around, trying to hide her curiosity. "Can't you read?" she demanded.

"Janice, I want you to come with me," I pleaded. "To prove that I was wrong."

She spun around so fast that she lost her balance. The beautiful green eyes glittered with surprise. "What?"

"I was a fraud, Janice," I explained. "Everything I found out was a fraud from Will Stalls to Jack Pazinsky. If you want the real story, there is only one place to get it. And you should be there when we get it."

"We?" She calmed her face down slightly and said, "I would like to have as little to do with the matter, and with you, Mr. Carmichael, as possible. I am, at least, willing to agree that you are a fraud."

"It's point one."

There was no particular reason why she should listen to me. Not unless she still had that strange craving for the case—her case—that possessiveness that had made her suspicious, and jealous of me. All I had to do was get her past a rather large, obvious, and apparently repellent obstacle. "Forget about me."

"I have tried, believe me," she said, clenching her teeth. "I was doing quite well until you broke in here just now. If you'll go, I can get back at it."

"Janice, listen to me, just for thirty seconds. Okay?"

Glancing at the technician with her, Janice sighed. "All right. For the time I saved not having had sex with you."

Which stopped me. Thirty seconds.

The technician coughed. "I'll be out..."

"Don't go far," Janice admonished him. To me, it was just, "Tick."

"Can we talk..."

"Tick."

"Maybe later," I said.

"This is later."

"All right. In twenty-five seconds: My solution to the Winter murder is an elaborate lie," I began. "It's not my lie, but I uncovered it so that it looked like the truth." I was wasting my substitute seconds. "Pazinsky isn't guilty! That sums it up."

Running her graceful, manicured fingers through that damned hair, Janice closed her eyes and bent backwards. "Anything else?" she asked when she the green reappeared.

I needed the right angle to entice her, to grab her, to awaken the fixation on the Winter case that had consumed her for nine months before I turned it off. "Will Stalls isn't guilty either. How's that?"

Captivated, in spite of herself, Janice carefully gnawed her upper lip. She went to the door without a glance at me. "Tell Carl I'm onto something, will you, George." She waited.

George, who obviously hadn't liked my frenzied look, had stayed just outside the room. He ducked around the door and eyed me, warning her, "He won't believe it. Not if I tell him who you're with."

Janice shot him a withering glance.

George's face fell. "Oh."

So, she didn't want me to know I was famous or, at least, that she had mentioned me to anybody. I felt momentum building.

"I'm with a source, George," she suggested, easing the door closed. She leaned against it, protectively, her eyes now on me. "I can tell when a sources is lying."

"Lying? Is that what you think?" I asked. "Janice, I wasn't lying in the first place. Just being the slow-witted idiot someone expected me to be. Come on," I begged her. I had to share it with her. It was our case. "Please, Janice."

Her smile answered before she did. "Where are we going?"

I produced two Allegheny commuter tickets. "To a small town just over the border," I said, cheerfully. "You've been there before."

"Elmira?" she asked.

"That is our first stop," I replied, opening the door. "If I'm right, Huntington is next."

Janice Simmons grimaced, which on her looked just fine. "Not Huntington! Neither one of us is very welcome there."

Taking her arm and leading her out the door to my waiting cab, I said, "That's all right. A parade would just slow us down."

~ ~ ~

During our short flight to Elmira, I explained to Janice all about my brainstorm.

"Brainstorm?"

"That's what it felt like."

"I'm sure."

"This is how it began," I said. "Sam Weil's feet were backwards."

Sitting close beside me on the small turbo-prop, Janice stiffened. "I beg your pardon."

If I lost her, I was done. I chose a new opening. "Okay. There were three things about this case that were backwards," I said. "The first one—or pair—is Sam Weil's feet. The second is my little black phone button, and," I paused dramatically, "The third is Harry Blair.

"Harry?" she asked, horrified. "What does Harry have to do with it?"

The strength of her reaction surprised me. "Harry."

"He's not part of this."

"He is, Janice," I said. "As much as the black button and Sam Weil's feet. As much as Will Stalls, and Jack Pazinsky."

She clenched one fist and punched me.

"Ow."

She said, "Stop it!"

"You hit me."

"Harry has nothing..."

"Harry has, like everything else in the case, two faces, two roles," I explained quickly, for fear of losing her for good. "One face has everything to do with it and the other has nothing to do with it. The problem was that I had him facing the wrong way."

Janice looked away. "You're wrong."

"Now, take the black button," I went on, diverting away from Harry. "It had less to do with the murder than I thought and yet, it had more to do with it than I thought."

She looked straight ahead as she said, coldly, "If you enjoy making a fool of me, go right ahead. It is your last chance..."

"That's two-sided, too, Janice," I interrupted. "There is one thing in the world I couldn't do—and wouldn't want to do—and that is make a fool of you. But that is exactly what I was hired to do. Not purposely, mind you, but it was what was expected of me."

"Congratulations," she snapped. "You've brought my ego up again. Miss self-important. I get it."

"You did. It is what you suspected all along," I reminded her. "You are the center of the world. At least, of my place in it. And I thought that you were just an beautiful side attraction."

"Oh, that's so flattering, Casey. Am I blushing?"

"I'm sorry, Janice. About the 'side' part."

She glared at me and then softened her expression to include forgiveness. "Oh, lord, Casey. I'm not handling this right at all," she said, putting her hand inside mine. "I like you even better when you're driving me nuts. It's a bit scary."

Her words came within an inch of derailing me permanently. I took a breath.

"Go on," she said.

"I had thought that it was my contact with Harry and my contact with the Hiller case that brought you to me. But it wasn't. That's what I meant when I said I had Harry facing the wrong way. It was that other side of him that really mattered, his connection with you."

"You mean, then, that I was right about you?" she asked, subdued. "That Diana didn't hire you just by chance?"

"Of course not. You were right. Pete Kline had only one detective to recommend, me," I emphasized. "Diana picked Pete's firm for that very reason."

"Because Pete Kline would, inevitably, send her to you," she said, taking the steps for me. "And you, through Harry, would get to me."

Finally resisting the impulse to be flip, I added, "And, ego or not, you were the one who counted. You were too convinced that Tony Hiller was innocent. You were too sure that the whole thing was wrong. I was hired to convince you that you were right about Tony. My accusation of Pazinsky would shut you off."

"It worked, didn't it?" she asked rhetorically. "It really worked. I was right about Tony, but wrong about everything else. I was too humiliated to think straight about it." She was dismayed at the thought. "Or you."

I enjoyed that for a moment before moving on. "Next, we have the party-line phone button. Playing the idiot Diana hired, I ignored its real significance. I ignored it to the point that I had to make up some new significance."

"I found it at the Hiller house," I continued. "Half buried in some dirt outside the door to Hiller's cellar. No one else bothered with it, but I knew it was important. I just didn't realize why. If it had been dropped on the night of the murder, then someone was carrying in it, probably in a shirt pocket. The only reason it would be in someone's pocket on that night is because someone removed it. That night."

The greens lit up as she said, "And then it wasn't used for recording before then!"

"Couldn't have been. It's only possible use was in enabling Alma Purcil to overhear a real conversation. A real, live conversation."

"Between Tony and Winter?" she asked.

I shook my head. "I don't think so. The person who would have tipped the phone into position would be one intending to reveal Tony's confession. Harold Winter is the most obvious, but he didn't know that the button was missing. He couldn't have known that he if he tipped the phone a few degrees,he would open up the line."

"And Tony wouldn't have because he didn't want anyone to hear the whole elaborate scheme," I concluded.

"Then who?" Janice had a look of wide-eyed bewilderment I had never seen before. And no one would like see again.

I had to pause in my explanation to remark, "My God, you are beautiful. Can't you do anything about it?"

A deep scarlet set off the greens quite nicely. "You don't have to look at me like that."

"I probably do, but we'll talk about that later."

"Good."

"This point is where the feet of Sam Weil come in."

"His backward feet," she recalled with a laugh.

"His backward feet," I said. "You see, Sam Weil had a limp, like Will Stalls' limp. But Becky Stockly told me that Weil had an elevated heel on his right shoe."

"To make up for the short leg," Janice agreed with a shrug. "I knew that, too."

"Ah, but Sam Weil had it backwards. There are two ways to look at it and either way is backward," I said. "I figured all this out on the street the other day. You see, William Stalls had one leg shorter than the other and that gave him a limp, like the limp that Becky told me about. The high heel was to correct the limp."

"So?"

"So," I declared as the plane hit the runway, "if Carol Burne meets us at the airport as she promised, we will be absolutely sure that Sam Weil and Will Stalls are not two names for one man, but two men with one limp."

~ ~ ~

We weren't two feet inside the tiny terminal before I saw the flashing blue lights through the door to the street. Under them sat a patrol car, like the one Bud Burne drove.

The young cop fell in step beside me, with an unpleasant expression on his face. Young faces seem capable of showing more contempt than older ones; maybe because there aren't any lines or cracks in their skin, the kind that mistakes and regrets etch over time.

Such was the stern attitude of Bud Burne that I didn't bother to ask him where he was taking us or why. I simply followed him to the door of the car and let him put Janice and me in the back.

Janice said nothing, but her face reflected a concern that comes from being swept up in someone else's problems.

"This is Carol Burne's husband," I explained. "I made the mistake of using his well-intentioned fib to my own not-so-well-intentioned purposes."

Starting up his car, Bud glowered at me via the mirror. "I warned you not to come here, Carmichael."

"He did?" Janice asked, starting to worry.

Bud Burne was a cop and too good a kid to do me much harm, so I didn't worry about aggravating him. "Come on, Bud," I said calmly. "You end I both know I'm trying to help this time,

"Carol has gotten sick over this business of yours, Carmichael," he said with feeling.

"I'm sorry," I responded, sounding less sincere then I was.

Bud Burne grunted. "Terrific."

No one said anything for a while. All the way into Elmira, the three of us sat quietly. Janice played with the handle of her purse until it broke. Bud Burne drove like a maniac, hissing at passing motorists. I enjoyed the scenery, because, before long, I could tell where we were going.

As we pulled up in front of the building with Will Stalls' reel apartment in it, I asked, "Is she in there, too?"

"No," Bud replied hoarsely. "Carol is sick."

Leading the way up to Will's apartment, Bud wearied of his hostility. "We can't sublet the place," he said.

Part of Carol Burne's problem, then, was that she had rented the dump for her "grand-uncle". It was probably more of a burden than she and Bud could afford, but I could understand how just seeing the place made her feel. It wouldn't help that it was the best she could do.

"I'm not surprised," Janice said grimly. To me, she had to whisper, "It looks like yours."

Her initial reaction affected Bud Burne, finishing off his fading belligerence. Half-responsible for supplying Will Stalls his dungeon, Bud shrank toward the door as Janice unconsciously shook her head in disapproval.

Leaving the others to their reactions, I began my search of the plastic bags that held Will Stalls' clothing and effects.

The first interesting thing I found was a box of documents yellowed with age. That I gave over to Janice, so that she would leave Bud Burne to suffer alone.

"I want anything that relates to that accident in the late fifties," I directed her. "Particularly insurance reports, hospital records. Things like that."

As she perused the papers, I continued my quest for a confirmation of my theory. It wasn't easy. The bags were huge and filled with tired, tattered clothes that seemed content to have nothing to do. Underneath all of that, I found hats of three or four different eras. The shoes were in the bottom.

Will Stalls had only one pair of wearable shoes and that pair only had enough leather left for a watchband. The soles had large ringed holes in them and were separated in half a dozen places from the body of the shoe. The heels, too, had been ground away, beyond the rubber and well into the layers of leather above.

I tossed the right shoe to Bud Burne, leaning against the door. "Bud," I asked, "does this look like his regular shoe?"

He nodded lamely.

"What about the shoes you buried him in?" The question sounded grisly enough to startle Janice.

"Casey."

"Bud?" I asked again. It could have been important, even if unlikely.

The young man gulped and spoke, his voice cracking. "He had a pair of new shoes," he said. "We bought them for his birthday, a year ago. He was saving them."

"Never wore them?"

He shook his head.

"Were they like these?"

"Exactly."

The old man had saved his only decent pair of shoes for his burial, which he knew would be coming before long. A lot of people did that, saving something for a time when it wouldn't matter anymore. It hadn't really occurred to me until then how foolish that could be.

"How about this one?" I asked tossing him the left shoe.

Bud just looked at it. "What?"

"The heel," I said. "It's built up."

He nodded again. "They all were. Since the accident."

"That's because," Janice interjected, "one leg, the left one was two inches shorter than the other. Here's the report to the insurance company."

The report was from 1959, about eighteen months after the Stalls-Stockly accident. His leg had been shattered near the top of the shin. In a way, he had been lucky, because his knee hadn't been involved. The result, however, was that his left leg was shortened by slightly more than two inches.

I had one more thing to do. Sitting down on the only chair in the room, I removed my right shoe. Janice and Bud stared at me, but I went on with my experiment. My pocket yielded a two inch thick, self-adhering slice of plastic I had brought for that purpose. It stuck nicely to the heel of my shoe,

When I stood up, I felt a tilt to my left. When I walked the tilt became a limp. "Is this how he walked?"

Bud replied. "It's a little exaggerated, but it was something like that."

Removing the artificial elevator from my right shoe, I felt jubilant. I took the pair of Will Stalls' shoes from a flabber-gasted Bud and announced that it was time to go.

"To Huntington!"

"Can I ask what just happened?" Janice asked, annoyed.

"Do you remember what Becky Stockly told me about Sam Weil's shoes?"

Janice sucked in her flawless cheeks and took Stalls' ele-vated left shoe. "She said it was the right shoe, not the left."

"Amazing." She grinned and said, "You didn't have to make a fool of yourself, Casey."

I pulled her out the door by the waist. "Just trying to even things out, Janice."

Bud Burne drove us out to the airport, where I picked up the car I had reserved. As we prepared to leave, the wan young policeman asked me plaintively, "What can I tell Carol?"

"Tell her thanks, Bud," I suggested. "And you might mention that a heel said the shoe doesn't fit."

~ ~ ~

"But, if they weren't the same men," Janice asked, after remaining silent all the way to Huntington, "who was Sam Weil?"

Taking my chair in the once-dark corner of the City Hotel restaurant, I responded by shaking my head. I was more interested for the moment in the bright new bulb installed over the table. The glare of the light annoyed me partly because I preferred the romantic shadows once dominant there and partly because Janice's freckles showed too clearly,

"I didn't know you had so many freckles," I said.

She stiffened her beck end frowned. "Excuse me," she said peevishly, "for having a freckle or two."

"No, Janice. I wasn't complaining about their existence," I told her. "It's just that I didn't notice them before and that's my job."

Cupping her chin in her hand, Janice stared straight at me. "No it isn't, Mr. Carmichael. Not with me."

She examined my face and added, "Besides, who are you to tell me about freckles?"

I ignored her implication. "Why haven't I seen them before?"

"I usually keep them covered," she admitted. "Especially on the air. They show up too clearly on TV for my taste. The lights reveal all." She ran her hand over her face. "It's good thing that I have an otherwise beautiful complexion."

The statement was true, but I failed to respond.

"Don't I?"

"How would your make-up look under this light? And, yes."

Huffy, she said, "I don't wear any make-up to speak of. If you were at all observant, you would realize that I happen to be naturally beautiful."

"Has someone failed to tell you that?" I asked.

"It took you forever."

"We've established that, at thirty seconds, I'm slow. Please answer my question."

Janice grinned and shook her head at me. "Nobody has ever treated me as badly as you do, but I'm sure it's the best you can manage." She glance up at the light with a squint. "It would look terrible. If I had any on, which I do not. Very much."

"Would it be obvious?"

"Why do you think we women love candle light, Casey?" she asked. "I could hardly seduce you if I looked like a clown, now could I?"

"Which clown?"

"You are awful!"

The lights above us had not been there the last time I had eaten at the City Hotel Restaurant. According to Becky Stockly, those harsh lights had not been there when Sam Weil had eaten at the restaurant either. And he hadn't eaten anywhere else.

I thought out loud. "Sam Weil was not Will Stalls and yet he looked and walked very much like him. It was not a coincidence."

"I'd like to eat dinner with you just once, just this once, without Sam Weil or Diana Winter or anyone else getting in the God damned way." Janice said, sighing. "I'm getting tired of him. Of all of this crap. I've been such a fool, all this...!"

Half listening, half thinking, I interrupted her. "Janice," I said firmly, "Sam Weil wore make-up. He was made up to look like Will Stalls, from the head to the heel. Son-of-a-bitch!"

"Enough Sam Weil, Casey!"

"Janice, this is important."

She was on her feet, angry. "Oh, it is, is it? Just this very moment?"

"It just came to me..."

"I can be something else, even if you can't. It's asinine being a fucking reporter all the time, and I'm sick of it!"

Before she could storm out of the restaurant, I seized her hand and held her back. "Please sit down."

Rubbing her elbow Janice relented with an angry clank. "Shit!"

Holding her in her place with my eyes, I said, "I'm only in this because of you, Janice. We have to see it through."

"This isn't a movie, damn it," she objected. "Don't give me this 'unwritten code' garbage."

"I'm not talking about any unwritten code, Janice. I don't have one any more and I doubt you do. We both do what we have to do."

"You were the one who followed this case, Janice, like you owned stock in it. I don't know why and it's none of my business. But because of you, I was dragged into it. And I responded, maybe out of habit, by putting another innocent man in jail. Truth or lies, right or wrong, that's not point."

She had her hand at her mouth by the time I was finished. Her pale cheeks pulsed from the pressure of holding her jaw closed. She relieved the pressure by whispering. "My God, Casey, I'm sorry." The two greens even moistened, glimmering in the hard light. "I don't know when I'm well off, do I?"

Under her gaze, I eased up. "We're on the verge of getting this off both our backs, Janice. Just sustain that passion for which you are so well known around here."

"Okay," she said, shivering a bit. "I'm listening now. Go ahead."

My neck felt uncomfortable in my collar as I spoke under her gaze "Okay. We have Sam Weil deliberately aping Will Stalls. The limp was the same, but we know that it was artificial. If the name Sam Weil is not an alias for Will Stalls, it is an alias for someone else."

Janice's attention did not seem totally focused on my words, but she nodded agreement.

"The question is: Who? A second question is why Stalls? Was he deliberately set up? Just as Tony Hiller was set up. Just as Jack Pazinsky was set up."

She smiled dreamily. "You skipped 'how,' Casey."

"That is what just came to me," I explained. "Our murderer was playing Sam Weil, Will Stalls with a fake limp and make-up and everything else."

"Make-up," she repeated quietly. "Oh. I'm sorry."

"He chose this particular table when he ate here because back in this corner, this table, there was hardly any light. No one would detect the make-up during the meal. The only time he couldn't get this table, he didn't eat anything. And I recall that several people mention his aversion to hot weather. That would also figure. In the heat, make-up would run with perspiration."

"Your mind is so devious, Casey," Janice said. "Did you know that you almost close one eye when you think, as though you're aiming at something."

Intentionally, Janice was distracting me, which annoyed and pleased me at the same time. She was drinking in what I said, her comments proved that, but she didn't take me so seriously anymore. Whatever had driven her to become enmeshed with the case as to become part of it, whatever had brought the two of us together, was gone. I was too uncertain about the consequences to think about it very much.

Then our waitress, a middle-aged women named Maureen, brought our dinners. I tried to concentrate on the food. In the bright light, it looked different from what I had ordered.   Janice was acting different, too, indulgent and understanding, instead of aloof and diffident.

"Something wrong, sir," Maureen asked.

Looking up, I could see that she was wrong too. She wasn't the same waitress. She wasn't Becky Stockly. The disorientation that had plagued me from the moment I took on Diana Winter's bizarre case finally overwhelmed me.

I found myself back in another restaurant, surrounded by people, young college people. We were all in the back, talking wildly, as we did in those days, about the future, our plans, our hopes. Foolish talk, stupid dreams. I could see the dozen or so rugged looking men who came through the door at once. I knew that they had guns, but I was shocked all the same to see them aiming straight for us.

Six of us were whisked away together, huddled in the back of a van.

Hank Bissel was there, madly gesturing and ranting, as he did when he was frightened. The others were quietly looking one another over, searching the signs of treachery. They never did find it. I was the only one who knew.

"Casey?" It was not a voice in the van...

"Casey?" Janice brought me back to my pork chop that looked like chicken.

"I was just thinking of some old friends," I dismissed the spell quickly "It's nothing important. Just something that happens to me once in a while."

Her words flowed gently as she spoke, "You terrified poor Maureen, Casey. She went to get the manager."

I laughed. "You should have stopped her. It's not serious."

Janice's searching eyes showed that she did not believe me. Green is a harder color than most and her eyes cut into me more easily than others. She smiled and let my lie stand.

Another voice droned, "Mr. Carmichael. I heard you were feeling sick."

Janice and I broke from one another and looked up to find Tony Hiller staring at us. He had aged several years since last I had seen. By this time, he had lost even the hint of robust good health I had detected during my visit with him at the hospital.

His clothes hung on him, far too large for what was left of a husky man. Like his attire, his mouth seemed too large for his words, which gave his speech a hollow sound. "Are you all right now?"

My voice felt like a dry wind as it came out. "Sure."

"And I remember you," he said to Janice. "Miss Simmons, isn't it? Yes. The pretty reporter."

Janice's expression bordered between shock and horror. Her voice didn't sound real when she said, "Yes, Mr. Hiller. I interviewed you last August."

"That's what everybody called you." Hiller's face couldn't support the smile that came and his mouth fell into an unintentional frown. "I remember,especially," he said, as though that were triumph enough, "you always had a tape recorder on your shoulder."

Starting to breathe again, Janice shook her head up and down. "I have an excellent recording of you if you'd like to hear it some day."

He gave out a sound approximating a laugh. "I hate my voice when I hear it on those things. I sound like someone else," he said, sounding, in fact, like someone else.

When I heard that I banged my fist on the table. That was it!

"Tony," I said, too loudly, "Will you keep Miss Simmons company for a minute."

I didn't give him time to object, not that he would have, as I jumped up and ran into the lobby.

Chapter Twenty-One

The phone was in the lobby. Harley Collins was on the other end. "You want what?"

"I want those tapes!" I shouted into the receiver. "I want those God damned tapes."

Collins, a patient man, reasoned with me. "Carmichael, those are evidence. I can't give them over to you. I have to sign for them myself."

"Do it!" I commanded. "I'll be at your office in twenty minutes."

"The hell you will!" Collins retorted, sharply. Then he calmed a bit. "Not without explaining first."

The telephone and I had never been good together, but lately even that relationship had deteriorated. The last thing I wanted to do was blow my revelation on the telephone. And believe me, that was sure to happen, considering the nature of the revelation. So, I said, "Harley, we are wrong! We are so wrong, that we're going to look damned foolish unless we straighten ourselves out tonight."

My sincerity apparently reached Collins through the long copper wires because he gave in. "I can't get there in twenty minutes, I have to get dressed first."

"Shit, Collins," I barked, "it's only 9:00. What the hell are you doing undressed at this hour?"

His hearty laugh hurt my ear. "It's more polite. See you in half an hour."

I was still glaring at the buzzing receiver when Hiller and Janice joined me in the lobby.

"What's wrong, now?" Janice asked tentatively.

Returning the receiver with a bang to its rightful place. "Not a thing. We're meeting Collins in thirty minutes."

She groaned. "Why, Casey? Let's go back to the motel."

Janice dropped into a chair when she saw that I had no intention of letting up. "All right, detective Carmichael. You can go, but I'm too worn out. Please take me to the motel before you meet Collins."

Hiller spoke up, sheepishly. "You could stay here, Miss Simmons," he offered. "If you'd like."

Despite her grateful smile, she said, "No, thank you, Tony. But I have already paid for a room near Franklin. It's a place I've stayed several times before and I'm too frazzled to adjust to new surroundings. I sleep better in a place I'm used to."

Hiller shrugged. "It's not much of a place to stay anyway."

"Tony's part owner, Casey," Janice told me. "Ned Cooper has transferred the hotel to Tony and Becky Stockly jointly."

"Only she won't come back," Tony added unhappily.

"Sooner or later she will," Janice assured him.

I doubted that, but didn't say so. Hiller looked too forlorn about it to need my opinion. "Let's go, Janice," I said instead. "And Tony, will you do me a favor?"

Nodding limply, Tony Hiller said, "I owe you at least one, Carmichael."

"Like hell, Hiller," I responded, knowing that what I did I did for myself, not anyone else. The thought made me a little resentful. "But do me one anyway."

"All right."

"First," I said, "Stay by the phone here for about an hour or so. I'm going to call you and ask you to talk."

"To talk?" The idea seemed ridiculous to him.

"Secondly, I'd like you to call Lewis Huntington and tell him to come down here tonight."

"Lewis?" he asked, becoming more confused. "But he's in Buffalo."

"I know," I said, trying to get the words right. "But I need to see him as soon as possible and I don't think he'll come here that quickly for me. For you, he will. Tell him it's an emergency."

"An emergency?"

"Any emergency. Tell him it involves Becky Stockly," I suggested. I had a feeling that would get Lewis into Huntington if anything would.

"Becky," he repeated, looking worried. "Is something wrong?"

Under my breath, I cursed everyone. They were all so damned concerned about the girl, now that it wouldn't help. "Don't worry, I made it up. Just tell Lewis that, all right?"

Something had happened to Tony Hiller. His eyes had gone blank and his mouth hung open, as though his mind had simply stopped bothering with his body. His posture sagged and he was headed for the floor. I caught him as he sank and straightened him out harshly.

After a blink and a couple breaths, Tony Hiller recovered the little that had slipped away in the previous moment. "I'll call."

Afraid that he had forgotten who, I repeated the instructions twice more and then pulled my trembling companion out the door.

"It's awful, Casey," she said, breathlessly, clutching onto the sleeve of my suit. "He's so different."

"He's different all right," I agreed. Different from the Tony Hiller we had met in the hospital, different from the Tony Hiller who had first come under Hanna Kish's treatment in September.

But more significantly, I knew now, he was different from the Tony Hiller who had pulled the trigger that had released Harold Winter's corrosive grip on way too many people.

Chapter Twenty-Two

As we rode to the motel that Janice loved so much, I recited my theory in full to a patient but only half-interested listener. While she seemed attentive enough, I could tell that Janice did not care much what I was saying. Her attitude irked me, but I didn't say anything about it in the car.

Proceeding directly to the room—she had already checked into the room she had had the last time—we sat down for a second, and talked.

"Janice, you aren't helping me very much at this point."

With a suppressed a smile, Janice replied, "I have come to the conclusion that I am now less of a factor in the case than I was. You have taken it over, Casey. My need of it is suddenly so much less important than yours that I don't feel the way I used to about it."

"That sort of drive doesn't just evaporate," I said. Yet, it had. Why?

Concentrating on the ceiling in exaggerated dismay, she said, "My 'drive' as you call it, Casey, is not really the issue. In any case, whatever it is, it is subordinate to yours now, and I don't really like the feeling of being a side-kick. Not even yours. I'm sorry, but it makes me very nervous, tagging along behind you..."

Since she was talking to herself and not to me, I let it go. I had other things to think about, things which she knew were important. Even as she spoke, therefore, I began to make my call to Lindsay McGuiness.

When Janice had finished, I shrugged and turned to talk to the motel switchboard. "Will you get the home number of Chief of Detectives Lindsay McGuiness in Franklin for me?"

"McGuiness?" the clerk said. "Okay, but let me call you back."

"Ring him first, will you? This is important official business."

Before I could put the phone back in the cradle, I could feel Janice close behind me, her hands running across my back. Involuntarily, my shoulders squared themselves and my neck snapped up hard enough to hurt.

She breathed in a deep sigh and exhaled deliberately against my taut neck. "I just want to feel the strength you must have in that back, Casey."

My quick turn did not seem to bother her. As we stood face to face, her expression remained studious, the one she had focused on me at times all evening: Her eyes bored into mine, while a curious smile played across the lips she would periodically scrape with her teeth. It was the kind of look you don't see much in younger women.

But I had to meet Collins in five minutes, and it would take me that long to get into Franklin. "Just one thing, Janice," I said. "I want you to talk to McGuiness when they get him. Tell him to meet me at Collins' office as soon as he can."

She didn't respond, so I went on. "Find out from him if this hick county has Voice ID Equipment in their lab. If they don't, get someone in Pittsburgh's lab to call Collin's office."

"Who?"

"If you don't know," I said carefully, "call an old friend of ours who does."

"Harry." The name sounded more resonant than I expected, or wanted it to.

"Will you do that for me?"

Janice laughed quietly, looking around the motel room. Then she shook her head. "This is such a nice room. I got

very used to it while I was up here in August and September.
And the other times," she stated. Then she sighed and added,
"Yes, Carmichael. I will do that for you. It doesn't sound like
much."

My "thanks" had a dull sound to it as I headed to the door.
Before I was out, she called after me.

"Casey," she said. "I hope you come back without that
hind-sighted monkey on your back."

~ ~ ~

I hauled the monkey, and my back, up the steps of the Venango County courthouse, before Jim Collins emerged from
the shadows of the darkened doorway. It didn't take much
of a shadow.

"We can't leave the building open to the public at this hour,
can we, Mr. Carmichael?" he asked.

"I wouldn't."

Pleased by my concession, Jim Collins used one of a ring
of keys to get us into the lobby. Another of the two dozen
keys took us up the elevator, while a third got us into the
DA's office.

After we had reached the receptionist's desk, Jim Collins
stopped and glared at the DA's door. His mouth twisted back
and forth as he said, "I have to go wait for McGuiness." Before I could say anything, he was gone.

The only door in the building that wasn't locked proved to
be Harley Collins'. Inside, the DA was on the phone. "I certainly did not, operator," he was saying when he saw me. His
hand instructed me to sit down. "Harry Blair? No, I don't
know him, either, but I think I know who does."

I nodded after he pointed at me.

"Connect him," Collins said. "Hello, Mr. Bortz."

Seeing the tape reel I had taken from the Elmira post-of-
fice, I got up again. Collins had a magnifying glass and a tape
recorder on his desk. He had played the reel half way
through.

Collins continued his conversation. "I'll call you back Mr. Bortz as soon as we are ready to go. And thank Mr. Blair for me. Good-bye."

"Did McGuiness call?" I asked.

Collins spun half way around in his chair. "He wanted to know what was going on over at my office at this hour. I expressed a somewhat similar sentiment."

Pointing to the tape, I said, "You must know part of it, already."

"You mean that the tape was spliced before the recording was made?" he asked.

"Yes."

The DA grinned as he hefted the huge magnifying glass. "As a matter of fact, Jimbo did that. My brother's eyes and ears are far superior to mine. The recording is so smooth in too many of the spliced sections, in his opinion, to have been the product of editing."

"We'll get a confirmation of that from Pittsburgh's lab," I told him. "They have the equipment there to tell us for sure."

"Bortz will be ready," Collins said. "What else do you have in the wind?"

Replacing the tape reels onto the recorder, I said, "We have several pieces of information now that we didn't have before."

"Most of which you have hoarded in a fit of '40's melodrama."

"First," I began, "we know that Sam Weil was not William Stalls, but an actor of some sort playing a character remarkably similar to Stalls in every way."

"Isn't that fine? And how do we know that?"

"I'll get to the evidence later," I advised. "But let me give you the conclusions first."

Collins shrugged, a quizzical smile on his lips. "Okay. Pazinsky will probably sue me no matter what I know."

"So, Weil is not Stalls," I began again. "That's Number One. Number Two is that this tape is a fraud, in that it was made after being spliced. That was so it would appear to have been edited. Which tells us that either Winter or Hiller made this tape, or some one who sounded like them made it."

"What?"

"Someone who could do Will Stalls and who could also do very good impressions of Tony Hiller," I explained. "Number Three is that Alma Purcil heard a real conversation over a party-line phone opened secretly by Sam Weil, our actor, specifically so that Alma would hear a confession by Hiller and the murder of Winter."

"A real conversation?" Collins demanded, incredulous. "Winter and Hiller?"

"Was it real?" I posed, "Yes. In a way."

"But if Sam Weil were there," Collins asked, rubbing his hand through the blond hair, "why would Winter call him 'Tony?' I don't see it."

"We are talking about an actor, Harley," I said. "A man who could do more than voices, he could do characters, like Will Stalls. Like Tony Hiller."

Collins' mouth fell open and his eyes bounded from the ceiling and down to the floor. "Christ. Are you serious?"

"The murder was so deliberate," I said. "The steps were carefully laid out in advance. Most of them, anyway. There were a couple of hitches. The audit was delayed, so Sam Weil staged a robbery that worked out just fine anyway. Weil, disguised as Tony Hiller would have had sufficient access to the books to set up the embezzlement. The audit would have exposed Hiller in mid-August, but Tony delayed the audit. Which came as a shock to Sam Weil."

"So with the audit out of the picture," I continued, "Weil needed an alternative: The robbery.

"To reveal the framed embezzlement," Collins finished for me.

"And the elaborate scheme to confess to everything before killing Winter. Tony was in a trap he couldn't get out of. He didn't know what was going on. Everything he said to exonerate himself had been set up against him by the confession Alma Purcil reported."

The DA covered his eyes and shook with laughter. "It's too incredible."

"The timing was vital. Will Stalls was a dying man. If he were to be used at all, as a cover, it had to be as soon as possible. He could have been dead even by mid-August. But if Weil waited until mid-September, when the audit was planned, there would be a greater risk that his cover would be dead when he was supposed to be roaming around Huntington. Weil got in touch with Stalls and gave him enough money to go visit his only close relative in Minnesota while he, Weil, would be in Huntington, impersonating Stalls..."

"But Carmichael," Collins interrupted. "Who is this damned Weil guy?"

The pause I took was more for breath than for drama. I had been talking so fast that my lungs hurt. I had really spilled all but my last conclusion. The last one had nothing to back it up. It couldn't, of course, because he had done such a good job. Not one frame, not two, but three stood between him and the murder. I knew there would be only one shred of evidence.

Just one and that one would not be admissible in court. Still it would be enough. Enough to tell us for sure, enough to free the thirteenth man I had put in jail, enough to clear a wretched dead man's name of a cloud I'd put on it.

"I'll tell you who in a couple minutes, Harley," I said. "But before I do I want Lindsay McGuiness here too. He's the man who will have to support you when the time comes, when you have to free Pazinsky and clear Will Stalls. Especially when you have no one else to offer."

"Whoa, wait a minute," Collins objected, "I've got Sam Weil. Don't I?"

"Forget him," I said. "There is no Sam Weil."

~ ~ ~

Once McGuiness came, I went through everything again, supplying the bits of evidence this time: The phone button dropped when it shouldn't have been dropped; the elevated heel of the wrong shoe; the pre-spliced tape recording; and finally the voices.

Bortz of Pittsburgh's crime lab had his phone tapped into the voice-print equipment that would tell us what we needed to know. The equipment. was highly advanced, if not yet recognized by the Courts of Pennsylvania as conclusive in determining voice comparisons.

After a quick call to the City Hotel to get a snatch of Tony's voice, we played the "edited" confession. With the tape reels spinning on Collins recorder, the three of us sat back while Bortz and his machinery did the work. In my pocket, I fingered the last ink in the chain. It was another reel of tape, a reel I had had made for me just before I put Pazinsky smack in the middle of a frame. I hadn't needed it then, because I had found the reel now playing, sitting in a box in an Elmira post office, inside an envelope mailed empty and only later stuffed with incriminating contents.

I barely waited until the faked tape had finished. Then I spoke to Bortz. "I have another one for you," I said. "I want the voices on this compared to the other two runs."

"Sure," Bortz said. "We can run it through the computer in no time. Set it up."

With the new tape in place, I hit the play button. After a brief leader, the voices began. First Lewis Huntington, then the others, Tom Winter, Jack Pazinsky and Diana Winter.

"What the hell is that?" McGuiness asked. The Detective Chief had been annoyed at me for getting him out of a bathtub. My story hadn't been appeased even a bit.

Calmly, I explained, "This tape was made a while back, at my request, to test Alma's hearing over the party-line phone. As it happened, I didn't need it at the time."

McGuiness' "Harrumph" summed up his displeasure, but he sat back and listened as the four voices engaged in a stilted conversation. Since Lewis Huntington had been in charge, his voice was the most prominent, the others sometimes barely audible.

"Shit," McGuiness snapped, "Lew is hogging the mike again."

Collins shot me a meaningful glance. "How long will this take, Carmichael?" he asked, feeling uncomfortable.

Checking my watch, I saw that it had passed 2:00 AM. "Not too long. I hope."

My error became obvious by 3:00. McGuiness wanted to go home, cold bathwater or not. I had asked Bortz to hold the information until he had it all. That had made for a very quiet, strained hour of waiting.

"Listen Carmichael," McGuiness finally barked, "I've been cooperative. But, Christ, I have to get up at 5:00 and I have enough late nights as it is. Why don't you just tell me and I'll go home. It's obvious that both of you know what you're doing here, but I'm done waiting."

With both palms held out, Collins said, "Come on, Lin. This is important."

Checking with Bortz, I found that he was ready with all but the final comparison. He would have that in a matter of minutes. "Okay," I decided. "Go ahead. What have you got?"

Through Collins' conference hook-up, we listened as Bortz related his findings. "As you suspected the tape was cut and spliced first and recorded later. It was spliced again in a couple places, probably for effect, but it mostly was a simple recording over spliced tape."

"Good," I said.

"Secondly," Bortz went on, "Neither of the voices on that first tape belongs to Tony Hiller."

McGuiness stood up. "What?"

"It is definitely someone else," Bortz repeated. "Obviously an impressionist, because it is superficially close, but there is no question that it is not the same voice."

The Chief was visibly shaken. "What does that mean?"

"Only that I was right in what I told you," I said.

McGuiness began to pace the room. "Shit."

I looked over at Collins, who would like to have enjoyed McGuiness' discomfort, but who obviously could not. To Bortz I said, "What about the last part?"

Bortz' voice came over bell-clear and confident. "It's coming through now. Give me another minute."

"Congratulations, Carmichael," Collins said, leaning back in his chair. "You were right. Finally." He laughed.

"Yeah. I'm told I'm slow."

"Got it," Bortz cut in, enthusiastically. "We've got our match."

My heart pounded as it hadn't for twenty years. "Are you sure?" Bortz gave the laugh of a man whose opinion is usually undervalued. "Absolutely."

"Who is it?"

Bortz paused, as though congratulating his computer. "Lewis Huntington's voice is the only one on both of the tapes!"

Chapter Twenty-Three

My bit was done, so I left Collins and McGuiness to ponder the problem of releasing Pazinsky without a replacement. Even though I knew that the evidence against Lewis couldn't be used in court, an overwhelming sense of relief carried me all the way back to the motel.

The motel itself was a modest two story affair, well kept for a non-name operation. Somehow Janice had wandered into it while covering the Winter case the previous August. In the dozen or so times she had returned to the Huntington area, she had stayed always in the same motel, always in the same room. Such compulsion about place in a girl so traveled surprised me. I wondered, lamely, if the room had any particular meaning to her.

Whatever else the room was, it was dark by the time I got there. Of course, it was about 3:30 by that time. The curtains were drawn and a weathered window air conditioner churned away against the still, humid night. I was almost afraid to disturb her.

I backed my rented Pontiac into the slot next to an old Mercury, which was chugging away noisily. Its open trunk was half-filled with suitcases and fishing gear and blocked the sidewalk in front of Janice's room.

The only light available to guide me to the door, barely, had to creep around the door left ajar by the owner of the Mercury. There wasn't much left when it got to me.

Tired as I was, I managed to get the door open in half the time it usually takes to open motel rooms. The fatigue probably suppressed the nervousness I felt about sharing Janice's special room with her.

As I felt my way towards the lamp on the desk, a wave of dizziness knocked me off my balance and into a chair. Relieved that the clamor had not awakened Janice, I switched the lamp on.

The small bulb illuminated the room through a dream-like haze. I tried to clear my eyes, but found that that was not the problem. Consciousness ebbed and surged as I looked around me. It was the air conditioner!

I watched, entranced, as the old air unit pumped exhaust from the Mercury into the room.

A quick look at Janice told me that the fumes had owned the room long enough. Weakening, I made for the door, fumbled with the nob and ran outside for a dozen deep breaths. My head a little clearer, I returned to the room and tore the covers off of a limp, unresponsive Janice.

The violence of my lugging her outside would have awakened anybody not damned near dead. Janice didn't even groan.

After resting her on the sidewalk, I flew into the room next door, with its door slightly open. Inside, I saw miscellaneous clothing and fishing equipment

The shower was running, but I knew that no one was inside. Ignoring the props, I used the phone to stir the night clerk, ordering an ambulance.

Stripping the beds, which looked only lightly slept in, I returned to Janice's side and draped the blankets over her. As warm as it was, there was nothing else I could think of doing but covering her with blankets. Maybe because I was numb and shaking.

By the time the ambulance arrived, I had stupidly watched the clerk feed her some oxygen from a cardiac emergency unit the motel kept just in case. The intern riding the ambulance checked her over quickly and assured us that she would be all right, but I didn't like the way he said it.

Once Janice was in the ambulance, my mind started whirring again. Grabbing the clerk's arm, I demanded, "Has anyone checked in tonight? Anyone?"

Bending away from me, the clerk timidly replied, "I'm the late shift."

With my other hand I seized his collar.

"I don't know who came in before me," he protested.

"Find the fuck out!"

Free of my grasp, the young clerk ran to the office. He beat me there easily. I hovered over him as he checked the book. "A couple and a single," he said.

"A single. A single what?"

He now backed away as he said, "A man. In 108. The other side."

Wrenching the key he offered me, I bolted. Nauseated and weak, I ran down the row of rooms. The doors with their numbers passed with increasing pain in my chest. By the time I stood in front of room 108, I had no breath left at all.

The master key worked on the lock, but not on the chain above the knob. Stepping back about five feet, I charged forward and hit the door with my right foot just above the latch. The crunch of screws pulling out of the wood brought the occupant to his feet.

The light switch beside me did no good, but suddenly the lamp by the bed went on, and we could see each other.

A touch of make-up base still on his face, Lewis Huntington shook his head and pointed a small gun at me.

~ ~ ~

"God damn you, Carmichael," Lewis said with a sigh.

I didn't bother with the gun. Instead, I went straight for his throat. My thrust lifted his feet off the floor and thumped him into the wall three feet back. The residue of make-up made it hard for me to get a decent grip. The bullet that stayed in my right shoulder probably didn't help.

The pain punctured my rage and Lewis knocked me over with a surprisingly solid elbow to the chest. He rubbed his eyes and shook his head again. "God damned you, Carmichael," he repeated, taking a towel from the dresser.

I didn't have any breath left for a reply.

Working the make-up off of his face, Lewis kept sighing heavily and pointing the little revolver in my direction. With the paint off, he looked years older than I remembered, more haggard. Like Tony Hiller he had aged a decade in the months since I had last seen him.

His face cleaned, he sat down on the bed, rubbing his reddened neck. "I didn't think it would be any problem," he said. "I hope you're not too badly hurt."

Since the wall was free of arterial spray, I replied, "A .22? "

"Smith & Wesson."

"Then one's my limit."

A smile coming to his face, he asked, "Why weren't you in there with her? You baffle me, Carmichael. If I had that woman in a motel room, I wouldn't go out for anything or anybody."

"I wanted to tell Collins all about your unheralded acting ability."

Looking at the Smith, he smiled. "I suppose you would," he said. "Then killing you wouldn't make things any better, would it?"

"Nope."

He grimaced and let the barrel droop. "I haven't much taste for killing. I had thought that blowing Harold Winter into little speckles on the wall of his study would do something for me besides making me sick." Rising he addressed the mirror over the desk. "Look at that. I'm almost as bad as Tony. You've seen Tony, Mr. Carmichael."

"What's left of him,"

Lewis shrugged. "When I think that I did that... and every-thing else, to Ned and Becky... I feel the same nausea that hit me when the shotgun went off."

Turning to me, he went on. "Killing Hal Winter seemed so right, so worth the planning, the risk, until then. After what he had done to my harmless, old grandfather, to Diana and everyone else, he really deserved to be remembered in mu-ral form."

"And," he continued, his voice losing inflection as he went, "I set it up pretty well."

"No argument."

"Everyone who merited a little punishment was written into it in advance. Tony who had claimed such ignorance when my grandfather's portfolio and his life collapsed. I didn't doubt him, Tony, but such neglect, such mindlessness deserved a bit of a jar, I thought."

"Pazinsky, too," the soliloquy drained on, "he had always relished his collaboration with Winter to bring us down, the Huntington's. I wanted him to share the final blame with foul old Will Stalls." Lewis let his mouth curl in disgust and animation returned to his voice. "I had to almost put that sot on the plane myself to keep him from spending his ticket to Minneapolis on bourbon."

To remind Lewis, and his gun, that I knew most of his story, and that Collins and McGuiness knew it too, I interjected a comment. "So you could use him."

He stared into the mirror. "I could play him now with far less makeup. I wouldn't have to worry about the heat so much."

My voice became nasty, which was dangerous. I couldn't help it. "And you used everyone else, too. Cooper, Tony, Becky and Diana."

"It was pathetic," he admitted, "the way they all lent them-selves to it. Ned was so damned blinded by the money that Weil, I, offered him—the money for Becky—that he didn't even hesitate when I asked him to remove the bulbs in the restaurant. Christ."

"The others, too. Tony paying so little attention to details that I could impersonate him without even much care. And Diana." He sighed. "Always so pliable. Needing help and wanting to please." He shifted his gaze in the mirror from himself to me. "Diana's changed."

"Everything's changed," he concluded, his eyes back on his own reflection. He ran one of his long fingers along the dark crease under one eye several times, as though trying to wipe it off. "Did I do that?"

"You recorded your meeting with Winter over the phone, too, didn't you?" I demanded. "While it was going on, while Alma was listening."

"Yes. I didn't expect it to come out, but it did. Well enough." Still going over his reflection carefully, only half interested in me, he said, "It was pretty good."

"Only Will Stalls fouled it up."

Nodding in the mirror, he agreed. "Yes. He did. He wouldn't die. He was supposed to die for sure sometime in October. With him dead, Pazinsky would have been ruined, even if they couldn't convict him. He would hate that, if they couldn't even convict him."

"It would have been so nice and pat. It wasn't easy. I went to so much trouble with the tapes and the makeup and all. I really did a very thorough job. I even risked that ridiculous bank robbery. It wouldn't have been a problem if Stalls had died when he was supposed to."

"I had to hold back until he died. I didn't intend to put Tony through nine months of that." Lewis shuddered. "I wouldn't have put Hal Winter through nine months of that."

Composing himself, he said, "Well, it is all done with now. I underestimated you, Carmichael. I figured that it would take you much longer to find the path I had hidden away for you." Scratching his head with the muzzle of the gun, he recalled, "Ah, but she was responsible. Miss Simmons. With Will Stalls living on like Moses and Janice Simmons' teeth in my tail, I had to do something. I had to get Pazinsky's frame into place and make everything stop there."

"That's where helped me out so nicely, Carmichael. I had put a detective on her, you know?"

My surprise must have shown.

"You were not so exclusive after all, my friend," he added.

"You wound me. Again."

"Sorry. Again. But I had to find out a few things. About her. And your friend Blair. She wasn't easy to reach. No friends, no lovers. With those looks? She wasn't close to anyone. Except for Blair."

"And Blair knew me," I said.

He nodded. "And, for some reason, trusted you. Some of that had to rub off on her. And it did. An unflattering scheme, I know and I apologize. But you didn't have much of a rep as a detective, so I was sure you'd stumble along, as I led you, until after Stalls died."

"Well, you did stumble and you found the proper clues—with the help of a hint I gave Janice Simmons about Cleveland—and you reached the proper conclusions along the way. But you didn't quit. Even she quit. Everyone else was satisfied. Why weren't you?"

That explanation might have made him feel better, so I punted. "It doesn't matter, Huntington. It's all past now."

"It is for you, at least," he agreed, staring down at me. He gave a weary shrug, his face full of reluctance.

Lewis tightened his grip on the pistol until the knuckles went white. The barrel jumped around as it pointed in my direction. He would have a tough time getting a clean shot off, I guessed and poised to strike after the first shot. It would have to come soon, my right arm couldn't hold me up long.

Grimly, he stared toward me. The look in his eye told me I could get him then, before the shot. He looked away, at the mirror studying his reflection. The gun jerked. Without a sound.

I was on my feet before he realized it, but my left fist stopped short.

The revolver was in his mouth.

Lewis' eyes flicked between me and the mirror twice be-fore he pulled the trigger. It wasn't much of a noise, but it wasn't much of a gun.

It was big enough, though, to screw up my shoulder. And it was big enough to drop Lewis Huntington into a pile in front of the mirror that had bothered him so much.

Chapter Twenty-Four

The two days I was in Venango County Hospital, I only had a couple visitors. Harley Collins came twice, once on each day, to review some aspects of the case so that he could talk coherently to the news media. The other one was Diana Winter.

She had come with Harley on his second visit, arriving as I gathered myself together for check-out. Diana stood silently while I tied my tie and brushed my graying hair. When I had finished, she said, "Do you forgive me?"

I didn't know what she meant, and said as much.

"The way I treated you," she explained. "At the end."

Squaring my shoulders, I said, "We were both mistaken about that."

She looked down. "Yes. This is the end."

"Well, we found out what we wanted to find out," I told her encouragingly, if unconvincingly.

"More," she agreed, "More than I wanted to find out. It's hard to feel like a... like that girl anymore." She looked at me intently. "Casey, I feel so old."

Several lines broke the smoothness of her forehead as she steadied herself. There was a sadness in her eyes, and with her smile.

"You've aged well, Diana." I missed something that had been in her, but not as much as I had expected. "Over the months."

"I'm trying to find Becky," she said, quietly. "I think she went to New York."

"I don't know if she will come if you find her, Diana. I doubt it."

Diana shrugged. "Tony asked me."

After pausing a long moment, she said, "I've decided to go to New York myself for a couple weeks. There are some things I have to think about and I can't do it around here. Jack's going to handle everything for me here. Bob finally gave in," she added with a laugh.

"Good."

A bit of smile, a fragment, crept onto her lips. "How's your friend?"

"Janice?" I asked. "She's still weak, but she'll be on screen in no time."

"I know that, Casey," she said, shaking her head. "That isn't what I meant."

"Other than that, I don't know, Diana," I admitted. "We haven't had much chance to talk about anything."

"But you do like her," Diana stated.

"Two or three times a day."

Diana looked at her watch and sighed. "You are a difficult man, Casey. Are you that way on purpose?" It was a rhetorical question and we both knew it.

Collins stuck his head in the door. "Time to go, Diana," he announced. "And I have to talk to Carmichael again."

With another shrug and a successful attempt at a farewell smile, Diana left the room.

Collins watched her leave. "What have you done to that poor girl?"

"Nothing, as far as I know," I told him. "What can I do for you?"

"Nothing," he said with his toothy grin. "But since you're leaving, I thought I'd ask you now to come up and go fishing with me next weekend."

I had to laugh at that. "Fishing? That sounds like what I've been doing all along."

The DA pursed his lips, "I know this doesn't matter, but," he began, "Tony Hiller's been readmitted over there, in psychiatric. They say he's had a break of some sort. Not the lucky kind."

"Shit."

He studied his fingernails. "I talked to Hanna Kish. I suggested that she take care of it properly or I'd go after her license."

"What'd she say?"

His laughter was harsh. "Nothing. She just stood there, tall and professional, staring at me. Then she started crying all over the place."

~ ~ ~

After I had signed all the forms necessary, I was told that I was a free man.

Visiting hours weren't quite up, so I wandered up to Janice Simmons' room. Peering through a crack in the door, I could see her eying a television, frown deepening with each change of scene. My knock brought a growl and an "Oh, come in."

When she saw me, she smiled broadly and turned off the television with a vengeful click of the remote switch. "It's about time you came to see me," she said, moving over to clear space for me.

I took the hint and sat next to her on the bed. "You missed out again?"

Janice threw her hair back out of her face, allowing her features more room to show off. "Not altogether, Mr. Carmichael. You may have deprived me last time, but this time, I got in my licks."

"Good," I said.

"Being part of the story didn't hurt, of course. The 'New Journalism.'" Her merry smile faded as she looked at me. She ran her hand up and down my left arm. "I was furious with you for running off that night to see Collins, did you know that?"

"No. But you've been able to fool me more than that once. Besides it worked out better, didn't it?"

For a change Janice bit her lower lip instead of the upper one. The only flaw in her long, finely defined lips was self-inflicted, her own teeth marks. Maybe that's the way it always is. "The near-death poisoning or the gunshot wound?" she asked.

"I liked the part where we both survived, because I wasn't with you, breathing heavily the whole time."

She looked me in the eyes and then her eyes shifted. "Are you going to kiss me, ever?" she demanded, the greens shifting back. "If you're going to look at my mouth that way, you really should. It is supposed to be irresistible, by the way. But since you came along, I'm beginning to doubt myself."

I first let her finish and then, to dispel her doubt, I let her have her way.

"Okay," she remarked after a while.

"A simple 'wow' would be nice."

"No. Sorry," she said, pulling back a bit. "How about 'much, much better than 'wow?'"

"I can live on that for a week."

She smiled and the greens danced for me. "Oh, you won't have to."

~

Acknowledgments

The Janus Murder, was initially inspired by a very real, very slowly draining, and, hence, flooded preserve. In that sense, the real bog deserves some credit here. The planned Ian Decker/Death by Condo series was inspired, if that he word, by living in a condo, the less said of that being the better.

In the Acknowledgment section for my epic 750 page novel *The Girl in the Coyote Coat,* I made the mistake of acknowledging the help of my sisters, Janet Nave and JoAnn Kiburz and friend Julie Kimball, for their alpha reading and editing assistance. Somehow, my compulsion to introduce two errors for every correction and rewrite they suggested may have made it impossible for them to get another similarly frustrating and non-paying gig.

So, *no one* helped me with *The Janus Murder.* Honest. And if anyone secretly did so, do not admit it.

I should add that this book is not autobiographical. I did endow Sebastian Decker with a few bits of my own background, more for fun than laziness, but Ian is his own man. Every other character or event in the novel is my own fabrication.

About the Author

Born in 1950, John Nicholas Datesh lived mostly in and around Pittsburgh, Pennsylvania until early 2009. At Brown University, he took many courses in writing as an institutionalized rationale for doing just that. Then, at Boston University School of Law, he learned to mix in words and phrases like *It Depends* and *Hereinafter*.

In Spring 2009, he moved cats Lila and Lucy Liu to a condominium one mile in from the east side of Naples Bay in Florida. He left his Pittsburgh career in law, business and product development in favor of concentrating on writing fiction, winging blogs and cultivating beach chairs, presumably in that order of dedication.

He began writing fiction with a pencil and published, on paper with actual ink, his first three novels, SF/Mystery *The Nightmare Machine*; Soft-boiled Detective *The Janus Murder*; and International Suspense *The Moscow Tape*. All three novels are *available* in virtual ink at e-book stores on the Web and in trade paperback.

Also *available* are short stories *The Pro Station* (WWII), *The Final Equation (SF), Reruns ad Infinitum* (SF/Fantasy) and Christmas short story, *You Could Call It a Christmas Story*, all published after the move to Naples.

He concocted a humorous and/or satiric blog at EmptyGlassFull.com shortly after moving. His *Christmas Story* started out as post to the blog, and he has e-published a collection its other early posts, grandly entitled *The Very First Blog Posts of All Time*. As novel writing began to take more of his time, he sent blogging on long vacation.

His 2013 novel, *The Girl in the Coyote Coat*, came to ignore the boundaries of mystery/suspense genre for which it was originally intended. No one would call it a romance, either. With a real estate and finance backdrop, the novel exposes how love, sex, money, scams, drugs, house-breaking and - shopping and fur coats can affect the lives of complex and intriguing characters and even kill a few.

November 2016's *The Janus Murder* is a Sunset Noir mystery novel. It is the first in the author's planned *Death by Condo* series starring prematurely retired lawyer Ian Decker.

His screenplay *The Last Three Minutes* was the first piece written partly on the beach and entirely in the Naples Bay scenery, though it is not set there. *The Last Three Minutes* has been adapted as a novel, if not a movie, by the author and was published in December 2016.

Author's Note on the novel
The Girl in the Coyote Coat
and *A Need Apart*

That heading is not an error. They are the same novel. So, why? To double sales? Not likely.

The novel *The Girl in the Coyote Coat* had a long, tortuous road to its final form, right down to the cover and the very title. It was published under that title after some serious consideration. The novel had gone through any number of working titles, as time allowed, from the 1979 original *The Real Estate Novel*. *The Girl in the Coyote Coat* was always my favorite, inspired, as it was, by an actual coyote coat on an actual model. In the end, that was the title I chose, in a close call (if only to me) over number two, *A Need Apart*, but I did not use the photo that initially inspired the title.

In 2016, I decided to try a little Amazon Kindle advertising. Amazon would not accept the somewhat racy cover. That rejection got me thinking. The novel had grown into what I must loosely call a literary novel, if only because it does not fit into any genre. Why not try a different cover for an ad? Then, I thought, why not try a different, more literary-sounding title. The result is the identical novel with a different name, *A Need Apart*, and a different cover.

Ironically, the *A Need Apart*'s cover uses the shot that originally inspired the working title *The Girl in the Coyote Coat*. Fortunately, I love both titles and both covers, equally. Oh, and both the coat and model, too, if not quite so equally.

www.ingramcontent.com/pod-product-compliance
Lightning Source LLC
Chambersburg PA
CBHW020737250626
47155CB00003B/802